Andrey Kurkov

THE SILVER BONE

Translated from the Russian by
Boris Dralyuk

MACLEHOSE PRESS
QUERCUS · LONDON

First published in the Russian language as *Samson i Nadezhda*
by Folio, Kharkiv, 2020
First published in Great Britain in 2024 by

MacLehose Press
an imprint of Quercus
Carmelite House
50 Victoria Embankment
London W1U 8EW
An Hachette UK Company

A CIP catalogue record for this book is available
from the British Library.

ISBN (Hardback) 978 1 52942 649 6
ISBN (Trade paperback) 978 1 52942 650 2
ISBN (Ebook) 978 1 52942 652 6

10 9 8 7 6 5 4 3 2

Designed and typeset in Sabon by CC Book Production
Printed and bound in Great Britain by Clays Ltd, Elcograf S.p.A.

MIX
Paper | Supporting
responsible forestry
FSC
www.fsc.org FSC® C104740

Papers used by Quercus are from well-managed forests and other responsible sources.

To Vsevolod Dmitriev,
a passionate archivist and idealist
who can't stand violence

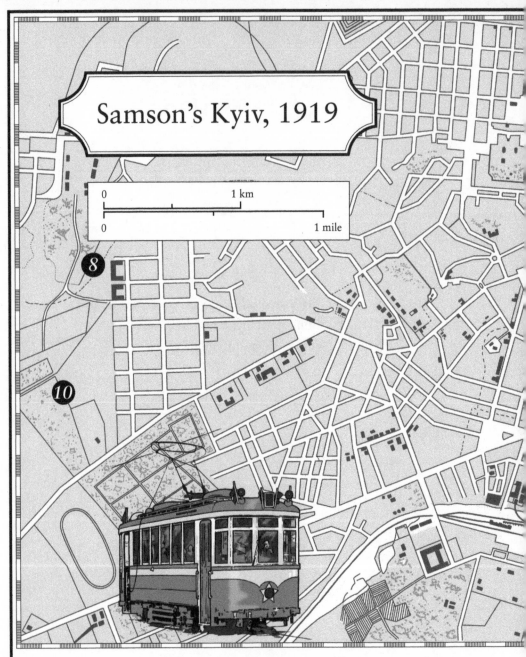

1. 3 Tarasivska Street: This was the location of the Lybid District police station, where Samson Kolechko unexpectedly found himself employed. Interestingly, the street's name never changed under Soviet rule or after.

2. 24 Zhylianska Street: Here the Kolechko family — mother, father, Samson and his younger sister — once lived happily. In 1919, the Red Army soldiers Fyodor and Anton were billeted in their flat.

3. 3 Baseina Street (located in the Pechersk neighbourhood, running from Besarabska Square to Shovkovychna and Hospitalna Streets): The address of Balzer the tailor, who plays an important role in the novel.

4. Naberezhno-Mykolska Street (now Hryhoriya Skovorody Street): Nadezhda's parents lived on this street, and so did she, until a certain time. The path from here to her place of work was dangerous, strewn with obstacles.

5. The Dog Path (now Mechnykova Street): The common name for this narrow path, which stretches along a ravine, stemmed from the fact that pilgrims making their way along it to the Monastery of the Caves in the centre of Kyiv were sometimes attacked by highwaymen and wild dogs.

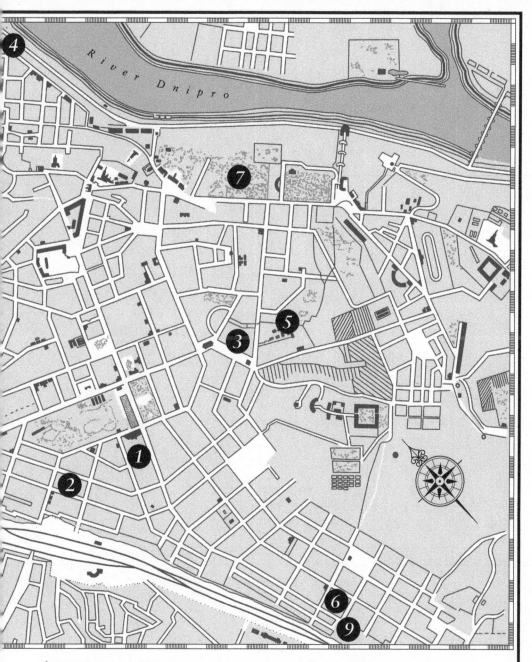

6. 36 Naberezhno-Lybidska Street (now Antonovycha Street): The home of Dr Vatrukhin, Specialist in Diseases of the Eye, where Samson showed up with his severed ear.

7. Oleksandrivsky Park (now Mariinskyi Park): Here the heroes of the Red Army, who perished in defence of the Revolution, were laid to rest, and Nayden made his speech over their mass grave.

8. Malo-Dorohozhytska Street (now Herzen Street): The surgeon Trattner worked on this street, at Iona Zaitsev's Jewish Surgical Hospital. It was a saying of his that set this whole tale in motion.

9. Nimetska Street (later renamed Telmana Street, now Nimetska again): The tailor Sivokon, who unwittingly aided Samson's investigation, lived here.

10. Dorohozhytska Street: The location of the Lukyanivka Cemetery, not far from what was once the firing range of the Kyiv Society for Proper Hunting, where Samson learned how to shoot.

Chapter 1

Samson was deafened by the sound of the sabre striking his father's head. He caught the glint of the flashing blade out of the corner of his eye and stepped into a puddle. His already dead father's left hand pushed him aside, so that the next sabre neither quite struck nor quite missed his ginger-haired head, slicing off his right ear. He managed to reach out and catch the falling ear, clutching it in his fist before it hit the gutter. His father, meanwhile, collapsed right onto the road, his head split in two. A horse stamped the body into the ground with a hind leg's shod hoof before its rider dug in his spurs and charged forward at a dozen townsfolk who were running and leaping into the gutters, realising what awaited them. Five more riders galloped past.

But Samson didn't see them. He was lying flat against the slope of the gutter, the palm of his left hand open on the wet earth and the fist of his right hand tucked under his head. His wound burned and burned, loudly and sonorously, as if someone were hammering a steel rail right above it. Hot blood poured down his cheek and seeped under his collar.

It started raining again. Samson raised his head. He saw before him the sole of his father's dark-blue English-made high button shoe, which, though splattered with mud, still looked noble. His father had worn them constantly and carefully for five years, since 1914, when a shoe dealer on Khreshchatyk, spooked by the outbreak of war, had lowered the price, rightly sensing that international hostilities didn't bode well for the sale of fashionable goods.

Samson didn't wish to see his dead father in full, with his head split open, so he crawled backwards along the gutter, tightly clutching the severed ear. He got out on the road, but couldn't straighten up. For a moment he just stood there, thin and hunched over, not allowing himself to turn round. When he at last took a couple of steps, he tripped over a corpse. Samson made his way around the body, but then an awful roar again assaulted his head, pouring like molten tin into the hole that had been his ear. He pressed his fist against the bleeding wound, as if trying to plug it shut, to block the noise that had burst into his head. Then he started running. He was simply running away, but it happened to be in the direction from which he and his father had come, towards Zhylianska Street, where he had been born and raised. Amid the general roar, he made out individual gunshots, but these didn't stop him. He ran past confused, aimless townsfolk, all of them staring blankly, and when he felt that he could go no further, that his legs were giving out, he spotted a large sign above the door of a two-storey house: DR N. N. VATRUKHIN, SPECIALIST IN DISEASES OF THE EYE.

Samson ran up and pulled the door handle with his left hand. Closed. He knocked with his fist.

"Open up!" he shouted.

Now he pounded the door with both fists.

"What do you want?" a woman's frightened voice asked from within.

"A doctor!"

"Nikolay Nikolaevich isn't seeing patients today."

"He has to! He's got to see me!"

"Who is it, Tonya?" a rich male baritone asked from deeper within.

"Someone out in the street," the old woman responded.

"Let them in."

The door opened a crack and the old woman peeked out at blood-stained Samson. She allowed him inside and immediately slammed the door shut behind him, double bolting it.

"Oh, Lord! Who did that to you?"

"Cossacks. Where's the doctor?"

"Let's go . . ."

The doctor, smooth-shaven and grey, silently treated Samson's wound, applied a gauze pad with ointment and bandaged his head.

Somewhat calmed by the noiseless flat, Samson looked at the doctor in quiet gratitude and unclenched his right fist.

"Can the ear . . . be saved?" he asked, barely audible.

"I couldn't say." The doctor shook his head sadly. "I'm an ophthalmologist. Who was it?"

"Don't know." The young man shrugged. "Cossacks."

"Red anarchy," Vatrukhin replied, heaving a heavy sigh. Then he went over to the table, rummaged in the top drawer, took out a powder box and brought it back to his patient.

Samson removed the lid. The box was empty. The doctor tore off a piece of cotton wool and lined its bottom. The young man lowered his ear into the box, closed it and stuck it into the patch pocket of his tunic.

He looked up at the doctor.

"My father's still out there," he said, wincing. "On the road. Hacked to death."

The doctor smacked his lips bitterly and shook his head.

"One can't even leave the house, these days," he said, throwing up his hands. "What are you going to do?"

"I don't know. I've got to go and get him . . ."

"Do you have money?"

"He did, in his wallet. We were on our way to the tailor's, to pick up a suit."

"Let's go, then," Vatrukhin pronounced, gesturing towards the door.

This time, the streets were deserted. The crack of rifle fire sounded in the distance. The sky seemed to be leaning lower and lower over the blood-engorged town, as if preparing to lie down for the night on its roofs and cemeteries.

When they reached Nimetska Street, where Symon Petliura's horsemen had overtaken Samson and his father, they saw ahead of them two carts and about a dozen men in peasant garb. Several corpses had already been lifted onto one of the carts, but Samson's father still lay on the side of the road. Only now he was barefoot – someone had taken his English shoes.

Samson bent over the body, trying to avoid looking at the head. Reaching his hand under his father's chest, he felt for the wallet in his coat's inner pocket and pulled it out. The wallet's plumpness surprised and somewhat embarrassed him. He slipped it into the pocket of his tunic, rose to his feet and looked back at the carts.

"Need me to take it somewhere?" asked the peasant holding the empty cart's horse by the bridle.

"Yes, I do." Samson nodded and looked back at the doctor.

"What is the closest funeral home?" the doctor asked.

"That'd be Gladbach's," the peasant replied. "Got money on you? I don't take any of them 'coupons' they're printing these days."

"We have Kerensky roubles," the doctor assured him.

"Alright, then." The man nodded. "Let me give you a hand with 'im – wouldn't want that mess all over your clothes . . ."

Samson glanced down at his dirty trousers and tunic, then he and the peasant both bent over his father's body.

On Tuesday, 11 March 1919, his life as he knew it was over.

Chapter 2

"I would advise you to take the coat," the clerk at the funeral home said in Russian with a Polish accent. "We don't bury people in coats. Coats won't keep them warm, where they're going. But I would put something on his feet."

Samson's father's body lay in a rough-hewn coffin. The head, covered with a square of purple Chinese silk, appeared to be unbroken. The undertaker had bandaged it well, reuniting its split halves.

"What about this board?" Samson asked, indicating with a glance one side of the coffin, which had obviously been intended for some other purpose.

"You know, we have our own sawmill near Fastiv, but it's impossible to reach now – and, if you do reach it, there's little chance of coming back," the clerk said. "Where we were short of good wood, we used planks from an old fence. Too many clients – the carpenter can't keep up. But perhaps it was a fence your father knew well from his walks . . ."

The usually deserted cemetery on Shchekavytsia Hill above the Dnipro was as loud as a busy street corner. Even the croaking of hundreds of crows, who had taken a fancy to the crown of a mighty oak in the section for Old Believers, was unable to drown out the din. Moaning, crying, anger – but these mournful voices came from the edge of the cemetery, near the cliff side. Samson, however, stood in the very centre, watching two peasants deepen a narrow pit between two old graves. From time to time, he would take a couple of steps back, so that the brown earth flying out of the pit wouldn't land on his shoes.

"Can't go any deeper!" one of the men shouted from below. "Hittin' coffins, down here."

In order to corroborate his words, he slammed his shovel against a wooden surface, which uttered a muffled, plaintive response.

Samson peered down.

"Will the coffin fit?"

"If we squeeze it in, sure," the man answered. "Might get a little squashed."

The darkened edge of Samson's mother's coffin showed on the right. They'd buried her five years ago. She'd passed away not long after his sister, Verusya, from whom she had contracted the lung ailment that took both their lives. Now Samson's father would lie next to them, the third, leaving Samson no space in the family grave.

His gaze rose to the tombstone – a concrete tree with missing branches, carved with the words VERUSYA KOLECHKO. ZINAI-DA FYODOROVNA KOLECHKO. REST IN PEACE. FROM YOUR LOVING FATHER, MOTHER AND BROTHER.

The inscription muddled Samson's thoughts.

The men lowered the coffin on their ropes. Its narrow foot easily reached the bottom, while the upper part got stuck a bit higher up.

The men worked at the brown earth with their shovels and the upper part sank down a few inches.

"Won't drop further now," one of the men said, shaking his head. "But it'll settle in time, always does. That's how it always is."

Samson nodded, and as he did so he felt the bandage slipping down his head. He felt for the knot above his severed ear, undid it, tightened the bandage and retied it again.

"Hurts bad?" one of the men asked solicitously.

"No," Samson answered. "Just aches a little."

"That's how it always is," the man commented, his uncovered head nodding up and down, slowly, in the manner of an all-comprehending sage. Then he drew a crumpled checked cap from the pocket of his wadded jacket and put it on.

Once they were paid, the men went back to their cart, leaving Samson alone. And then the sun peeked out from behind the clouds, its rays pacifying the whole cemetery. The crows fell silent. The weeping and shouting on the cliff side died down. All seemed to be hiding, holding its breath. All aside from the cool March breeze.

The brown patches of earth on the old, hardened snow around the fresh grave looked to Samson like bloodstains.

Having cleaned off its collar and padded shoulders, Samson hung his father's soiled but solid coat on the left side of the wardrobe. The right side was occupied by his mother's clothes, including her beloved grey fox fur coat.

He went into his father's study. Before now, he'd hardly ever set foot in this small, cosy room, with its single window overlooking the street. His father kept his writing desk in German order. On the right edge of the tabletop lay an abacus, a gift from the owner of the trading company whose accounts his father had kept right up until it was closed down last year. The abacus's walnut frame was inlaid with ivory, and its beads too were noble – made from the bones of a "sea creature", as his father liked to put it.

A stack of cardboard folders, stuffed full of documents and fastened with string, usually sat on the left side of the desk. But, when the trading company closed, these folders had migrated to the floor. Samson's father had been in no hurry to get rid of them. He used to say that life could not sustain itself without air, water and trade, and so he held on to the belief that the trading company could reopen as soon as "those who were dissatisfied became satisfied".

On the walls to the left and to the right of the desk, another three dozen abacuses – a whole collection – hung on nails. Previously, they had all seemed the same to Samson, but now that he was alone in the flat and able to examine them more closely, he saw many differences in shape and shade, as well as in bead colouring. The small number of photographs in wooden frames looked strange and silly on the abacus-bedecked walls. One showed Samson's grandfather and grandmother, another his father and mother, and a third showed himself and Verusya as small children wearing sailor suits.

Samson moved closer to the photograph of himself and his sister. His hand reached for the abacus hanging directly beneath it.

With some force, he pushed one of the beads towards the empty left side of its rod.

"Verusya," he said glumly. Pushing the next bead in the same direction, he said, "Mother," and then, sending a third bead after them, in a completely deadened voice, "Father."

He separated a fourth bead from those remaining on the right and slid it back and forth across the rod.

Uttering a little grunt, Samson walked away and sat down at his father's desk. He pulled out the top left drawer and took out their family passport. The photograph showed all four of them. The passport had been issued on 13 February 1913. His father had secured it with the idea of taking the family to Austria-Hungary, to the spas. Now, there was no more Austria-Hungary, no more Russian Empire and no more Father – only the passport.

Samson closed the little grey booklet and slipped it back into the drawer, placing beside it the powder box containing his ear. Then he raised his hand to his right temple and palpated the wound beneath the bandage. It really was aching dully rather than hurting badly.

He snapped his fingers near the wound and the click seemed loud and resonant.

Well, at least I can still hear, he thought.

Chapter 3

On the ninth day after his father's murder, Samson looked at himself in the mirror, at his sunken eyes, his sunken cheeks, his stained, frayed bandage.

The days flowed past like rainwater down Volodymyr Descent, noisily, underfoot. Samson never once went out into the street, only glanced, from time to time, out of the windows of his father's study and the living room. Those in his own room, like those in Verusya's room and that of his parents, overlooked the courtyard, revealing the still-bare branches of the old maple tree. But Verusya's room might as well have not existed now. Its door was completely blocked by a sideboard. Two days earlier, Samson had also hidden the door to his parents' bedroom with a wardrobe. These rooms, closed off from the outside world, somehow concealed the pain of his losses, making it a bit easier for Samson to bear the thought of his departed parents and sister.

The rain gave way to sleet, the sound of feet squelching through puddles was now and then overpowered by the clatter of horse-shoes on cobblestones, and sometimes the noise of an engine would swoop in like a gust of wind, drowning out everything else, but never for long.

After polishing off a plate of yesterday's porridge, a source of sustenance he'd grown quite sick of in recent days, Samson brushed the dried mud from his father's coat and put it on. He looked in the mirror again. No, the coat didn't make him look any more like his father, whose face radiated wisdom and self-confidence even as his brown eyes shone with imperturbable placidity. The coat, with its air of respectable significance, simply emphasised, by contrast, Samson's frightened, unshaven countenance.

He put the brushed coat away in the wardrobe, but these thoughts about his father, which had rightly welled up inside him on the ninth day, when Orthodox tradition decreed that the dead be mourned, demanded action. Should he ride over to the cemetery? No, that course of action Samson immediately rejected – too far, too dangerous.

Even if you lined up Red Army men with rifles along the entire route, it would still be dangerous. Who knows what might get into their heads, whom they might suddenly see as their enemy? Should he go to church, then, and light a candle? This, of course, was possible, but neither his father nor he himself had ever been particularly pious. His mother used to attend services on feast days, but she barely mentioned it, let alone spoke of it at length – too shy.

Samson retrieved his father's wallet, sat down at his desk and listened to the sounds of Zhylianska Street filtering in through the closed window. He pulled out and counted the Kerensky and Duma roubles that had been issued by the Provisional Government. The wallet also held three business cards; a certificate of membership for the Kyiv Society for Proper Hunting; a tailor's receipt, folded many times, for the entire cost of the fabric, the cutting and the sewing of the suit, and confirmation of the accuracy of all measurements taken; several stamps for paying various duties and fees; and an oval-shaped photograph of Samson's mother.

The previous evening, when it was already dark outside, the yard-sweeper's widow had knocked on his door and told him that a peasant woman was selling milk and butter in the back wing of the building. He ran down in time to buy half a pound of butter and a quart of milk. And when the bottom step of the wooden staircase creaked under his foot, just outside the yard-sweeper's cubbyhole of a flat, the widow, a woman of about forty-five, with a fondness for modest, inexpensive headscarves, invited him into her kitchen. The stench from that kitchen was terrible, viscous, as if someone had been frying onions for hours. But Samson accepted the invitation with no complaints and sat down at the table for a cup of tea.

"You're an orphan now," she said in a pitying, partly questioning tone. "Can't go on that way for too long . . . It'll kill you . . ."

"What can I do?" Samson asked, intending simply to prolong her verbal participation in the discussion of the situation in which he, thanks to fate, had found himself.

"Marry," she said firmly. "Marriage drives away orphanhood. And you'll eat regular then, too." She examined his face critically, apparently passing judgement on his hollow, stubbly cheeks. "If it's a good match, you'll put your suffering behind you . . ."

"I'm still young," Samson responded, after giving it some thought. "Too early for me."

"Whaddaya mean, early?" she objected. "I got hitched at fourteen!"

Samson finished his tea. Lifting the bottle of milk and pack of butter from his lap, he rose to his feet and thanked his neighbour.

"If I spot someone who's right for you, I'll be sure and tell you," the widow promised as she closed the door behind him.

The milk and butter now took their place on a windowsill in the living room. The cold tiled stoves were asking for firewood, but it seemed to Samson that the air in the flat was still warm from the last time he'd stoked them. Before going to bed, he burned half an armful of wood in the stove responsible for heating both the living room and his bedroom. The air in his father's study, of course, was prickly cold, but still not as frigid as on those winter days when they'd been left with no firewood at all. Yet he and his father had managed, somehow. And at winter's end they'd found out that someone had hidden a huge amount of firewood in their cellar. Stolen, apparently. Whoever it was had disappeared, allowing the building to live in warmth. But the sun was already turning towards spring, and natural warmth was just around the corner.

When the light outside grew grey and twilight was approaching, Samson put on his old high-school greatcoat, slipped the tailor's receipt into one of its pockets and set off for Nimetska Street.

Everyone he passed seemed to be proceeding with utmost caution, trying not to look around them, as if afraid to witness something unpleasant. As he walked, his wound reminded him of its existence. After adjusting and retying the bandage, he went on down the path that had turned out to be his father's last. At the place of the murder, he stopped to look at the gutter and the edge of the road. He remembered how he had returned here with the doctor. His head began to buzz, as if the blood had risen in his thoughts.

And these thoughts of his grew heavy and sluggish, taking on the taste of blood. They seemed intent on engulfing him with their heaviness and sluggishness, and so Samson moved away from the scene with decisive steps, turned onto Nimetska and only stopped when he reached the tailor's residence, which bore a sign reading, SIVOKON, TAILOR. SUITS. MORNING COATS. TAILCOATS.

The light in the workshop's window wasn't bright. A brighter one shone from the two windows on the first floor. Samson knocked loudly and waited.

The tailor, whom Samson had only seen a couple of times in his life, opened the door just a crack and asked, without saying hello, "What is your business at this odd hour?"

Samson introduced himself and slipped the receipt through the gap, which the door chain kept from spreading any wider than a fist.

The tailor let Samson in and heard him out, nodding sympathetically.

"You're slighter than your dear papa was," he said with a sigh. "I can recut it, of course ... But now's not the time. My hands are trembling. Better to wait. You can take it, if you want. Or I can keep it a while longer, if you're afraid to carry it at night . . ."

"I'll take it," Samson said.

It wasn't yet so very late and scary when he set off for home. He even passed a pair of young women, both neatly dressed in sombre colours. He heard one of them whisper to the other, "Look, what a handsome dark-haired fellow – wounded, like a hero . . ." He stopped and followed them with his eyes, then adjusted his bandage, which had begun to slip again. It occurred to him that, in the dark, no-one would see that the bandage was old and dirty.

The suit was folded, wrapped in paper and tied with twine. He carried it under his arm, pressing it close to his body, so as not to attract the attention of passers-by.

At home, he placed the suit, without unwrapping it, at the bottom of the left half of the wardrobe, beneath his father's coat.

He spread his greatcoat over his blanket and went to bed in his warm undershirt and long underwear. He lay there, waiting for his body to warm up, but could not fall asleep. Then he thought he heard a rustle, like that of a mouse gnawing on paper or cardboard. He got up, lit a kerosene lamp and peered into every corner of his room, yet failed to discover the source of the susurration. The sound accompanied him all through his search for the unseen mouse, which was surprising, since mice usually fell silent as soon as he began to look for them. When he stopped, he realised he could still hear the rustle. Now he was sure it was coming from elsewhere, outside his room. He went out into the hallway; the rustle, sounding louder and more distinct, seemed to be emanating from his father's study, even though that room's heavy walnut door was supposed to keep its noises concealed from the outside world.

Samson entered the study and identified the source of the annoying rustle – his father's desk. He approached, abruptly pulled out the upper left-hand drawer, and the sound disappeared. The mouse darted deeper into the drawer and also vanished. By the light of the kerosene lamp, Samson saw that the powder box now had a hole in one of its corners, wide enough to fit a finger.

He picked up the box, removed the lid and looked at his ear. The side where it had been cut was caked with blood, but the ear seemed alive, not at all dried up. Amazed, Samson touched it with his finger – and simultaneously felt the contact with both the finger and the ear. He touched his left ear and experienced the same sensation.

Confused and sleepy, he closed the box and took it into the kitchen. There, he found a round tin that had once held boiled sweets from Montpensier; he stuck the box inside it and brought the tin with him to his room. He at last felt the desire for sleep overcoming the coldness in his body.

Chapter 4

Nikolay Nikolaevich Vatrukhin did not seem at all surprised to see Samson at his door.

"Let's have a look at that ear. Come with me," he said, inviting the young man into his office and nodding to his housekeeper, Tonya, who was peering out from behind the visitor's back, after letting him inside.

Having removed the dirty bandage from Samson's head and tossed it disgustedly into the wastepaper basket, he brought his face closer to the bare earhole.

Samson noticed that a mother-of-pearl-handled magnifying glass had appeared in the doctor's hands.

"Well, well, well." The doctor nodded thoughtfully. "Healing up very nicely indeed," he drawled, as if surprised at the discovery. "No need for a bandage now. I'll apply a bit of ointment, but after that . . ."

"Could you wrap it up just one more time?" Samson asked.

"Certainly, but, as I say, there's no need. The wound ought to breathe at this point."

"It's just that it's damp and cold outside," Samson responded, somewhat flustered. "To be honest, I'm afraid to walk down the street without an ear, where everyone can see . . ."

"Alright, alright," the doctor said, relenting. "I don't want you to think that I'm reluctant to expend gauze on you – though of course it's impossible to come by, these days. My supply is dwindling. How's the hearing? As I told you, I'm no expert, but let's have a look."

Before re-bandaging Samson's head, the doctor used both hands and a good deal of force to turn the bare earhole towards the window.

"No visible damage. Can you hear well enough?"

The young man sighed. "Too well, sometimes. Hard to fall asleep."

"That makes sense, my young friend. You now have omni-directional hearing on this side – quite different from the left. We are given ears not simply to hear, but, above all, to listen. Directional hearing retrieves what we need from the general hubbub of life, while omnidirectional hearing clogs our attention. You understand?"

Samson nodded.

"Is there anyone at home to help you with the bandaging?"

The young man shook his head.

"In any case, you can always bring the gauze to a barber – they know how to do it. And I'd advise washing the bandage every two days. It should last you a couple of weeks."

"May I also consult you about my eyes?" Samson asked, having worked up the courage.

"What's the matter with them?"

"Some things appear redder than usual ... I was looking at a candle in a church recently and knew that the flame ought to be yellow, but what I saw was red."

The magnifying glass reappeared in the doctor's hands.

"Please look out the window."

Samson trained his gaze on the unwashed panes. Wet snowflakes crawled down the glass, leaving behind grimy grey trails.

"Do they sting?" the doctor asked.

"A little."

"You have spots on your cornea ... Reddish particles ... We'll flush them out."

The doctor went over to a metal cabinet with white enamelled edges. Its door creaked.

"Now, look up at the ceiling," he said.

The young man raised his head and opened his eyes wide.

"Good Lord," the doctor gasped.

"What is it?" Samson asked with fear in his voice.

"It must be your father's blood. And a fragment of his brain. Don't worry, we'll get it all out."

The doctor put drops in the young man's eyes.

"Just sit still a while. Let your eyes take their bath."

Samson walked home slowly, looking down at his feet. "Don't expose your eyes to the snow," the doctor had warned him sternly. "Flush them with warm water five times a day. Today is Wednesday. Come back Friday. We'll get those corneas clean."

Behind him he heard the shoes of a hurrying horse clattering against the pavement. Taking fright, he rushed towards the nearest house. A glance back revealed that the rider was a Red Army man, peering intensely in the direction of his steed's flight. The clatter was now receding and someone else leapt out the way, yielding the road to the new regime's mounted guardsman.

The thought of a new regime made Samson chuckle bitterly. When there was one regime, albeit an old one, life seemed unsightly, comprehensible and routine. That regime was also routinely disparaged, although, even after the outbreak of the World War, the difficulties people experienced under its rule were, in comparison with what was to come, not so much difficulties as inconveniences. Yet the old royal regime had collapsed, and in its wake came many petty furious ones, replacing one another with much shooting and hatred. It was only during the time of the German garrison and the invisible Hetman of Ukraine, Pavlo Skoropadskyi, that life seemed to grow relatively safe and quiet again, but this lull ended with the terrible warehouse explosions and fires in the Zvirynets district that left hundreds of Kyivans dead and thousands crippled and homeless.

Back then, in June 1918, the air of Kyiv settled on the tongue and prickled the nostrils with the scent of burnt gunpowder. Now, at every hint of a thaw, the icy snowdrifts of rubbish piled up at the corners of residential buildings began to smell of warm manure. It was as if the first thing to sense the approach of spring was the horse dung, with which the wooden shovels of yard-sweepers generously supplemented the rubbish. The manure served as the hard mass of the expanding snowdrifts and was therefore always closer to passers-by than the rubbish of early winter, which lay buried in the cold depths of these black, frozen Kyivan Appalachians.

As soon as the bottom step of the wooden staircase creaked, the door to the yard-sweeper's flat swung open. The widow beckoned Samson into her never-ventilated realm of heavy, viscous odours.

"Red Army men were here for you," she said. "Came to demand a contribution. I told them you were an orphan. They seemed to like that, but they'll be back anyway. They've got the whole list of tenants ... Planning to evict you."

"Why would they do that?"

"All about justice, you know. A person deserves a corner, not a whole flat. Oh, and they asked whether you had any musicians in the family ... They're requisitioning instruments now. Want to make music themselves."

"We had a violin," Samson recalled. "I'm happy to give it up. My father was the only one who knew how to play."

"Listen, that's not why I called you in here. Given any more thought to marriage?"

The young man, taken aback, looked into the widow's eyes. "No," he admitted.

"I've got one in mind for you. Comes from educated folk, but she's handy, can do it all. She'll help you hold on to the flat too, keep you from being evicted."

"How would she do that?" Samson asked dubiously.

"I'm telling you, she's no shrinking violet. Soft as butter one moment, hard as iron the next. You ought to see her. A wife like that is as good as a rifle. She'd make a soldier quake in his boots. You know what, come by for some herring tonight. I'll get her over here too, so's you can have a look for yourself."

Perplexed, Samson went up the stairs. Without taking off his shoes or overcoat, he walked around the flat, which now really did feel cold and lonely. He stopped in front of a stove, next to which lay three birch logs, and sighed heavily. He would have to fetch more from the cellar. Three logs would only warm up the stove's cast-iron door – it would take ten to heat its tiled walls.

His gaze fell on the sweets tin from Montpensier that he had selected to protect the powder box from the jaws of rodents. He carried it back to his father's study and dropped it into the desk drawer. No mouse alive could gnaw its way through tin.

Then, swapping his overcoat for his father's old wadded jacket, he set off down the stairs for firewood.

Chapter 5

When the birch logs were already crackling with all their might inside the stove that served the living room and Samson's bedroom, there was a rude knock at the door. And immediately after the rude one came a polite, enquiring one.

Samson found himself facing two Red Army men of different heights but of approximately the same age, both wearing crumpled overcoats that looked several sizes too large for them. Just off to their side stood the yard-sweeper's widow. He realised that the rude knock had come from the soldiers, the polite one from her. She must have wanted to demonstrate how civilised urban folk behave.

"A different pair, these two," she said to Samson, nodding at the Red Army men, who stared at him with a mix of confusion and hostility. "I told them there wasn't any sewing machine up here, but they wouldn't believe me. Show them, would you?"

"Why would you need a sewing machine?" Samson asked, and, just in case, he looked at their hands barely peeking out of the wide sleeves of their overcoats. They had large peasant fingers, not the slender ones of musicians or tailors.

"We've got orders," answered the taller one, with as much gruffness, it seemed, as his voice could carry. He looked to be the same age as Samson.

"Come in, look around." Samson shrugged. "None of us ever did any sewing."

Glancing apprehensively to right and left, the Red Army men made their way through the hallway and the living room.

"What about in there?" the shorter one asked, stopping in front of Samson's father's study, and, without waiting for permission, he opened the door.

"Why'd you cover the whole wall with these?" he asked, turning to Samson.

"Just decoration," Samson responded. "Father loved to count . . ."

"Where is he?"

"He was recently killed."

"Out on the street?"

"Out on the street," Samson confirmed, and then realised that both Red Army men were now staring at his bandaged head.

"And you was wounded, eh?" asked the short one.

Samson nodded.

"Boy, is it nice and warm over here," the taller one said, changing the subject and placing his palm against the tiled wall of the stove.

"Getting cosy, are you?" the yard-sweeper's widow, who had stayed in the hallway, shouted at them. "You see there ain't no sewing machine, so move along!"

"Hey, don't be nasty," the short one said, taking the rifle off his shoulder. "We'll see how nasty you are when I plant one in your forehead."

Fear flashed in the widow's eyes – that Samson noticed – but not a single muscle twitched in her face.

"Oh, sure, you'll plant one! I treated your commissar to kvass! I'll go and tell him all about this!"

The short one slung the rifle back over his shoulder.

At the same time, the tall one stretched out his hand and ran his fingers along the sleeve of the wadded jacket Samson hadn't removed after going down for firewood.

"Your father didn't leave behind any undies, did he? Warm ones?" he asked. "Your winters go on for ever up here, not like at home."

"Where are you from?" Samson asked.

"From the south, Melitopol."

Samson hurried to his bedroom, opened the chest in the corner, took out a pair of his own long underwear and carried it out to the soldier. He noticed the short one glancing with envy at the tall one and swallowing his saliva unpleasantly.

"Go on, then, get out." The yard-sweeper's widow began to shoo them out the door. "And make sure you report that there ain't no sewing equipment anywhere in this flat . . ."

The Red Army men left without saying goodbye, while the widow lingered a moment. She reminded Samson that he was welcome to come over for herring in the evening.

An hour before the herring, Samson found himself in a romantic mood. He was preoccupied with a question that hadn't bothered him for two years: what should he wear? The first thing he did was find a white shirt. The trousers of his school uniform made him nervous because they hadn't been hanging in the wardrobe but lying in a canvas bag inside the chest, wrapped up with his summer sandals. He'd never needed a belt to keep them up before, but now they sagged. The belt, too, he'd found at the bottom of the chest, with its buckle missing. A further dig turned up an old bronze buckle from school, embossed with two diverging laurel branches and a large letter S against a fan of calligraphy nibs. Finally, he tried on his tunic and calmed down when a look in the mirror revealed a heroically attractive young man with a bandaged head.

Before going downstairs, he shaved his cheeks to a shine with a cut-throat razor and doused himself with Brocard's floral cologne – then immediately regretted having done so. The excessively close shave made him look more like a victim than a hero. And the young woman might perceive the scent of bourgeois cologne as a sign of weakness or, worse, as a protest against the odours of the new life. After washing off the cologne with soapy water, he dried his face and neck with a cold, damp-smelling towel.

The air in the widow's kitchen proved even thicker than usual. A saucepan was boiling on the kerosene stove, and there was no need to look inside to see what it contained – no question that the saucepan was filling the whole kitchen with the warm aroma of potatoes. The round table, draped with a white linen cloth, bore a dessert plate, a side plate and dinner plate from the same service, and next to each lay a crude proletarian fork. In the centre, at an equal distance from all the plates, sat a porcelain butter dish in the shape of a roosting hen.

"Nadezhda isn't here yet, but she promised she'd come," said the widow, seating her guest at the table.

Beautiful name, thought Samson.

"Forgive me, I didn't want to bring those soldiers to your door . . . I usually tell them to beat it and they listen, but these two insisted on checking for themselves. I said to them, 'You fellows and I are of the same feather; why don't you believe me?' But they wouldn't listen."

"Oh, it's no problem," Samson responded soothingly.

"And, as for you, next time, don't go giving them what they ask for. Because, later on, when you get a visit from people you oughtn't say 'no' to, you won't have anything left to give. I swear, you're just like your papa, may he rest in peace . . ."

The sound of knocking distracted the widow and imbued her body with graceful agility. She fluttered up from the table and soon the door creaked open.

"Nadezhda, my dear! I'm so glad you made it – come in, come in!"

A girl of excessively athletic appearance entered the kitchen, her wooden shoes scraping against the wooden floor. Her face was round, her frame large but not fat. She wore a black sheepskin coat that seemed to strain against its buttons, and an austere below-the-knee skirt. Before taking the seat the widow had offered her, she unbuttoned her sheepskin coat, which sprang open to reveal a bright maroon plush blouse done up to her neck. It made her look like a flower. Then she untied the grey Orenburg shawl on her head, undid the top button of her blouse and finally sat down, giving the smiling Samson a friendly look.

"Nadezhda," she announced, holding out her hand over the table.

The young man introduced himself, felt her firm handshake and gazed into her green eyes amiably and somewhat plaintively.

"Everything smells so delicious," Nadezhda said as she turned to their hostess, who was standing over the stove.

"It's almost ready, almost – here, hand me your plate."

Three roughly peeled, steaming potatoes landed on the dinner plate that had been assigned to Nadezhda. Another three ended up on Samson's side plate. On her own dessert plate the widow placed two. Once she was seated, she lifted the cover from the hen-shaped butter dish and eyed her guests with pride. Before them lay an uncleaned herring cut into large pieces and garnished with a few green leaves.

"Goodness, where did you get the salad?" Nadezhda marvelled.

"That's no salad – they're geranium leaves! I just thought I'd dress it up a bit." The widow's voice took on an apologetic tone. "Don't eat them. They're bitter."

Then she plucked the leaves from the herring, took them over to the windowsill and dropped them into the pot whence they came.

"Will you take a little glass?" she asked.

Nadezhda nodded. "If the wine isn't sour."

"Not sour." The hostess chuckled. "It's the clear, bitter kind."

The first five minutes of the meal passed in silence, but then the conversation began to flow of its own accord, starting with the cold weather and the herring, and gradually rising above the problems of everyday life and nutrition.

"New employees are a headache," Nadezhda complained. "They show up and claim they can do anything you need, but then it turns out they were just looking for a warm place to sit. They can't even write properly."

"So they keep your office well heated?" Samson asked, perking up.

"Yes, fairly well. But the stoker complains that almost everyone tries to steal firewood, hiding at least one log under their coats. Lately, I've even taken to checking people as they leave for the day. I tell them it's a shame to steal from yourself."

"We got lucky," Samson sighed. "We have a pile of birch logs in the cellar from the time the Directorate was in power. They must have requisitioned the firewood from somewhere else, and then they requisitioned our cellar to store it. But the cellar remained ours. And so did the firewood, outlasting the Directorate."

The widow threw a sharp, disapproving glance at Samson, and he realised that he was blabbing.

"We're running out, of course," he said, cutting himself off. "And who knows where we'll get more?"

"Firewood comes from trees, so one would find it where trees grow," Nadezhda responded with a shrug. "And what is it you do, Samson?"

"Coping with the misfortunes that have befallen us," he began to say, but was diverted by another sharp glance from the widow. "My father was killed, and I didn't escape unscathed . . ."

"Bandits?" the young woman asked.

"Cossacks on horseback . . . Cutting people to pieces, right out on the street – for nothing!"

The widow nodded. "Too much disorder, these days."

"Yes," the young woman agreed. "Without strong leadership, people grow feral . . . As soon as the state tightens its grip and shows its teeth, it will all quieten down. But what's your profession, Samson?"

"I studied electrical engineering at the university. And you, Nadezhda?"

"Pharmacology. Now, though, I collect data for the Provincial Bureau of Statistics."

"Do you find it interesting?"

"Work shouldn't be interesting," the young woman said, her voice suddenly cool. "It should be important and necessary for society."

"I admire your determination," Samson ventured a compliment and immediately caught the widow's approving glance.

Nadezhda seemed to blush. She touched her short brown hair, checking the evenness of her fringe, which ended about half an inch above her thick eyebrows.

"I try to set an example as a person of the future," she said softly. "A person of the future should be determined, hardworking and kind. My parents, though they themselves belong to the world of the past, agree with me."

"Where do you live in Kyiv?" Samson asked.

"In Podil. But I work near here, just a few houses down."

"And you walk to and from work every day?"

"Sometimes I walk, other times I take the tram."

"Nadezhda, you should move in with us," the widow cut in. "Samson's all alone now. He'd gladly give you a room."

"Oh, my salary wouldn't allow me to rent a room," the young woman said with genuine regret in her voice.

"You can stay for free!" Samson suggested. "Consider it a room requisitioned for the purposes of work."

"Well, my superiors would need to prepare the proper documentation," the girl said, quite seriously.

"I was joking about that!"

"You know, Samson," she sighed, "walking home from work in the dark is no joke . . ."

Samson apologised and repeated his invitation, though it had actually been the widow who had first extended it.

As they were drinking tea, a shot rang out outside and someone ran off screaming.

"It's time to go," Nadezhda announced nervously.

"Please stay," Samson said.

"No, I have to go, or my mother will be up all night worrying."

She rose to her feet, buttoned up her sheepskin coat and tied the warm shawl around her head.

The widow stared questioningly at Samson. He leapt out of his chair.

"I'll accompany you," he said firmly, in military fashion.

"Thank you," the young woman assented.

"Just give me a moment to wrap up."

Chapter 6

Night-time Kyiv, through which Samson walked back from Podil, amazed and frightened him no end. While accompanying Nadezhda home, he had joked and even ran along Khreshchatyk after a tram carrying, instead of passengers, some bags guarded by Red Army men, promising Nadezhda to bring it to a stop and convince the driver and the soldiers to take them at least as far as Duma Square, but his lighthearted mood gave way to fear as soon as the young woman vanished behind the green front door of a two-storey building on Naberezhno-Mykolska Street. He managed to reach Oleksandrivska without mishap, walking along streets that terrified him with their sudden emptiness. But then a volley of rifle fire burst out above his head, forcing him so far down to the pavement that he could almost touch it with his hands. Failing to determine the source of the fusillade, he remembered Dr Vatrukhin's explanation that the orifice of the ear, freed of its auricle, admits all noises indiscriminately, regardless of direction. He knew, at least, that the volley had come from somewhere on the right. Forcing himself to straighten his back, he picked up his pace so as to cross the open square as quickly as possible.

Just then, from the left, came the ring of an approaching tram. The hour was getting late, so it could only be heading to one of the depots. Pausing under a tree and merging with its trunk in the darkness, Samson watched the vehicle draw near. To his surprise, it wasn't empty, but rather full of people who looked excessively identical – Red Army men. Passing the stop without slowing down, the tram continued on to Mezhyhirska Street, vanishing behind the dark hulks of two- and three-storey buildings.

After letting a minute pass, Samson scurried along the left side of the enormous complex of Hostynnyi Dvir, with its dozens of shops, and from there went up Andrew's Descent.

Here, another shock awaited him. The brief and angry shouts of male voices made him stop and hide behind the corner of a one-storey house with dark windows. From that position, he saw the door of a house on the other side of the Descent, a little higher up, swing open. Red Army soldiers emerged carrying items of furniture. A man in pyjamas leapt out after them and grabbed one of the soldiers by the sleeve. Another soldier unslung his rifle from his shoulder and ran the pyjamaed man through with his bayonet. The man first sank to his knees, then fell face down onto the cobble-stones. A horse snorted. "Load 'er up!" someone yelled, and the horse pulled its cart into the dim light of a street lamp. The soldiers threw a set of chairs onto the cart, then lifted a small dining table, probably for four people, and set it down with its legs in the air.

The door to the house remained wide open. The coachman whipped the horse and turned it uphill, towards St Andrew's Church. Ever so slowly, she pulled her load, and the Red Army men – there may have been four of them – jumped up on the cart too, saving themselves the trouble of walking. The coachman tried to dissuade them by raising his voice, but he quickly fell silent, having received in return a promise to help him part with his life.

Once the cart had disappeared around the gentle curve of the slope, Samson ran up to the man in pyjamas. He was no longer breathing. Then Samson poked his head into the doorway and shouted, "Anyone there?" Without waiting for an answer, he went inside and stepped through another open door into a small flat. Everything was scattered on the floor. A broken cup crunched under his foot. Samson saw the wire of a chandelier stretched along the wall. He found the switch, flipped it, but nothing happened. The flow of power to private households had been cut off that night.

After spending another minute or so over the body of the

murdered man, he gave a heavy sigh and hurried up to Mykhailivska Square. He hurried, yes, but paused every now and again to listen closely, not wishing to overtake the cart bearing the Red Army soldiers with their expensive requisitioned furniture.

He came home just after two, shrouded in the unpleasant scents of uncleaned streets – scents that had congealed in the humid night. Removing his padded jacket, he gave it a sniff and recoiled with a fright. It seemed to have absorbed all those aromas that had irritated his tired soul. Be that as it may, he had to keep warm, so he put the jacket on again. He only had enough strength to light three logs, which would of course produce merely the smell of warmth and no actual heat. But he couldn't very well stay up all night, stoking the stove. He took off his jacket and trousers and went to bed in two pairs of long underwear and a knitted jumper, which he'd pulled on over a thick winter shirt.

Yet sleep never came. As soon as a watery March dawn began to colour the night grey, there was a rude pounding at the door. It sounded exactly like the pounding of the day before, when the Red Army men had come to register privately owned sewing machines. But their rude knock had been followed by a courteous one – the widow's. This time, it appeared she had not accompanied the knockers.

Samson staggered out into the hallway, opened the door just a bit and was immediately pushed aside. Whoever it was brought something into the flat. This all transpired in the morning gloom. The power had yet to be restored, the sun had yet to rise and the sleepy host had not thought to light a candle.

Nevertheless, he noticed that his visitors were once again Red Army soldiers in mouse-coloured overcoats. The thump of their boots accumulated in Samson's head, making it ache. He pressed a finger against his bandaged bare earhole and stepped back. Then a match flared in front of his face and someone peered into his eyes. This short, squinting someone seemed familiar.

"How goes it, landlord?" he said. "We came to see you yesterday, remember?"

Samson nodded.

"We brought our things – three boxes. Hands off, understand? We'll be moving in soon. Commander gave us a paper and everything. All legal, like."

He handed Samson a crumpled sheet of paper.

Silence descended over the flat, but out in the street a horse neighed and cartwheels creaked.

After washing, Samson dressed, went downstairs and knocked on the widow's door.

She was awake and met him on the threshold with a kerosene lamp in her hand, but didn't invite him in.

"They said they're moving into my flat," Samson complained.

"Well, what can I do?" she said with a sigh. "Maybe one of your papa's friends can help?"

"Never mind. I'm sorry I troubled you." The young man turned to go. The first step creaked plaintively beneath him.

As soon as he returned to his flat, the power came on. In the hallway, against the wall, stood three military boxes, without locks. Samson opened the one nearest him, revealing a velvet curtain. Lifting it aside, he saw a silver candlestick, wooden shoe lasts, a cobbler's hammer and a photo-camera.

Samson remembered the sheet of paper he'd received from the shorter soldier. It read: *I hereby confirm that the Red Army soldiers Anton Tsvigun and Fyodor Bravada are to be billeted in 24 Zhylianska Street, Flat 3. The residents of the flat are obliged to feed them and provide them with three changes of underwear, not counting two changes of bed linen.* Beneath that was the word *Commissar* and an illegible signature covered with a smeared stamp.

Samson wilted. What would he feed them? he wondered.

He counted all the Kerensky and Duma roubles remaining in

the house, as well as the locally issued coupons, and also found a few tsarist banknotes and coins. No-one in Kyiv would accept the latter, of course, but – who knows? – rumour had it that Denikin's troops were advancing, edging closer and closer. Denikin was a tsarist through and through – if he should win, he'd certainly restore this double-headed eagle money. The old banknotes were still the largest and most attractive of the bunch. And they were so crisp that their crunch echoed in Samson's head like a bite into a fresh apple. By contrast, the Kerenskys, Dumkas and coupons didn't crunch at all. And their small size said more about the crisis in the paper industry than about their buying power. Although it also said a thing or two about their buying power, if you counted how many of them could fit on a single tsarist three-rouble note.

Maybe I ought to get a job, Samson thought, realising that the money he'd gathered wouldn't last long and remembering how Nadezhda had spoken of her position. It didn't seem to be a burden on her. In fact, she liked being useful. And this way he'd receive a state salary, not to mention ration cards for bread of the first category, rather than the third.

Samson wanted to consult someone who was comfortable with the new regime. There was no point in approaching Dr Vatrukhin, who was clearly in hiding from everything new. Of Samson's fellow students, it was only Babukin whose revolutionary fervour had burned hotter than his hunger for knowledge. He decided to go and see his old friend on Stolypin Street. Samson had never refused Babukin a loan in the old days, so he was sure he could count on his help now.

Inspired by his decision, Samson breakfasted on some porridge from his pantry reserves and washed it down with tea he had recently bought for a hundred Kerenskys, the package for which, with its little elephants, summoned his thoughts to India.

As he was getting ready to go out, the two soldiers whom the commissar with the illegible signature had assigned to his flat showed up at his door.

"I was just leaving," he murmured in confusion as they lowered their rifles to the floor with a thud, stocks down, and rested them against the wall.

"Don't let us stop you. What do we care?" the tall one assured him.

"You must be Fyodor?" the young man ventured, recalling the names on the sheet of paper.

"Nope, I'm Anton – that there's Fyodor." The tall one indicated his partner.

The removal of their overcoats unleashed a wave of body odour.

"No, first I should show you where you'll be staying," Samson suggested, thinking that they might otherwise claim his bedroom.

"Oh, we know where we'll be staying – that room with the counting frames all over the walls," Anton declared. "We don't need much space and we wouldn't want to cramp you."

Samson nodded. "Then I suppose I'll go?" he asked.

"Go, go – you're the landlord around here. Just leave us the key. And, don't worry, if we go, we won't lock the door," added little Fyodor.

The front door of the three-storey building on Stolypin Street was shut tight, and no-one answered Samson's polite knock. Growing angry, he began to pound on it with both fists. It occurred to him that this was exactly how the Red Army men now billeted in his father's study had banged on his own door. He stopped. Just as he was turning for home, the door shyly opened a crack and an old face, its frightened mouth slightly agape, peered out.

"Who are you here for?" the old man asked, his voice trembling with high notes.

"Alexander Valentinovich Babukin."

"He's at work. Should be back by seven."

"Is that so?" Samson was overjoyed. "Then I'll wait."

"Go right ahead. Over there." A hand reached out of the door and pointed to the left. "You'll find a Soviet cafeteria on the corner of Chekhov Lane. They keep it nice and warm."

Chapter 7

No fewer than fifteen Soviet cafeterias had already sprung up in the centre of town. The yard-sweeper's widow had told Samson all about them, including the fact that civil servants could get meals there with special vouchers, but that bread was not included.

Inside, Samson was greeted by the appetising smell of lightly burnt millet porridge. He cautiously approached the cook, who stood on the other side of the serving table.

"Do you serve food without vouchers?" he asked.

"You on the list of the Provincial Executive Committee?" she asked in response, as her eyes began to search for something under the table – apparently, this very list.

"No, I'm just hungry."

She glanced around the room, empty but for one lone woman who was loudly slurping spoonfuls of soup.

"Alright," she said softly and gave a little sigh. "Millet porridge with gravy and tea. Six fifty."

"Six fifty . . . of what?" Samson asked cautiously.

"What do you have?"

"Kerenskys."

"Then twenty," she said in a whisper.

The millet porridge with thick brown gravy was hard to chew, but seemed delicious. The spoon was made of a strangely light, grey-coloured metal, possibly impure aluminium, and its handle was stamped with a five-pointed star. The spoon kept distracting Samson from his food, demanding he examine it closely. His hand, too, accustomed as it was to heavy, noble cutlery, held the spoon uncertainly, even condescendingly. And he also felt that the spoon had its own rusty-sour taste, which remained on the lips after each insertion. Samson washed away this aftertaste with tea, which, with its sweetness, pushed the porridge deeper down his throat and oesophagus. As the plate – inscribed round the rim, in blue, with the words *Soviet Cafeteria* – grew empty, Samson's stomach filled up with weight and a sense of calm. His thoughts gradually shifted from food to other topics, namely, to Nadezhda, whom he'd imagined, before their meeting, as fragile, thin, airy. Although the dinner had flipped this image completely, it hadn't disappointed him at all. He saw in her thickset, athletic build – even in the fact that her black sheepskin coat strained against its buttons – an incredible, almost acrobatic stability in response to the challenges of everyday life, from which all stability had fled.

How can I give her a room now that those soldiers have moved in? he asked himself, not without bitterness. Maybe they'll be transferred somewhere else soon. The army can't live in citizens' flats forever, can it?

Babukin answered the door with some suspicion, but allowed him inside. Of course, after the two revolutions of 1917 and all the blood spilled in 1918, everyone who met an acquaintance, even a friend, whom they hadn't seen in the last two years, was forced to wonder, forebodingly, what that person had been doing all that time.

"You're still over on Zhylianska?" Babukin asked cautiously, straightening the wispy tips of his moustache, which had drooped. He was trimming it differently these days, not the way he used to. Previously, it had been curled into thin sharp brushes pointing up on either side of his nose.

"Yes, same place," Samson responded, sitting down on the chair to which Babukin had pointed, beside the chess table. "But all alone now. Father was recently killed, and Mother and Verusya died of a lung infection."

"Awful," Babukin said with a solemn air, chewing his thick lips.

He seemed to have retained his weight, despite the myriad food crises that succeeded each other, in name if not in effect, with surprising regularity. The milk crisis had supplanted the bread crisis, soon ceding to the butter crisis – butter to meat, meat to cereals, then back to bread again.

"Has the new regime settled anyone with you?" Samson asked, looking around the spacious living room. His attention rested on a tall grandfather clock, which displayed a time that could not have corresponded to reality.

"No, Radomitsky saw to that. He issued me an exemption from requisitions, mobilisations and so on . . ."

Upon hearing the name of another of his former comrades, Samson raised his head and peered with evident curiosity into Babukin's eyes, as if pleading with him to say more.

"He's head of the railways now," the host added. "And railway workers are protected from anything undesirable."

"So, you work on the railways now?"

"What? No, I work at the power plant."

Samson looked up at the single electric bulb glowing in the four-armed chandelier above them.

"Is that so?" he marvelled. "Lucky you! Using your education!"

"Some luck!" Babukin scoffed. "Do you pay for electric power?"

"No," said Samson. "I never get any bills for it."

"None of the citizens pay! The city does, a little, for the trams, and also helps out with fuel – but that's it. And, even then, there's barely any fuel left. We're making electricity with firewood now, if you can believe it. We have two barges of it left, out on the river, but then what? Should we start dismantling wooden bridges?"

"Yes, yes." The guest nodded sympathetically. "I notice we only get power in the evenings – and not every evening, either. Water only in the mornings and evenings, but not every day. Listen, I came to speak to you about something else. Maybe you can find some work for me at the station? I'd like to make myself useful."

"Oh, there's plenty of work." Babukin chuckled. "And the salary's top notch. Only it's never paid."

"What do you mean?"

"Just that. No-one gets paid. Instead, you get vouchers, cards, tickets for pieces of fabric and whatnot. But there's almost no actual money. Because citizens don't pay for electricity ... If that kind of job suits you, I can arrange it."

"I'd have to give it some thought ..." Samson sank in the chair and his host smiled again, this time bitterly.

"Go on, take your time. There's no rush. It's only the people erecting plywood monuments who ought to hurry."

"Why should they hurry?"

"They get paid in currency for each head. A two-headed bust brings in double the money. Artists are in an enviable position, these days – unlike us engineers."

Chapter 8

Back home, in the dark hallway, Samson first tripped on the military boxes, then on a rifle that stood against the wall like a broom. It fell and went off. The young man dropped to his haunches and heard, through the echoing roar, doors slamming shut inside the flat.

When silence was restored, he flipped the switch, just to make sure there really was no power. Then he went into the living room and found matches and a candle where he always kept them. With the candle in hand, he glanced around, wondering where the Red Army men might have gone. He decided to check his father's study. There they were, sitting on the floor in the corner, their faces looking spooked and therefore even more dramatic in the candlelight.

"What the hell was that?" Anton asked in a trembling voice, rising to his feet.

"It's dark," Samson answered guiltily. "One of the rifles fell and went off."

Anton turned and glared angrily at his comrade. "You left yours loaded?"

"What? Mine wasn't loaded!" Fyodor responded, also rising from the floor.

Samson was no longer listening. He was trying to figure out how they would spend the night in the study, where there was only one couch.

"Maybe you'd better sleep in the living room?" he asked.

"Big room's no good," Fyodor replied, scratching his unshaven cheek. "Hard to defend."

"Defend from what?" Samson asked.

"From attack. We've got to be ready to defend our ground. This one's smaller, easier." |

"But how will you defend your ground if your rifles are in the hallway?"

Detecting no irony in the question, the Red Army men exchanged glances.

"We'll bring them in for the night," Anton declared. "But we'll need a mattress and warm blankets, too."

Samson got two narrow mattresses from the wardrobe and some bedclothes out of the chest. He even found a big pillow that reeked of moth repellent.

And so, a double bed took shape on the floor of the study. When the soldiers lay down, their heads touched the desk and their feet hit the couch.

"Alright, time to sleep," Anton said, dismissing their host.

Samson left. He stoked up his stove a bit, all the while listening to the rustling coming from the study, then turned in.

For quite some time, however, the dull, droning wind outside the window kept sleep at bay. When it at last died down, Samson slowly drifted off to the realm of Morpheus. He could already feel its warm waves on his cheeks when a whisper suddenly pulled him back.

"Hey, move over." The voice clearly belonged to Anton.

"I'm on the edge – nowhere to move," the other soldier replied.

"Mattress is damp. We ought to dry it on the stove."

"These stoves aren't worth a damn, not like the real ones at home. All they can do is warm up the air. Too small to sleep on."

"You're right. And they don't even do that. Must be he don't want to waste firewood on us."

The clarity of what he heard alarmed Samson. He opened his eyes and lifted a hand to his bandage: it had slipped off, exposing his earhole.

"Should we just kill him?" Fyodor whispered. "Fellow's useless, but the flat's grand. I'm sure we'd find plenty of stuff."

"Go to sleep," the other responded. "Killing's your answer to everything. What will you do when they ban it, now that you've got so used to it? Join up with bandits?"

"I ain't used to it. It still hurts to see folks dead."

"What did the commissar tell us yesterday? Remember? No accidents."

Samson adjusted his bandage and cautiously sat up in bed, focusing entirely on his sense of hearing. It became increasingly clear to him that his severed ear, which lay in the drawer of his father's desk, was warning him of danger. Otherwise, how would he have heard these whispers?

Should I run? he wondered, and immediately shook his head. There was nowhere to run. He might go down to the widow's, sit there until the morning. She'd let him in. But then what? And, after all, this was his house, his flat – why should he run? Maybe he ought to take one of those rifles and kill them instead? But how would he check whether the one that hadn't fallen was loaded? And if there was only a single cartridge, then the second soldier would kill him. Unlike him, they knew how to kill – the army teaches a person that much. Or did their army only recruit those who'd already learned how to kill on their own? Just look at how many corpses had littered Kyiv's streets a year earlier. Later, too. And when his father was killed . . .

Samson got up without making a sound. The cold wooden floor pricked his bare feet. He felt around for his slippers, put them on and his feet grew warmer.

"No need to kill him," Anton whispered again, and for a moment Samson felt grateful to him.

"It was just an idea." Fyodor yawned loudly.

"You wouldn't want to live with a corpse in the flat, would you?" the tall Red Army man went on. "And we're not supposed to throw bodies out on the street anymore. The yard-sweeper will kick up a fuss, plus the patrols . . ."

"It's so goddamn cold . . . And these lice just won't quit . . . Little bastards must be cold, too," Fyodor said, and yawned again.

"Why should they be cold? You're still alive – keeping them warm."

After that, they fell silent, and a minute later Samson heard snoring. At first, he was afraid that he'd have to listen to it all night long, but then the snorer turned to a more comfortable position and brought peace to Samson's head.

He went into the living room and stood in the dark. The cold air made him shiver. Then he got dressed and, with a candle in one hand and an empty sack in the other, went down to the cellar for firewood. He gathered about fifteen logs and, taking care to avoid the creaky first step of the staircase, returned to his flat.

He stoked up the stove that warmed the living room and his bedroom, and then decided to stoke up the second one, the back of which heated his father's study. He didn't skimp on firewood, placing even more in that burner. His hope was that the Red Army soldiers would sleep longer if they were warm, and would, perhaps, wake up in a good and peaceful mood.

In the morning, they did indeed emerge from the study in a benevolent manner. After taking their turns washing and snorting in the bathroom (the plumbing worked, surprisingly), they slung their rifles over their shoulders and left without a word.

In the clear light of day, Samson saw that the bullet from the fallen rifle had split the thick oak door leading into the living room and had got stuck in it. The damage was unpleasant to the eye but hardly noticeable, since it was so low down, about an inch from the floor.

As his thoughts turned from the evening's mishap to the present moment, Samson realised that it was Friday – the day Dr Vatrukhin was to wash out his eyes.

He set off to see the doctor in his padded jacket and untidy, wrinkled trousers, so as not to attract attention on the street. And this time he locked the door behind him, on the assumption that the Red Army service day ended late.

Along Zhylianska, puddles squelched beneath the boots of passers-by. The drifts of frozen rubbish were especially pungent, which meant that spring had again begun to battle winter for its rightful calendrical space. March reluctantly approached April. From somewhere nearby came the clanging of a tram, and in a moment it emerged from Volodymyrska and kept clanging as it sped along Zhylianska towards its final stop.

The sound of hammer blows stopped Samson in his tracks at the corner of Kuznechna. He looked around and spotted a worker atop a wooden ladder propped against one of the houses. The man was nailing a square of plywood over the street sign. The plywood bore an inscription in black: PROLETARIAN STREET.

On reaching the doctor's house, Samson was seized with a certain uneasiness before he could determine its cause. The long signboard announcing that a specialist in diseases of the eye was seeing patients no longer hung above the door. Samson's heart sank and Fyodor's night whisper surfaced in his mind: *Should we just kill him?*

These terrible forebodings, however, did not turn Samson back. He overcame them and knocked on the door politely, as if nothing were amiss.

The doctor's elderly servant let him in at once. She didn't look well. Her face was pale, and the dark circles around her eyes spoke of a sleepless night.

"Oh, yes," the doctor exclaimed, evidently delighted to see Samson. "You didn't forget! Come on, come on. Tonya is just tidying up in here."

The old woman was indeed sweeping up broken glass. The doctor was wearing a warm dressing gown, but sawdust and other minor carpentry debris clung to the fabric on his shoulders and chest.

"We had an unpleasant adventure here last night," said Dr Vatrukhin, brushing off the dirt he seemed to notice only now, thanks to Samson's persistent gaze. "Two soldiers burst into the house and dragged me out of bed. One of them pointed his rifle right at me and shouted, 'Fix it!' It turned out that, in the heat of a political dispute, he had gouged out his comrade's eye with his bayonet. Then, as ill luck would have it, he saw my sign . . . So, here he was, pushing this poor fellow with his leaking socket towards me and shouting, 'Fix it, bastard!' I tried to explain to him that there was nothing left to fix . . . In any case, I took the one-eyed fellow into my office and treated his wound, while the other one kept on shouting and poking me in the side with his bayonet. I explained that I had done everything I could. The important thing now was to prevent sepsis, keep the socket dry. But the irate soldier wouldn't have it. 'Fix it,' he shouts, 'or I'll fix you good!' More bad luck: he spots an artificial eye in my medicine cabinet – an advertising sample, purely decorative, which I'd kept in memory of my late friend, a great prosthetist. The soldier smashes the glass with his bayonet, grabs the eye and hands it to me, saying, 'Get it in there and save my comrade.' I explain that artificial eyes are made to order, sized individually for each patient, and are only inserted after the socket has healed. In the end, he shoves the eye into the pocket of his overcoat and takes his comrade away, threatening to come back and leave no stone unturned. Once they were gone, I woke up the yard-sweepers from the houses on either side and the three of us took down my sign. The men took the sign in payment, for kindling. Enough about that. I've already recovered, caught my breath. The only thing left to do is to repair the lock on the door. Now, show me those eyes."

The doctor freed Samson's corneas of foreign particles and carefully examined the retinas.

"Less red?" he asked.

"Less," Samson answered.

"I see you never did wash the bandage," the doctor said, shaking his head. "I can't give you a new one – it would be of no medical use."

"That's fine. I'll ask my neighbour to wash it," Samson responded. "There just wasn't enough time. I've been looking for a job, but so far nothing has turned up."

"A job? Under them?" Vatrukhin asked doubtfully. But then his voice softened a bit. "Maybe that would be best. They say it's easier to work under them than under the tsar. No-one is exploited. No-one looks over your shoulder, watching your every move. Salary, cards, vouchers . . . To be honest, I myself thought of getting a job at the Oleksandrivska Clinical Hospital. I went over there, and some twenty-year-old student told me that medicine was free now, which meant that doctors should treat people without expecting a salary. Doctors, he said, had earned enough under the tsar. I was a citizen of a hostile class, he told me, third category, and was entitled to no more than half a pound of bread. They should have assigned me to the second category – after all, I'm not a merchant – but, no, it turns out I'm an exploiter, because I have a servant. It didn't matter, of course, that I had told Tonya to go, that she was free . . . 'Your time has come,' I told her. But she said, 'Nikolay Nikolaevich, I have nowhere to go. I'll stay here with you.' If they at least restored order, got rid of the bandits and soldiers, that alone would be worth it . . ." The doctor sighed.

Just then, Tonya appeared at the door, having returned after taking out the broken glass. "I'll make you some tea," she said firmly.

"Do, do," the doctor responded approvingly. "Tea is the one medication that has no side effects."

Chapter 9

That night the Red Army men didn't disturb Samson with their whispering. All he heard was Fyodor's complaint that he missed his mother and that she'd never cope with the crops without his peasant hands.

In the morning, the sun peeped into Samson's room through the dirty window, its rays emphasising both the griminess of the panes and the general mess for which his parents, had they still been alive, would have reprimanded him in the strongest terms. The resonant crows of Kyiv cawed vigorously and joyfully out on the street.

The silence in the living room led Samson to believe that the soldiers were still sleeping. He retrieved a broom and dustpan from the cupboard and went back to his room to sweep the floor.

Suddenly he heard a polite knock at the front door.

As he made his way through the hallway, Samson noticed that the rifles were gone.

He opened the unlocked door.

"Been ordered to give every tenant this here 'directive'," the yard-sweeper's widow announced, thrusting a yellowish sheet of paper into his hands. "Also, today's a community work day. We've got to clear the rubbish off the streets. No getting out of it. We start at ten."

The news about the work day didn't darken Samson's light, sunny mood. The directive, on the other hand, which had been printed with minimal ink, gave him pause.

Citizen residents, as of 22 March this year, the city of Kyiv will begin requisitioning excess furniture for the purposes of equipping Soviet institutions. The requisitions will be carried out by the Red Army and representatives of the Provincial Executive Committee in the presence of authorised house committees. In exchange for the furniture taken, each citizen will be given a document confirming the list of requisitioned items with a stamp and signature.

Items deemed necessary for living and not subject to requisition are: a chair and a bed for each family member or tenant, as well as one wardrobe, one dining table and one desk per family. Kitchen furniture not mentioned above is not subject to requisition.

Having read and reread the directive, which had been signed and stamped by the chairman of the Provincial Executive Committee, Samson decided to check his father's desk and cautiously entered the study. The Red Army men were gone, but the two mattresses, sheets all crumpled, still lay on the floor, surrounded by the soldiers' things. And their smell, too, stood immobile, like a pillar – a strange mixture of mustiness, tobacco smoke and machine or gun oil.

The first thing Samson did was check the top drawer. The tin was where he'd left it, as were the other papers and the family passport. Order still reigned in the bottom drawer as well: the German pencil holder on the left, next to the old paid bills, and the old unpaid bills on the right.

Samson pulled out the unpaid stack and leafed through them. They all dated back to 1917. There were bills from the urban water-supply system, the power plant and the mineral-water shop that had closed long ago, as well as one for a pair of horn-rimmed spectacles and another for a medicated foot ointment.

He slipped the bills back into place and, in the depths of the desk, found the vial of Lain ointment his father had used to treat the eczema on his feet. He turned it in his hands a couple of times, then put it back and closed the drawer.

Leaning over the desk, he opened the window, hoping to dilute the Red Army aroma with a bit of fresh air. A hubbub unusually loud and garrulous for a Saturday burst into the study. On the other side of Zhylianska, two well-dressed elderly men were chipping away at the edges of their rubbish drift, one with a shovel, the other with a short crowbar.

"Work day," remembered Samson, and closed the window, but not completely, so that the street and the study could exchange breaths.

Donning the most workmanlike, nondescript garments he could find, Samson went downstairs and saw the yard-sweeper's widow hand his neighbour Ovetsky a big heavy crowbar.

He himself was given a coal shovel, a tool imperfectly suited to cracking frozen drifts. But he had no alternative. The sounds of spring resounded up and down Zhylianska. The sun was surprisingly steadfast in the sky, eroding the iced-up rubbish with its rays. Cars, carriages and carts rattled past over the cobblestones. Cart drivers hurled curses as clumps of black snow and chunks of dirty ice flew under their horses' hooves. The frost that had held captive the frozen effluvium of the city's disorderly winter was receding, letting the stench of rubbish escape into the air. But this process was gradual, so that people had time to get thoroughly used to the smells of sour kvass and last year's mould, and then to other smells, none of which made them yearn for roses in the countryside or overturned powder boxes. Everyone was diligently destroying the drifts in front of their houses and, it seemed, rejoicing at the opportunity to do some physical labour on the weekend. Several times already this had been declared "holiday" work, yet it wasn't clear to Samson whether work could be a holiday – and, if it could, how exactly should it be celebrated?

About thirty yards away, towards Kuznechna, several women were working at a substantial drift – and they actually did seem to be treating the occasion as a holiday. It was almost as if they were dancing. Samson would glance in their direction every time their cheerful, perky voices cut through the din directly around him.

From time to time, Red Army patrols passed by, stopping briefly at each drift, examining the work-day participants and either commenting or joking among themselves through their moustaches and black teeth, as evidenced by the sometimes sunny, sometimes malevolent gleam in their eyes. Needless to say, at their approach, all the participants would redouble their efforts. Even Ovetsky, who was barely strong enough to handle a broom, much less a crowbar, would strike at the drift with renewed vigour.

By means of head-shaking and various hand gestures, the latest patrol expressed uncertainty that the day would end in victory for Samson and his neighbour.

Samson threw another envious glance down the street, at the cheerful ladies, whose drift was by now almost gone. And suddenly it seemed to him that, among the sonorous workers, he recognised Nadezhda.

He lowered his shovel onto the cobblestones and decided to walk over and check whether his eyes had deceived him.

But, no, it really was Nadezhda. And the building was none other than the Bureau of Statistics, where she worked.

"Well, how's it going?" she asked affably, recognising the young man.

"Terrible," Samson admitted. "It's just the two of us. The yard-sweeper's widow didn't even come out to help."

"Well, we'll help you – that's our way!" she exclaimed mischievously, looking around at her friends. They nodded.

The beautiful ladies, all invigorated by their Saturday labours, accompanied Samson back to his building. Brand new steel shovels glinted in their hands. Neighbour Ovetsky decided to get out of their way and catch his breath, while Samson picked up the crowbar and set about stabbing the drift with its heavy tip. Work was going well, now. The widow's astonished face appeared in the ground-floor window, and across it spread a kind, friendly smile.

"Why did so few of you come out?" Nadezhda asked, shovel in hand.

"There just aren't that many of us. The Guzeevs from the second floor rode off to Odesa back at the beginning of February, and my next-door neighbour's wife is nursing her child."

"Yes, that makes sense. You're in a residential building, while we have an entire institution, with lots of people. Oh, look!" she exclaimed, her attention drawn by something behind Samson's back.

Four Chinese Red Army soldiers approached the drift with brisk steps, talking loudly and cheerfully in their language. They gestured to the young women to step aside, took their rifles from their shoulders and began to inflict significant bayonet blows upon the frozen rubbish. Having crumbled the mound's upper layer, they waved their hands, smiled and left.

There was little left to do. Having dismantled the drift and covered the whole pavement with its fragments, the weekend workers dispersed to their homes. Nadezhda and Samson, however, were invited to the widow's flat for tea. She summoned them directly from her window. And, after tea, Samson asked the young woman whether she would like to take a walk with him through the Merchants' Garden. She readily agreed, since the Garden was on her daily route to and from work anyway.

The sun had already hidden behind the clouds, but the air was still warm. Two trams were standing at the terminus in what used to be called Tsar's Square. A crowd of would-be passengers bustled about them. The stairs leading to the observation platform and the summer theatre were also crowded. Samson in his overcoat – he'd run home after tea to change – and Nadezhda in her sheepskin were as kindred spirits to all these promenaders enjoying a sunny Saturday afternoon.

"It's amazing how one doesn't feel history here," the girl suddenly observed.

"What history?" Samson asked.

"The history that's changing the world this very moment. One doesn't feel the war here, and yet our army is preparing for a decisive battle – a battle against all enemies. Do you understand?" She looked inquisitively at her companion.

Samson nodded. "I understand about the enemies," he said. "But here the soldiers billeted in my flat miss their village, their land. You shouldn't take so many people away from their land . . ."

"Yes, the only thing on peasant minds these days is what the harvest will look like," Nadezhda agreed. "But that's precisely what should inspire them to defeat the enemy! That way, they can go home sooner. After all, workers also want to return to their factories and families. This impatience for victory should aid us!"

Samson sighed. They were approaching the edge of the observation platform. Twilight was just around the corner and most of the promenaders were already turning back towards the head of the stairs beside the former Merchants' Hall. By the time Samson and Nadezhda reached the platform, they were alone.

"Can you see your house from here?" Samson asked.

"No," she answered, shaking her head. "But isn't it beautiful, how the smoke rises from the chimneys?"

"It is," Samson replied.

"I love it when the air smells of chimney smoke in the winter," Nadezhda intoned dreamily. "But, to appreciate it, you have to go to the dachas, where the air is clean. Not so long ago, the smoke would rise in columns that looked like they were propping up the sky, but now the wind blows it away too quickly . . ."

"People used to burn coal, and coal smoke is denser, more stable," the young man explained. "Nowadays they burn firewood, sometimes even books, and wood smoke is light, shapeless – dissipates with the slightest breath."

"Oh, the street lamps have come on!" Nadezhda pointed down at the lights of Podil. "I wonder where they get the electricity?"

"Also from firewood." Samson chuckled. "Only there isn't much to go around. A friend of mine from the power plant was complaining that their supplies were running low. When all the wood is burned, the lights will go out."

"Oh, come now," Nadezhda scoffed. "Kyiv is surrounded by forests!"

"Yes, there are plenty of forests, but no lumberjacks. They've all been mobilised into the army."

"That's alright. If need be, they'll announce a weekend work day, issue everyone with an axe and take them off to the forest on the number 19 tram," the young woman declared confidently.

"Will they issue you with an axe?"

"Of course they will! What makes me any different?" she responded, turning round and giving Samson a confident smile. "Oh, I forgot!" She opened her purse, which hung from the crook of her elbow. With a bit of rustling, she pulled out something wrapped in newspaper and unfolded it, revealing an odd bread-like item in the form of a hammer. "Do you prefer sweet or salty?"

"Sweet," the young man confessed.

She broke off the head of the hammer-bun, leaving the handle for herself.

"The Red Bakery made this for us – a gift for our weekend work day. It was a weekend work day for them, too. The head has a filling of plum butter, the handle of stewed cabbage."

Nadezhda took a bite of her savoury piece and her eyes lit up with joy. Samson carefully bit into his part as well, but failed to reach the butter.

Chapter 10

On returning from Podil to Zhylianska without incident or danger, Samson spotted a cart lined with straw parked in front of his building. Its driver was in the process of unfolding a tarpaulin and spreading it over the straw. The double doors of the front entrance slowly opened and a Red Army soldier exited backwards with something in his hands. Samson stopped in his tracks when he realised that his guests, Anton and Fyodor, were bringing out his father's desk. They set it down beside the cart. After them came another military man, older and wearing a black leather jacket instead of an overcoat.

"Excuse me –" Samson hurried up to them – "What do you think you're doing? That's my desk!"

"We told you it was in our way," Fyodor tried to explain, in a guilty voice.

"Citizen, your desk has been requisitioned," the man in the jacket said, turning to Samson. "The yard-sweeper was tasked with informing you. We lacked the means to transport it earlier. Load it up!"

The soldiers pulled themselves up, lifted the desk and placed it upside down on the tarpaulin. Samson distinctly heard the objects in its drawers rattle like coins in a jug.

"But those are my things! My documents!" he shouted, feeling the same helplessness he had felt the day his father was killed.

"The drawers are sealed. Nothing will be lost," said the man in the jacket.

"What do you mean, nothing will be lost? Where are you taking it?"

"To the police station on Tarasivska."

"The police station?" Samson asked, taken aback, recalling how he and a friend from university had been brought there two years ago for participating in a demonstration in Tsar's Square, near the monument to Alexander II. They had been accused of stealing the silver wreaths from the fence around the statue, but the wreaths were quickly found; it turned out that they'd been taken by some workers from the Arsenal factory. And so Samson and his friend hadn't even spent the night at the station, but he remembered the setting well: plump leather sofas of incredible size and weight, and equally massive desks littered with folders and topped with lamps on marble columns.

"But they have plenty of furniture!" Samson declared, gazing with sudden resolve at the man in the jacket.

"The station was cleaned out. The robbers took axes to whatever they couldn't fit through the doors," the man responded. Then he shouted to the cart driver, "What are you waiting for? Go!"

The driver whipped the horse and pulled on the left rein. The cart began to turn around, its wheels creaking and throwing fragments of frozen rubbish at the men's feet.

That was the cue for Anton and Fyodor to go back inside. Samson followed them with his eyes, then turned and watched the man in the jacket jump onto the cart. For a minute or so, he felt once more as if he'd been violently deprived of an important part of his body, but then some force pushed him in the back and he set off after the cart. When the horse sped up, Samson did too, so as not to fall behind and let his father's desk out of his sight. At that moment, it seemed to him that he was running behind the cart that had taken his father's coffin to the cemetery on Shchekavytsia Hill.

Soon the cart pulled up in front of the familiar brick police building. The man in the jacket went inside and emerged with three soldiers. They took the desk off the cart and carried it as it had lain, upside down, into the station. The driver jumped down from his box, poked his head through the open doors and shouted something about his fee. In response to his cry, the man in the jacket came out and handed him a piece of paper the size of a Kerensky rouble, but clearly not money. The driver brought the paper close to his face, turned it every which way, then looked enquiringly at the representative of the police. His eyes hurled an obscene gaze and he walked away.

As he watched the empty cart drive off, Samson gathered enough courage to approach the station and step inside.

"Where you going?" asked a Red Army soldier standing inside the doorway, his right hand on the barrel of a rifle resting butt-down on the floor.

"They've just brought in my desk," the young man tried to explain. "I don't know where exactly they took it."

"Up there," the soldier said, nodding towards a wooden staircase with beautiful red railings.

"May I?" Samson asked.

"Sure," the soldier replied, looking respectfully at the visitor's bandaged head.

Samson ran up the steps and came face to face with a man wearing an old green tunic and blue trousers. The tunic and trousers were from different uniforms and Samson failed to put them together in his thoughts – nor did the man's tired, irritated gaze give him much time to try.

"What do you want?" the man asked hoarsely.

Concisely but haltingly, Samson explained the purpose of his visit, mentioning the "directive" concerning the requisitioning of excess furniture, which stated that one desk per family was not excessive and promised that a document would be given in exchange for any items seized. He hadn't received any document, and the desk had clearly been requisitioned on the basis of a complaint made by his two guests, whose sleep this piece of furniture had disrupted.

The man beckoned him into a room and pointed to a desk,

which Samson immediately recognised. Its drawers were indeed sealed with mastic.

"That's the one?" the man asked.

"Yes." Samson nodded.

"Well, then, take a seat and write out a detailed report about the entire incident," the man said, then fetched two sheets of paper and a thick, unsharpened pencil. The word he had used in relation to the requested document inspired respect and trust, and even a touch of hope for a positive outcome.

Samson moved a lone chair from the corner of the empty room up to the desk, sat down and glanced critically at the ceiling, from which a dim lamp just about shone.

The man silently brought a table lamp from another room and plugged it in.

Now there was nothing left for Samson to do but to write the report.

"Start with a bit about yourself – surname, brief biographical information, address," the man suggested.

Samson laid everything out, sparing no detail. He certainly did not neglect to mention the death of his father, hoping that this might reflect well on him personally, since victims are seldom regarded as negative characters in life.

A short time later, the man received two sheets completely covered in neat handwriting.

"You go on home," he said with a sigh. "I'll read it in the morning."

"Why not now?"

"My eyes need a rest. Come back in the morning, at ten. I live here, so you won't miss me. Ask for Nayden."

"And ... they won't take it somewhere else?" Samson asked, nodding at the desk.

"They won't. I promise," the man with the strange surname assured him firmly.

Samson straightened the bandage on his head, tightening it with an automatic movement of his fingers, and went out to the staircase.

The flat's open doors immediately reminded the owner, upon his return, that he was no longer the owner. Two bayonetted rifles stood propped against the wall, like brooms in a yard-sweeper's cupboard. Next to them was a sack, stuffed to capacity. Samson flipped a switch and the lightbulb flashed on, but almost instantly went out again, its faint glow trembling like a candle's flame. He looked inside the sack and pulled out a piece of fabric. It turned out to be a pattern for a vest, with bold chalk lines indicating the future seams. Clearly the Red Army men had wasted no time and had paid a visit to a tailor. Cold damp air wafted towards Samson's face from the living room, forcing him to go down to the cellar for firewood without changing his clothes.

After stoking up the stove that warmed his bedroom, he turned to the one that warmed his father's study. That was where the soldiers were sleeping now, having freed up the space in the most underhand fashion.

Anger bubbled up in Samson's thoughts, but he tamped it down and dutifully stoked their stove, only this time consciously skimping on firewood.

He couldn't sleep all night. On several occasions, when he seemed to perceive their secret, conspiratorial whispering, he would approach the door of the study on tiptoe, press his left and only ear against it and hear nothing but silence or solitary, meaningless snoring.

Towards morning, he imagined that, when he saw them face to face, he would not hesitate to express all his unpleasant thoughts directly. And they, being common folk, would be unable to offer any explanation – their response would be violence. What then? Would he pit more of his reason against their violence? Provoke them to greater violence? No . . .

He decided to leave home early and take a long walk before going over to Tarasivska to meet Comrade Nayden.

As he descended the stairs, Samson intentionally placed his foot on the first creaky step. He knew that the sound would draw out the yard-sweeper's widow, and that it did. She invited him in for tea.

In the end, instead of taking his long walk, he sat for more than an hour in the widow's warm kitchen, which overflowed with the smells of the simple life. He told her of his promenade in the Merchants' Garden with Nadezhda, but he didn't mention his desk and was somewhat surprised that she didn't ask him about it. She couldn't have missed the Red Army soldiers carrying it out of the building. Yet their chat over tea didn't touch on the ill-fated item. Meanwhile, the street outside awoke and began to bustle.

"If you need to hide something, you can always give it to me for safekeeping," the widow said at parting. "They'll be coming round again tomorrow – after more free quartering. You'd better save what needs saving, you hear?"

Chapter 11

"Vasyl, get the tea going!" Comrade Nayden shouted, seeing yesterday's desk-minded visitor climbing up the stairs with the red railings.

Nayden led Samson into the same office and the young man was amazed at the changes that had taken place overnight. Now, in addition to his desk and the old chair, a bookless bookcase stood against the wall, with two impressive club chairs on either side of it. There was also a chess table in front of the chair on the right.

"Take a seat," said Nayden, pointing to that very chair. "Let's have some tea."

Samson carefully lowered himself into the chair, which accepted him softly and respectfully, as if he were a person of great significance. For a moment, he felt he was.

"I read your report." Nayden exhaled thoughtfully. "You write well."

A greying, round-shouldered man came into the office with two mugs of tea. He handed one to Nayden, who had sunk into the second club chair, and the other to Samson.

"Your write well," Nayden repeated, after Vasyl stepped out. "It's been a long time since I read something so smoothly written. You express your thoughts accurately, in detail."

"Thank you," Samson replied, expecting Nayden to change the subject and get to the point.

Nayden did, but the visitor was not pleased.

"I am forced to turn down your request," he said, after a pause. "The officer who requisitioned the desk will be punished on two accounts – requisitioning a desk that is not subject to requisition and failing to issue a document concerning the requisitioned desk. But the desk itself –” Nayden threw a thoughtful glance at the subject of their conversation – “that we need, badly. The cases are piling up, yet we've got nothing on which to do the work – and almost no-one to do it . . .”

He turned and faced Samson expectantly.

The young man wilted, realising that the previous evening's strenuous efforts to trace a convincing argument on paper had been in vain.

“I see it is dear to you,” Nayden added sympathetically.

“It was my father's desk. In the drawer . . . our family pass-port . . .”

“Well, those documents will soon be useless. We'll be issuing new ones,” Nayden assured him. He took a sip of tea and grimaced, having apparently scalded his lip on the rim of the mug. “How did you feel about Denikin when he was in charge?” he asked, forgetting about his lip.

“Not good.”

“And about Skoropadskyi?”

“The same as everyone else,” Samson answered cautiously. “Like we felt about his Germans.”

“I see,” Nayden nodded. “And did you sympathise with the Directorate?”

“Why would I?” the young man responded in a surprised voice.

“Well, how about our workers' regime?”

Samson suddenly looked at his interlocutor with real pity in his eyes.

“I sympathise with you,” he said, referring specifically to the sleep-deprived man before him, whose way of life had almost obliterated his facial features.

Nayden was silent for a while, then went over to the desk, fetched Samson's report and sank back into his chair.

“I can only help you if you're willing to help us,” he pronounced.

"How can I help?"

"We must put a stop to all the banditry and disorder out there. To do that, we need a cadre of determined –" Nayden glanced at Samson's frayed bandage – "of determined and competent people . . . If you agree to join us, this will be your work desk. The whole office will be yours. We'll also put in a couch, so you can get some rest without leaving the premises."

"I don't understand . . . What would I do here?" Samson looked around, trying to imagine his future in the office.

"Well, we'll decide on the exact position, but your duty would be to combat crime and restore order. We'll provide you with everything we can. I can give you vouchers for the Soviet cafeteria as soon as tomorrow, if you agree."

Samson hesitated. The sabre that had killed his father flashed up in his memory, as did the sabre that had cut off his ear – the ear that now lay here, in this office, in the upper left-hand drawer of his father's desk. It appeared that the desk itself had moved from his flat to the police station in order to avenge the death of its owner, to take part in the struggle for order, which was nowhere to be seen, not even in Samson's flat, now shared with Anton and Fyodor.

"Will I be given a weapon?" the young man asked, or rather nearly demanded, looking at his interlocutor intently.

"Of course!"

"Then I'm in," Samson said, his lips immediately going dry. He desperately needed a sip of tea, which had had time to cool down.

"Good man," Nayden said with a nod. "I'll bring some paper and we'll make it official, in accordance with regulations."

"And will I be allowed to retrieve my possessions from the drawers?"

"It's your desk – you can take out anything you like, or keep it there. But Comrade Pasechny must be the one to remove the seals, since he was the one to affix them."

Chapter 12

"Nadezhda told me about you," Trofim Sigismundovich said with a smile as he shook Samson's hand. He was a short, slightly stooped man of about fifty, white-shirted, with a waistcoat arresting his belly and a blanket thrown over his shoulders. "My daughter and I have no secrets. Do come in. Mila, dear, put on some tea!" This last was directed at his wife, who scurried out of the room to fulfil her assignment.

Nadezhda's father seated Samson on a soft chair and sat down on the couch beside it.

"She should be back any moment, our Nadezhda. She went to pay a visit to her aunt, who lives just a few doors down."

Sensing, in Nadezhda's absence, a cautious distance between himself and her parents, whom he was meeting for the first time, Samson spoke little and slowly. To remain completely silent, of course, would not have been polite.

"It's a bit cold in here," he said, his eyes roaming the room in search of a stove. He spotted it in the opposite corner – a slender column, covered with emerald-coloured tiles.

"You mean your home is warmer?" Trofim Sigismundovich asked with some surprise, covering his legs with the sides of the blanket. "We're almost used to it by now ... But we are indeed looking forward to spring."

"No, it isn't any warmer," Samson responded, rubbing his palms together. His gaze shifted to the door as his hostess, who'd been sent to make tea, came back into the room. "But spring is fast approaching. They're already clearing the rubbish off the streets."

Nadezhda's father nodded. "Do you have a dacha?" he asked.

"A dacha? We had one, near Vasylkiv ... I've no idea what's become of it."

"You haven't been there in some time, I gather?"

Samson's heart sank as he realised with horror that he hadn't even thought of his family's dacha – the cosy summer house of his sweet childhood – in two years. After his mother and sister had passed away, his father never mentioned it. Now, he recalled the long road there by horse-drawn carriage, as well as his father's lists of things needed for the summer, with ticks next to each packed item. Lord, how can so seemingly recent a past feel so distant, as if one had read it in a book and not lived it?

"Yes, a long time," Samson responded.

"You seem sad, young man," Trofim Sigismundovich said, gazing with sympathy into his guest's face. "Was your dacha ... robbed?"

"I couldn't even say," Samson admitted, hearing in his own voice something like tears for the past.

"Don't despair. As soon as things settle down, you'll go and have a look. The ocean can be stormy for months, but eventually it grows calm, throws dead fish ashore – nature cleanses itself and rests."

Samson gave a faint smile. Nadezhda's mother brought in a kettle and began to set the table. The sound of heels striking against the wooden floor reached them from the hallway and Nadezhda appeared at the door. She wore her sheepskin coat and had a warm kerchief round her head.

"We have a guest?" she asked excitedly, her eyes sparkling at Samson. "Had I known, I would have come back earlier."

"Well, I showed up without warning," Samson said, wanting to give her an excuse. "I have some good news to share."

"What news?" she asked, as she removed her kerchief and hung it neatly on the back of a chair. Then she unbuttoned her coat and sat down.

"I've found a job," the young man announced.

"Is that so? Where?"

"With the police – Lybid District."

"Oh, that's not far from your flat, on Tarasivska! How convenient," she said, smiling broadly.

"On Tarasivska?" Nadezhda's father repeated, turning to his wife, who was already filling cups with tea. "That's where we would go to visit the Savelyevs, you remember?"

"Not the Savelyevs, the Trushkins," his wife corrected him. "The Savelyevs were on Nazarivska, and the Trushkins lived near the Mariinsky Children's Home, on Pankivska."

"Ah, yes," the head of the family conceded. "I've got it all mixed up."

Without removing the blanket from his shoulders, Trofim Sigismundovich moved over to the table. They all arranged themselves in a friendly circle.

Seeing that nothing edible had been offered with the tea, Samson felt a slight pang of hunger. But then a great noise burst into his head, as if a bird, its wings frantically aflutter, had tried to fly into his bare earhole through the bandage. He covered his right temple with his palm, eliciting questioning looks from both Nadezhda's father and mother.

"Has the wound not healed?" Trofim Sigismundovich asked sympathetically.

"It still hurts sometimes," Samson answered, lowering his hand and feeling rather awkward.

But then he heard the noise again and looked around, searching for its source. He caught another shyly curious glance from the hostess.

Suddenly, against the background of this incomprehensible noise, two shots rang out – as if right inside Samson's head. They made him leap up and, for some reason, rush to the window. He looked out onto the street from the height of the first floor, seeing no movement and not a soul below.

"Did you hear that?" he asked no-one in particular.

"Hear what?" Nadezhda's father responded.

"The gunshots!"

"No," Nadezhda said, with obvious concern. "I didn't hear any."

The noises continued to pile up in Samson's head. Now, he heard the drawn-out creak of furniture being dragged across a wooden floor. At last, he guessed the source of all these sounds, and the possibility both frightened him and made him profoundly uncomfortable in front of Nadezhda's family.

"Excuse me, but I have to go," he announced as he turned his back to the window and quickly made for the hallway. He leapt down the wooden steps to the front door and really did take off running down the street, feeling both strength and fatigue in his legs, and trying to avoid the frozen rubbish scattered across the cobblestones – fragments of the drifts the weekend workers had apparently struggled with all over town. After several minutes, he slowed down against his will, sensing an unbearable weight descending onto his shoulders. Then he saw a horse-drawn cab by the side of the road and jumped in.

"To the police station on Tarasivska!" he shouted to the motionless galoot on the bench seat.

The man wore a fur hat with its earflaps down. He turned his head, revealing hostile eyes, a twisted mouth and a watery beard.

"Nothing doing," he hissed. "I can't feed my bay with your vouchers – I work for oats."

Samson pulled from his coat pocket a forty-Kerensky-rouble note. The cabby's thick hand emerged from the wide sleeve of his baggy, many-folded, red-belted, dark blue coat and snatched the money. Immediately, it seemed as if both his shoulders rose, but in reality he only raised his right hand and whipped his bay, shouting, "Giddy-up!"

The cab's wheels rattled on the cobblestones, while Samson, trying to catch his breath, looked around and also ahead of them.

The cabby pulled at the reins and shouted, "Whoa!" Samson jumped down before the horse could stop. He dashed through the open doors of the police station and up the stairs, gripping the red railing with his left hand. When he reached the door of the office that Nayden had assigned to him, he saw a Red Army soldier lying face down in front of his father's desk. On the floor to the right, leaning his back against one of the club chairs, sat Nayden. His palm was pressed against a wound above his heart, which had darkened the upper part of his tunic with blood. Two more Red Army men were for some reason standing idle to the left of the scene. They glanced sideways at Samson, who rushed over to Nayden.

"What happened?" he cried out. "Are you injured?"

"They're getting a doctor," Nayden got out. "These fools brought in a deserter but didn't bother to search him. He pulled out a revolver and fired off a shot before I killed him."

Feet pounded up the stairs, and a moment later a young fellow with a yellow bag in his hand was pushed into the office. Behind him, breathing heavily, came the man in the black leather jacket who'd requisitioned Samson's desk.

"There, fix him up!" he barked at the young fellow, nodding towards Nayden.

"Who is that?" Nayden asked.

"A doctor! Straight from the university."

"A student?" Nayden asked, with indignation in his voice.

"Final year. Knows all he needs."

Nayden's painfully contorted face told Samson that the man was barely restraining himself from saying something offensive.

The student knelt beside the wounded man and opened his bag. A blade flashed in his hand.

"What is that?" Nayden asked.

"A surgical knife. I have to expose the wound."

"Don't you dare," the wounded man wheezed. "I'll show you,

74

cutting people's clothes ... Just help me take it off. Who'll make me a new jacket? You?"

Nayden raised his arms with a groan, indicating that the right sleeve ought to be pulled off first. Samson rushed to help the student. They undressed the wounded man quickly and carefully, causing no additional pain.

"Lie back on the floor," the student instructed, taking a few vials and a paper bag of bandaging materials from his bag.

Samson rose to his feet, went over to the dead deserter and noticed that his father's desk was spattered with blood. This made him a bit sick, as if he could taste the foreign blood on his lips. He wanted to spit.

He looked around and saw that old Vasyl was peeping in through the doorway.

"Bring a rag and some water," he told him.

"I brought the doctor that water, there. Don't have any more at this hour. Just some tea in the kettle."

"Bring the tea, then," Samson said.

While the young policeman was scrubbing the already drying blood from the desktop and drawers, the student doctor was binding Nayden's chest with a snow-white bandage. Even just watching them out of the corner of his eye, Samson felt uncomfortable about his own bandage – so dirty and tattered.

"Strip him, Vasyl," Nayden suddenly commanded, his voice sounding firmer, more resolute.

Vasyl squatted down beside the deserter, pushed him away from the desk and turned him onto his back. The bullet seemed to have pushed the dead man's face into the back of his skull. It must have struck him just under the nostrils, or perhaps right in the nose.

"Not a mark on it," Vasyl whispered rather loudly, examining the overcoat and extracting the dead man's right arm from its sleeve. "Smart shooting."

The man in the leather jacket came back into the office, and his surprised eyes halted on Samson, who was scrubbing blood from the left-hand drawers of the desk.

"We requisitioned that thing from you," he said, furrowing his brows. "What are you doing here?"

"He'll be working with us, Kostya," replied the bandaged Nayden, whom the student had just helped into one of the chairs.

"Would you like to keep the bullet?" the student asked the wounded man, showing him a small red object pinched by a pair of tweezers.

"He will," the man in the leather jacket answered for Nayden. "I've already got two just like it."

Nayden nodded.

The student lowered the bullet into a kidney-shaped enamel tray, which already held a bloody surgical knife and two other instruments Samson could not identify. He then doused the bullet with the liquid from one of his vials and wiped it off with a piece of cotton wool.

Having finished stripping the body, Vasyl looked back at the two Red Army men standing in indecision.

"Leave your rifles here and take him down to the door, but don't put him out on the street, you hear?" he commanded, nodding at the naked corpse defaced by a well-aimed bullet.

Samson got the attention of the man in the jacket.

"You were the one to seal them, yes?" he asked, nodding at the drawers.

"That's right. The name is Konstantin Pasechny. You can call me Kostya."

"Can you take them off?"

"Certainly," Pasechny responded. "But you should seal them yourself overnight – to maintain the internal order."

"You mean you have thefts here too?" Samson asked in surprise.

"Little things. It happens." Pasechny exhaled with regret. "But we'll put a stop to it, once and for all. Isn't that right, Comrade Nayden?"

Nayden nodded from his chair. His face was pale, and his bare shoulders, slightly blue from the cold, trembled slightly.

"We need to cover you up," Samson said with concern in his voice.

"I'll go fetch a blanket. We've got plenty. We have to sleep here sometimes," Pasechny said.

He went out and quickly returned with a thick blue blanket, which he spread over Nayden up to his chin. Then his gaze fell on the dead deserter's clothes. He picked up the overcoat and draped that over the wounded man too, on top of the blanket. Then he ordered Vasyl to arrange some hot tea.

"I'd like to hear some music," Nayden intoned dreamily.

"There will be music," Pasechny declared confidently. "Don't you worry."

Chapter 13

When Samson arrived home, Anton and Fyodor immediately retreated to his father's study. They didn't want to face their host. While he was rummaging through the chest of clothes in his bedroom, he heard hurried footsteps and realised that the Red Army men had left the flat.

He decided to make sure and went out into the hallway. There were no rifles, but another sack had been added to the one from the day before. Sticking out of its opening was a lady's reindeer-fawn hat. Samson pulled out the hat, slipped his hand deep inside the sack and pricked his finger on a fork. He extracted the item, which was made of silver and engraved with the monogram of its owners – its former owners.

A lump formed in Samson's throat. He thought of the boxes in the living room, filled to the brim with other people's goods, and wondered why their appearance hadn't shocked him right from the start. After all, these were people's possessions, which had been stolen or taken by force – by the force of the Red Army, in this case represented by Anton and Fyodor. It was Anton and Fyodor, too, who had given his father's desk to the police, just so that they could stretch out at night – not exactly robbery, but still a low, vile act.

A wall came down in Samson's mind between him and these Red Army soldiers – a wall that seemed to be founded on class. Their thievery and vileness made him feel that he was superior to them, cleaner and more honest. And this inspired another unpleasant feeling in his soul – the feeling that he had no right to think badly of them. Weren't they the ones fighting and dying? They probably felt terribly out of place and on edge here in the city, where the war had stopped – with people walking around, trams running and cars honking as if everything were fine and dandy. All around were posters of bourgeois with bayonets plunged into their thick bellies – posters that seemed to call on them, these Red Army soldiers, paralysed for lack of war, to find a fat bourgeois specimen, run him through with a bayonet and tear the reindeer-fawn hat off his wife's rotten capitalist head. What right did he have to judge them?

Growing agitated, Samson reined in his thoughts, but then he remembered the dead man who had wounded Nayden. He was also a Red Army soldier, only a deserter. Or maybe he had just felt that the war was over for him, since he was no longer called into battle, and he simply had no change of clothes. But wasn't that how soldiers became deserters?

Hunger distracted Samson from these ruminations. He drew the meal vouchers he'd received from Vasyl out of the pocket of his overcoat. Then he carefully examined three other pieces of paper he'd been given, with their portentous blue stamps. The first gave him permission to walk around the city at any time of night. The second assigned him to a one-day course in marksmanship. The third directed him to the military clothing warehouse, to select an appropriate uniform.

The course was scheduled for the following day, but he needed to deal with the food and uniform questions before then.

In the Soviet cafeteria on Stolypin Street, which he had recently visited as an ordinary citizen of the third category, Samson now proudly handed the cook a meal voucher. He got everything except bread – pea soup, millet with gravy, warm milk jelly – and sat down beside a loudly munching citizen in greyish attire. There were no other seats available. As soon as he started on his soup, familiar voices sounded in his head.

"Have you checked the old card cabinet?" Pasechny's voice enquired.

"Of course," responded Nayden's. "He was once detained for vandalising the monument to Tsar Alexander. Nothing more. And he writes well."

"Uses pretty words?"

"No, writes clearly and competently. Better than you."

"I didn't study to be a clerk. Accurate shooting is more important. How's he with a gun?"

"Useless, for now. I assigned him to a course."

"Uh-huh . . . What sort of family does he come from?"

"His father was an accountant, so he's probably no slouch at arithmetic, either."

"And what's the matter with his head?"

"Cossacks were fooling around – hacked his father to death, then lopped off his ear."

And then a long heavy creak told Samson that one of the speakers had pulled out a desk drawer.

"Look at that fancy passport . . . This must be his father . . . Mother's not bad looking . . . Has a sister, I see," Pasechny's voice drawled.

"All gone. He's the only one left."

"Pogrom, eh? So he's Jewish?"

"No, Orthodox, but not a believer. Got that clear, right off the bat."

"What are those sweets, there?"

"Hands off, Kostya. Don't get used to ferreting through people's things."

"Heh-heh," Pasechny sniggered. "Isn't that our job?"

"To put it bluntly, our job is to ferret out crimes, not to ferret through things."

The desk drawer was slid forcefully shut.

The cook had under-salted the soup, which just went to show

that Soviet cafeterias weren't especially well stocked. Salt, of course, had been in short supply for a while. At this point, cabbies would probably accept it in payment for rides.

Samson's head grew quiet. Nayden and Pasechny must have moved away from the desk.

The sweet milk jelly gently coated his unsalted tongue, like a warm blanket covering a baby.

Samson again heard his neighbour's loud champing, but wasn't annoyed by it. The man was eating the last of his porridge, having apparently finished his jelly before Samson arrived.

The sun, which had been invisible half an hour earlier, now shone through the cafeteria's windows. Samson hurried through his lunch, eager to meet its rays. He had to take the tram to the military clothing warehouse, but he spent a quarter of an hour strolling towards the stop.

Khreshchatyk flashed past the tram's windows. First came endless Oleksandrivska Street, descending to Podil. He changed trams on Oleksandrivska Square, and then Kyrylivska Street, with Richert's brewery and the Church of St Nicholas Jordan, rushed by him on either side. Soon he was racing through Kurenivka – dirty, single-storeyed, not at all like the rest of Kyiv. There were more horse-drawn vehicles here. Carts rolled by, their wooden wheels clattering and – to Samson's surprise – splashing through puddles. This meant either that it was warmer here than in Upper Kyiv, or that the sun had begun to bake in earnest everywhere.

The tram kept stopping abruptly, and, every time it did, Samson, holding tight to the hanging leather loop, swayed to and fro like the clapper in a bell.

There were fewer and fewer passengers left, which gave the young man the sense that the tram was nearing its destination. He had already taken a vacated wooden seat when it occurred to him to ask the tram driver about the warehouse.

"Stop after next, behind the dachas," the driver answered.

The warehouse occupied a brick building that looked like a factory. Five carts loaded with sacks were parked in front of the gate. Slavic and Chinese Red Army soldiers stood nearby, in separate groups. An empty cart drove out of the gate and one of the five loaded ones slowly moved towards the building's wide doors.

Samson followed it. The cart stopped about a yard from the entrance and three soldiers in belted military shirts came out to meet it. Each threw a sack over his shoulders and briskly carried his burden inside.

"Where you going?" The cabby stopped Samson, who had tried to follow the soldiers into the building. "That there's the trade entrance. Yours is over on that side." He pointed to the left.

Samson rounded the corner of the building and saw an ordinary office door. He showed his stamped paper to the soldier on duty, who summoned one of his comrades – freckled and very young. That second soldier led the visitor into the warehouse, where he was handed over to a clerkish man in a grey suit, with three sharpened pencils sticking out of his breast pocket.

The man studied the paper, then examined the visitor carefully and nodded. A second nod instructed Samson to follow him.

The huge space of the warehouse was divided into two parts. One was littered with sacks and bales, the second looked more like a bathhouse dressing room: several rows of wooden benches bearing long underwear, shirts and overcoats. The clerkish man led Samson to these benches. There, he picked up a shirt, shook it out, placed it against Samson's torso and nodded contentedly. He picked out another, measuring it by eye.

"Take them," he said.

Then he chose a pair of long underwear and a warm undershirt and placed those against the young man's body. The sour smell of medicated soap tickled Samson's nose.

"You probably need a jacket, not an overcoat," the clerkish man suddenly pronounced, narrowing his eyes. Without waiting for a response, he stepped over two benches and took from the third a leather jacket with a hole cut in its sleeve. "It's solid," he said. "Can sew that up with a thick needle in three minutes' time. Now, let's see about boots."

He led Samson to the other side of the warehouse. The young man winced at the smell of mould and rot emanating from the bales and sacks.

"This must all be disinfected and washed," the clerkish man explained. "You can steam the boots or treat them with kerosene yourself. We never have enough."

In the far corner, to the right, a Chinese Red Army soldier was shaking boots out of sacks and trying to arrange them in pairs.

The clerkish fellow bent down, pulled one pair closer, picked it up, examined it, then looked at Samson's decent shoes.

"Hold on to those," he said thoughtfully. "You won't find a pair like that anymore. Now, try these on."

Samson lowered the clothes he'd received to the floor and squatted down. The right boot gave him trouble at first, but, once it was on, it seemed to instil confidence into his leg. He pulled on the left boot and stamped about for a bit.

"Not too tight?" the fellow asked.

"No."

"Don't take them off," he said. "I'll give you a sack for the clothes."

On the tram back, Samson caught passengers eying his sack and his boots intensely – at times, it seemed, with hostility. He wanted to get to Oleksandrivska Square as quickly as possible. There, he would transfer to the number 2, the passengers of which demonstrated, even at this difficult time, greater neatness and friendliness than those encountered on the lines to the outskirts of town.

Chapter 14

Only when he returned home did Samson realise that, of all the items he had received at the warehouse, the only ones he had tried on were the boots. And those had fitted nicely, straight away. He recalled the clerkish man in the grey suit, with sharp pencils sticking out of his breast pocket – recalled how the man had measured him with his eyes, as if they were scopes belonging to the most precise German-made surveyor's levels. Apparently, his self-assurance had momentarily rubbed off on Samson, and so the young man hadn't even thought of trying on his new clothes.

Now, however, lowering his sack onto the dining table and wanting to take advantage of the fact that he was alone – no rifles in the hallway, the flat completely silent – he decided to put on the uniform and examine himself in the mirror. First, he pulled on the navy-blue trousers, which needed ironing but still looked respectable, then the green cloth shirt and finally the leather jacket. The lengthwise slit in the jacket's sleeve immediately bulged out. Samson saw that it ran right along the back of the elbow, and he could easily imagine how it got there. The former owner must have been trying to defend himself by raising his forearm, but what good is a forearm against a sabre?

Tears welled up in Samson's eyes. The last moments of his father's life flashed through his mind, along with that second sabre, which had descended on his own head but had failed to reach its goal thanks to a final, posthumous act of fatherly love. The poor man hadn't even had a chance to raise his arm to protect himself – and that was the only reason his clothes had remained intact . . .

Samson wiped away the tears with the back of his hand, then

slipped the hand into his jacket pocket and felt paper. He extracted the object: the stub of a hand-rolled cigarette. He checked the other pocket: empty. Then he reached into the inner pocket and withdrew an envelope, which turned out to contain a photograph.

A woman's attractive face, slightly inclined towards her right shoulder and surrounded by an oval border, looked up at Samson with love and sadness.

On the right, beneath the oval, was an inscription: *To warrior Peter, from his loving wife Nastya, in painful memory.*

A heavy sigh escaped Samson's mouth. The sounds of human presence reached him from the hallway. The Red Army men had returned, placing their rifle butts on the floor with a thud. They entered the living room and froze at the sight of the owner with a photograph in his hand.

They approached Samson and saw that his eyes were wet. Anton glanced down at the photo, nodded sadly, and in an unusually gentle manner drew a photo of his own from inside his overcoat. He held his wife's face so that Samson too could examine it. This photographer had not been so sophisticated. And yet, though no oval border accentuated its romantic character, the face of this young peasant woman, her hair drawn tightly back and the collar of her blouse or sweater reaching right up to her neck, still struck Samson as pretty.

He carefully took the photo from the soldier's hand, turned it around and read the inscription: *To my dear husband Anton, in faithful memory.*

Fyodor also reached a hand into the bosom of his overcoat, but then suddenly pulled it out and shoved it into his side pocket.

"Sorry again about the desk, but it was hurting our heads," Anton said. "Hey, how much did you pay for that jacket?" he asked, trying it on with his eyes.

"Nothing," Samson answered. "Came with the job."

"You got a job?" Fyodor asked, wide-eyed. "Where?"

"At the police station."

The Red Army men exchanged tense glances. Anton nodded and they went into the study, closing the door behind them.

Samson looked himself over in the mirror again, sideways and full face. The jacket seemed a little stiff to him. On the other hand, a person facing danger needs a stiff, protective outer garment – though this one hadn't done much to protect its previous owner, otherwise he'd still be wearing it.

Samson didn't know how to sew. He went down to ask the yard-sweeper's widow for a favour.

After inspecting the thickness of the leather at the site of the cut, she shook her head.

"I'd never get the needle through," she said. "Don't have that kind of strength."

Samson put the jacket back on and decided to visit his father's tailor on Nimetska Street.

The tailor received the young man amiably and treated him to tea. He quickly sewed up the rent on his machine, then covered the elbow with black polish and brushed it to a shine. Now, the sleeve looked solid.

On the way back, Samson stopped in front of Dr Vatrukhin's house, which now said nothing about its inhabitants. No new sign hung above the door, while the old one had disappeared along with the rubbish drift that had, until recently, sat frozen on the pavement to the right.

Samson knocked and Tonya immediately opened the door.

Nikolay Nikolaevich looked awful and had developed a cough. He wore a warm dressing gown with a blue cardigan peeping out over the top of its overlapping sides.

"I only need a minute of your time," Samson informed the doctor as the housekeeper led him into the office. "Just one question."

"Still haven't washed your bandage," Vatrukhin said, regretfully and reproachfully.

"Never found the time."

Samson sat in the chair for patients at the side of the desk. The doctor lowered himself into his own chair and assumed a professional, attentive expression.

"Ask away," he said.

"When the Red Army men broke into your place, they stole an artificial eye. Correct?"

"That's right – they requisitioned it," the doctor confirmed sarcastically.

"But this eye, it only masks the real one's absence, right? It can't actually see, can it?"

"Of course not! It's only meant to give the patient peace of mind."

"Do you know of anyone who makes artificial ears?"

"Honestly, no," the doctor said with a shrug. "One could make it out of plaster easily enough, but how would you attach it?"

"That would give me peace of mind . . . Then I could take off the bandage."

The doctor looked up at the young man's bandaged head.

"You should take it off in any case. There's no telling how many viruses and bacteria are crawling all over that thing. God forbid you should suffer blood poisoning."

"But how can I walk down the street with a hole where my ear should be?" Samson asked in an almost martyr-like tone.

"Oh, don't be naive," the doctor responded. "The weather is still wintry. You can wear a hat with earflaps – no-one will see your wound. Later, you can find another kind of hat, or have one made for you. All that bandage does is draw attention to itself!"

The doctor's suggestion lit a joyful fire in Samson's mind. Why hadn't he thought of that himself?

"I can't tell you how grateful I am," he said to Vatrukhin. "How strange that it never occurred to me . . ."

"Nonsense," the doctor responded, with a wave of the hand. "What about your eyes? Giving you any trouble?"

"No trouble at all! And tomorrow I'll test them at the firing range!"

"Firing range?" the doctor repeated, leaning back in his chair as if to better examine his visitor.

"I've found work – at the Lybid police station. Tomorrow, I'm taking a marksmanship course with the Society for Proper Hunting, out past Kurenivka."

"I know the place," the doctor responded, nodding thoughtfully. "I once dabbled in hunting myself. So, what, you've decided to become a Bolshevik?" He eyed Samson's jacket.

"No, absolutely not," the young man hastened to assure the doctor. "I'll be fighting to restore order."

"Order comes in many varieties, these days," the doctor said, before absentmindedly chewing his lip. "There is the order of the Bolsheviks, the order of Makhno's anarchists, the order of Denikin. None of these is written down on paper, and they all change like the weather in England. Nothing is settled. Yet that's precisely what life requires – a settled order, established by law, so that the same rules apply to everyone . . ."

"That's what we'll have," Samson promised the doctor. "We will. I should go."

"Very well, off you go. Establish your order," Vatrukhin said, somewhat gloomily, as he rose to see the young man off. "And, if your eyes give you trouble, I'll be here. Medicine has adhered to the same law and the same order for millennia now. Diseases don't care a whit whether you're with the Bolsheviks or with Petliura."

Chapter 15

With his ear no longer in his father's study, Samson was too worried to sleep. He kept sneaking up to the door and trying to make out whether the billeted soldiers were whispering something or other. Only when the distinct sound of snoring reached him did Samson calm down and stretch out in bed, his whole body aching.

He greeted dawn with eyes open. Tea with a slice of bread brought him to his senses, while putting on the uniform he had received the previous day gave him confidence. The only thing that concerned him was that he hadn't been given a cap. Rummaging through the wardrobe, he dug up his father's beaver hat – thick, without earflaps – and, although it clashed with the rough leather of his jacket, he resolutely donned it, after removing his tattered bandage. His head was smaller than his father's, so the hat covered both his left ear and what remained of the right. Wearing his boots and leather jacket, he stepped out into the street in a completely new way, not at all as he'd done, time and again, in his high-school greatcoat and English shoes. His stooped back, for which there was no-one at home to scold him, straightened itself, stretching out under the jacket like a bowstring. The boots required a special gait, and his feet found it themselves, as if they instinctively knew how to walk in this or that footwear.

A lightweight White Motor Company truck was parked outside the police station. Pasechny stood near the cab, smoking and chatting with the driver through the lowered window. The driver was also smoking – a little cloud floated out of the cab. Samson approached and greeted the men.

"We're waiting for another comrade," Pasechny announced straight away.

"How's Comrade Nayden?" Samson enquired.

"Resting. The doctor looked him over last night and told him to stay off his feet for a while."

"So, he's at home?"

"This is his home," Pasechny said, nodding at the door to the police station. "He's on the couch in his office." Then, raising his eyes to the beaver hat: "Say, why didn't they dress you properly?"

"This was my father's. They didn't offer me anything yesterday."

"Right, we can't have you wearing an army cap," Pasechny granted. "Never mind, we'll find you something. And the workshops will open any day now, too. We've already requisitioned thirteen sewing machines – soon the seamstresses will get down to it, spreading their song far and wide . . . What, you don't smoke?"

"No," Samson admitted. "I tried it once in high school – didn't like it."

"Ah." Pasechny chuckled. "So, you only do what you like, is that it?" Suddenly his attention shifted to something behind Samson's back: "Here comes Comrade Kholodny!"

Samson turned round and saw a heavily built, jowly man with surprisingly white skin on the lower part of his face. He wore a brown leather jacket and baggy black trousers.

"This is Samson Kolechko, another new colleague," Pasechny announced, nodding in Samson's direction.

"Sergius Kholodny," the man introduced himself.

"Sergius?" Samson repeated.

"Sergius, Sergey, doesn't matter," the man answered. "Just call me Comrade Kholodny."

"Comrade Kholodny was a clergyman," Pasechny explained. "Then he realised that religion was a sham and renounced God. He wanted to fight real evil, so he signed up with us."

Samson examined the former clergyman's face with renewed

interest and deduced why the lower part was so white. He must have worn a beard for a very long time and shaved if off only recently. The skin, which the beard had shielded from the light, seemed ashamed to bare itself before the world.

"Alright," Pasechny said, taking a watch from his pocket and snapping open its protective silver case. "It's time. Hop in the back."

Kholodny and Samson sat down on wooden benches, facing each other. The truck started off and the rigidity of those benches made itself felt. Although the driver was no speed demon, the cobbled street knocked them up, down and sideways. Samson was sorry they hadn't taken the tram instead, but it wasn't up to him to decide how they would get to the former Society for Proper Hunting.

After passing through Galitska Square, the driver manoeuvred through strange little lanes until they emerged, some forty minutes later, at Kyrylivska Square and began to move slowly along Kurenivska Street, now and then getting stuck behind peasant carts and sometimes successfully overtaking them by driving onto the tram tracks, at which point Samson's and Kholodny's hands would grip the benches of their own volition.

"I was here yesterday," Samson said to Kholodny, indicating a tram heading towards Podil.

"At the firing range?"

"No, the military clothing warehouse. If you don't mind my asking, what was your rank in the Church?"

"I was a priest," Kholodny readily responded, outshouting the traffic noise. "In the Chernihiv province."

"Is your family still there?" Samson asked.

"Family's still in Chernihiv, yes. Nowhere to house them here. As soon as they give me a flat, I'll bring them over. Although things are more stable back home, and it's closer to Moscow. At first, I thought I'd go to Moscow to renounce God, but there are too many of my kind over there."

"Yes, I haven't heard of anything like it in Kyiv," Samson admitted.

"And how about you, Comrade Samson? Have you renounced God?"

"I've been an atheist since my school days."

"Ah, so you didn't have to ... Well, I'll tell you honestly, my heart goes out to you. It's a shame you haven't had the chance to enjoy the great spiritual cleansing I experienced."

The firing range of the former Society for Proper Hunting looked more like a forest preserve. Here and there, among the pine trunks, stood plywood targets some incompetent artist had painted to resemble various enemies of the revolution. Atop the painted nose of each of these enemies sat a painted pair of spectacles or pince-nez. Every third figure was of a bearded priest.

Shots as short as full stops echoed in the crowns of the trees, the work of a group of four novice Cheka agents. The instructor had lined them up and, after correcting their stances, allowed them to fire at the plywood targets in turn.

Then, for about half an hour, the instructor worked with some young women wearing long black skirts, black leather jackets and leather berets. These uniforms appealed to Samson, but he reserved his judgement; the sight of young women firing Nagant revolvers inspired caution, especially since, as it turned out, this wasn't their first time at the range – they were crack shots. Once, it seemed to Samson that one of the young women turned her eyes from the sights of her revolver to cast an enquiring glance at him. He quickly turned away.

At last, the instructor approached Samson and Kholodny. Keeping the revolver level turned out to be harder than Samson had expected. To make matters worse, the instructor forced him to take off his beaver hat, claiming that such headwear seriously interfered with shooting. The young man's hand hurt, but he tried to follow all the instructions. It was easier for him to shoot with his elbow bent than with his arm outstretched. All the same, his bullets kept whizzing past the painted plywood. Kholodny, meanwhile, hit the prototype of the enemy right in the face with his very first shot, and he held the revolver so firmly and confidently that it seemed he might have been born with a gun in his hand. Samson felt a twinge of envy towards the former priest. After working with Kholodny, the instructor returned to the young man and, in the end, achieved some measure of success: Samson's last five shots hit their plywood target.

Before they left the firing range, Pasechny led the new recruits into the lodge and handed each of them a handwritten sheet of paper bearing a purple stamp. Samson stared at his: *Issued to Samson Theophilovich Kolechko for completion of the Red marksmanship course on 22 March 1919.*

"Take care to keep that in your pocket at all times," Pasechny admonished them. "In general, the more documents you've got in your pockets, the better."

"Will we be given new passports too?" Samson asked, remembering the old family passport that had been issued to his father, whose murder had rendered it useless for all the other members of the family, living and dead.

"Yes." Pasechny nodded. "As soon as the bounds of our power are determined, there will be passports."

On their return to the police station, Samson and Kholodny each received a revolver with a belt and wooden holster, as well as a dozen rounds of ammunition and a handwritten firearm licence.

Samson girded himself and felt a pleasant weight at his right hip. Now, he thought, life would change. It always changes when a person is given a weapon.

"I put a couple of case files from the tsarist police on your desk, to help you figure out what detective and intelligence work really means," Pasechny told Samson. "Get to work. Comrade Kholodny and I have other matter to discuss."

Back in his office, Samson enthusiastically sat down at his father's desk and examined Pasechny's seals, which were still intact. He tore them off, opened the upper left-hand drawer and gazed tenderly at the Montpensier tin and the obsolete family passport.

Then he pulled up a file that bore an inscription in a beautiful, sweeping hand: *The case of the murder of factory owner S. P. Kornienko and members of his family at 47 Zhylianska Street, third floor.*

Before Samson's eyes appeared a familiar building, which stood two blocks from his own home. Searching the cover for a date, he found that the case had been opened in January 1916. He opened the file and began to read the first handwritten sheet – a report on the crime – while trying to recall whether he'd heard about the murder when it occurred.

His memory reminded him that, in those years, he had tried not to hear about any murders at all, because they seemed to occur constantly, making life feel fragile, like a Venetian glass vessel in need of a protective case. Yet, now, with the weight of a revolver at his right hip, the report on the murder of an entire family who lived close to his own home, on the same street, didn't disturb or frighten him quite so much.

Chapter 16

Trofim Sigismundovich didn't immediately recognise Samson as he opened his door and took fright. When he did, he took fright once again, but nevertheless let him inside.

"That high-school greatcoat suited you better," he said, waiting for his guest to hang up his holster belt and jacket.

Nadezhda, for her part, wasn't especially surprised by Samson's new attire. He did, however, read pity in the young woman's eyes and realised right away that its cause was the bareness of his earhole, which was no longer disguised by the bandage. This made him shrink inwardly. He'd left his hat on the hook too – he couldn't have worn it to the table, after all . . .

Lyudmila, Nadezhda's mother, poured the tea and put out gingerbread in a fancy porcelain bowl.

"Pardon me, but I've forgotten your patronymic," the young woman's father admitted, looking into Samson's eyes.

"Theophilovich."

A smile of approval swelled on Trofim Sigismundovich's lips. Nadezhda's eyes twinkled ironically.

"People should have the right to free themselves of their constraining pasts," she commented slyly.

"I don't feel the need to free myself of anything," her father retorted.

"Well, I do," she said, in a stubborn but cheerful voice. "What about you, Samson?"

The young man contemplated the question. "I would rather get back something I've lost," he said cautiously, and, fearing that Nadezhda might ask him to elaborate, he immediately decided to change the subject. "We have a new employee at the police station – a former priest!"

"Defrocked?" Trofim Sigismundovich asked, perking up.

"Yes, he says he's renounced God and wants to help restore order."

"Watch yourself around him." Nadezhda's mother spoke with concern. "When a man becomes his opposite, his ideas of good and evil may get jumbled."

"That can happen to anyone," her husband declared with a wave of his hand. "These days, it's all too difficult to discern good from evil. For example, I now know that Petliura's men are evil, but the Hetman? I just can't say. And Denikin? His army will come to Kyiv – are they good? Evil?"

"They won't come," Nadezhda angrily cut him off. "Kyiv isn't a boat, to be rocked this way and that."

"You say that, but the Bolsheviks are here for the second time, now," Trofim Sigismundovich pressed on.

"And God loves a trinity," his wife added, then covered her mouth with her hand as she realised how inappropriate it was.

After tea, Samson put on his hat, jacket and firearm, and took Nadezhda out for a short stroll.

The evening seemed remarkably calm. Crows cawed rhythmically. The steel wheels of trams went clanging along their rails.

"Where are you taking me?" Nadezhda asked.

She clearly liked the way passers-by looked sideways at Samson's holster – some with interest, others with apprehension.

"You'll find out soon enough," Samson answered, playing for time.

They walked past the iron shutters of shop windows, past street lamps illuminating crossroads and past advertising columns plastered with theatrical posters that caught their attention with titles of plays they'd never seen. Eventually they reached the northern edge of Oleksandrivska Square.

"To Khreshchatyk, then?" Nadezhda again enquired as to the aim of their stroll.

"No. And we're almost there."

They stopped before a deserted little market sprawled out near the Fountain of Samson.

"What's this?" she asked, looking around in disappointment. "I thought you were taking me to a café?"

Samson sighed. "Take a better look."

She pirouetted playfully, like a ballerina, then fixed her gaze on him. "Just tell me, will you?" she asked.

He went to the fountain and pointed at the sculpture of Samson prising open the lion's mouth. "Do you know who that is?"

"Samson," she answered, and immediately burst out laughing. "You wanted to show me your namesake?"

"Yes," the young man replied. "This is where my parents first met. At the market. Then they tossed a coin in the fountain. And they named me Samson in his honour," he added, nodding at the funny figure. "If it wasn't for him, I might not exist."

"How pietistic!" she exclaimed, clasping her hands to her heart. "You really are so sweet." She touched the shoulder of his jacket, as if wanting to draw him closer, but then moved her hand away.

"I think it's important to hold on to family stories, so that the heart doesn't grow cold," Samson said in a serious, somewhat didactic tone. "Today I was reading about old murders ... I don't want to spoil your mood ... But afterwards a wounded comrade told me that every person one day finds themselves witness to evil or to some sort of crime – and that, in the end, everyone pays for this either by becoming a victim or by being named an accomplice. He said that I should always look twice, carefully, in order to spot the evil that I may not consciously notice at first ..."

"And where did you spot this evil?" Nadezhda asked, somewhat offended. "At our home?"

"No, of course not! I like your parents very much! The evil I see is in my own flat, right there in my late father's study. That's where they talk all night of desertion – of getting home in time for the sowing season . . ."

"Who's 'they'?"

"Anton and Fyodor, two Red Army men," Samson explained. "They brought in three boxes of requisitioned or stolen goods. And a sack of clothes and patterns from some tailor . . ."

"Well, maybe those goods really were properly requisitioned."

Samson shook his head. "Now I know that the requisitioned items are taken to warehouses – not to flats where soldiers happen to be billeted."

Nadezhda fell silent, thinking as she stared at the waterless fountain and the rubbish-strewn market with its lopsided, cracked wooden stalls.

"If I were you, I would ask them directly," she suddenly pronounced, raising her resolute eyes to meet Samson's.

"Tomorrow, I'll open a case against them, describing my suspicions in detail. I'll pass it on to Comrade Nayden and he'll write out with his own hand what ought to be done."

"See? You worry your head off, but we already have procedures in place. You just have to remember to follow them."

"You're right," Samson agreed. "May I take you home?"

"Certainly!"

When they came to the corner of Mezhyhirska and Spaska streets, the electric streetlamps suddenly went dark.

"There we are." Samson exhaled sadly. "The power plant has run out of wood."

"Can you get out your revolver?" Nadezhda asked, frightened by the darkness.

Samson unfastened the top of his wooden holster, pulled out his weighty gun and showed it to her. "Don't be afraid," he said softly. "I can protect you."

His eyes soon adjusted to the dark. They walked more slowly

than usual, listening for footsteps not their own, and passed a tram car abandoned by its passengers and driver, which had apparently stopped due to the sudden loss of power.

Nadezhda took Samson's arm and pressed herself against his side. They stopped.

"Can you fire just once?" she whispered conspiratorially.

"What for?" he asked.

"So that, instead of us being afraid, people will fear us."

Her warm breath blew right into his left ear.

Samson loaded his revolver, looked up at the darkened sky, which seemed to be hiding inside itself, and fired in its direction. The shot set the air ringing, raining echoes onto the roofs of nearby houses and beyond. Then came the sound of someone running away, their feet loudly slapping the cobblestones.

"Thank you," Nadezhda whispered into Samson's left ear. And then the same ear felt the touch of her tender, slightly sticky lips.

Chapter 17

Samson had been surprised to discover that Nayden's office was half the size of his own, but he only worked up the courage to ask about it the next morning, when he knocked on Nayden's door with the intention of opening a criminal case.

Nayden was sitting on the couch behind his desk, reading some handwritten documents. The expression on his face was that of someone who'd accidentally swallowed a fly. His left arm, bent at the elbow, hung motionless, suspended from his neck by a linen belt. Or maybe it was a rifle sling. At the sight of Samson, his face took on a look of goodwill. In response to the young man's harmless everyday question, he nodded at the pot-belly stove by the window.

"Cosier here," he said. "The room warms up faster, which makes it easier to concentrate. Like in a prison cell."

"So, it's harder to work in a larger office?"

"The walls don't bear down on you there. Nothing stimulates thought like walls closing in. Less daydreaming, more work."

"My office is very large," Samson said in confusion.

"We'll pack you in tighter soon," Nayden promised. "What can I do for you? I've got this chicken scratch to decipher . . ."

"I need your advice," Samson admitted. "Do we still open cases as they did under the tsar? With a written report?"

"You already have a case on your hands?"

"I've had it for a while, though I didn't realise it until we spoke. You said that we all live among criminals and crimes, but we try not to notice them until we ourselves become victims."

"Right."

"Well, I have two Red Army men billeted in my flat. They've

brought in three boxes and two sacks of loot, and now they're planning to desert and return home for the sowing season."

"What did I tell you?" Nayden said, shaking his head. "Alright, buckle up."

"So . . . do I report on them . . . to myself?"

"No, we don't bother with reports anymore. Write out a statement about the crime to the Criminal Investigation Department of the Lybid District, then bring it to me and I'll endorse an investigation. Understood?"

Samson nodded and went back to his desk. When he took off his holster belt and placed it on the floor to the left of his chair, he immediately began to breathe easier. Now, fresh thoughts freely entered his mind, as though they had been afraid to approach him while he was armed. He called out to Vasyl, asking for tea and paper. The man brought him a file of tsarist police cases.

"No new paper yet," he said. "Fillet these and write on the clean sides. I'll be back with the tea."

Resisting the urge to pore over the tsarist materials, Samson chose a few sheets that contained only a little text and laid them on the part of his desktop covered with tightly stretched dark-green leather. He got out the pen and ink, and, at the top of the first sheet, wrote: STATEMENT. The first sentence came easily, as if he'd been composing statements all his life: *I hereby state the facts concerning the criminal activity of soldiers Anton and Fyodor, who are preparing to desert from the Red Army and are suspected of robbery and illegal requisitioning . . .*

But here the ease departed. He realised that he didn't know his guests' surnames, which he had only glimpsed briefly on the billeting order and immediately forgotten. Furthermore, he didn't know to which detachment or regiment they belonged. In fact, he could indicate nothing specific in his statement except for the address of their stay – that is, his own address. But he didn't want to bother Nayden again so soon . . .

Samson decided to list from memory the contents of the sack and boxes he'd examined. At the end of his short statement, he added, *I urge the arrest of the above-mentioned citizens for the purposes of a detailed investigation and the determination of proper punishment.*

Then, after a cup of tea, he went back to Nayden.

"You write well," Nayden declared, after reading the statement. "But too little. Not enough detail. Of course, these types fill in the blanks themselves under interrogation, but do give it some thought – you might remember something useful from your conversations."

Instead of going to the Soviet cafeteria for lunch, Samson slipped the Montpensier tin into his pocket and went home. The Red Army men were out. He went into his father's study, which smelled of tobacco and sweat, and found that his guests had violated the order of the beads on the abacuses. He also noticed two more sacks in the corner. Rummaging through them, he discovered only clothes, including a large satin waistcoat. With a huff, he walked over to the bookcase, opened it and tucked the tin with the ear between the books and the top of the second shelf, leaving the door ajar.

He also looked through the wooden boxes again and reviewed their contents more closely, trying to remember everything he saw.

On the way back to the station, he was nearly run over by a cab. The driver turned and swore at him, capping off his curses with "Bolshevik scum".

As a result, Samson returned to his office with a sour expression on his face. And this expression apparently remained in place, against his will, for at least an hour, because, after one look at him, Vasyl asked whether they'd finally started salting the soups and porridges in the cafeteria properly.

At that very moment, a shout reached them from the ground floor and Vasyl, without waiting for an answer, disappeared. Grabbing his revolver, Samson too went downstairs. There, he saw his fellow agents taking two bandits, hands tied behind their backs, down to the prison cells in the basement.

Climbing back up the stairs, Samson ran into Nayden, who must have decided to examine the catch with his own eyes or, perhaps, to check with his agents about this or that case.

"Well, how goes the writing?" Nayden asked.

"Coming along," Samson responded.

And, indeed, after returning to his desk, he began to fill the back of another tsarist police report with prompts and questions that would allow him to learn more about the soldiers' misdeeds. He knew, of course, that his questions might arouse anxiety and suspicion in the minds of his guests, but this too could prove useful. The more anxious they grew, the more they would whisper at night, and their whispering was bound to be far more revealing than any open conversation.

When he left for the day, he decided to leave his holstered revolver at the station, hiding it in a drawer. This was the only drawer that he secured with his own seal, which Vasyl had given him the previous day.

He walked home empty-handed and was surprised to discover that he felt less afraid without his revolver than he did with it.

This time, the air in the kitchen was akin to the air in his father's study. It too smelled of tobacco and dampness, only this dampness wasn't natural, but the sort induced by the wrong way of life. Samson opened the window. It was dry outside, and the smells of the kitchen were joined by a waft of coal smoke, which had apparently descended from the roof of one of the adjacent buildings. No-one knew what their neighbours used to heat their flats. Some were long out of firewood, while others were still working through old reserves of coal.

Samson had a cup of tea, then crushed some millet groats in a cast-iron mortar with a heavy pestle, poured them out into a mug and covered them with boiling water. His dinner would be ready in half an hour, though all such a meal does is to deceive the stomach with its weight. Perhaps he should have gone to the Soviet cafeteria after all. But, no, Vasyl was right: they skimped on the salt there, and under-salted food just isn't satisfying.

The Red Army men tramped into the hallway and put down their rifles.

Anton peeked into the kitchen. Catching sight of their host, he nodded indifferently.

Samson finished his porridge, fetched firewood from downstairs and stoked both stoves: the one that warmed the Red Army soldiers and his own. At the sound of the creaking stove door and crackling logs, Fyodor came out of the study. He rejoiced as he realised that he and his comrade would be warm that night.

A couple of minutes later, Anton too stepped out into the living room.

"We had a lecture on health today," he said. "A doctor came and told us how you can beat illness and avoid typhus."

The soldier's intonation immediately told Samson that he hadn't brought up the lecture for no reason. And, indeed, after a pause, Anton continued: "He said that a stove's as good as a nurse. You just need to know how to use it."

"Was this about lying on a proper Russian stove as big as half a hut?" Samson asked.

First Fyodor shook his head, then Anton.

"No. Turns out all diseases are carried by parasites, and these parasites are carried by people," Anton explained, shifting his gaze between the piles of logs in front of the two stoves. "They're all afraid of heat, these parasites. Doctor said you can fire up a stove till it's blazing hot, then move the coals aside and put your clothes in their place. Add some water, then close the door and just make sure the stuff doesn't catch fire or get singed."

"This is about lice, isn't it?" Samson asked, beginning to understand.

"Both fleas and lice. Little bastards can't survive the stove. But you need lots of firewood," Anton went on, glancing sideways at the logs in front of the stove that heated Samson's bedroom.

"So, you have lice?" the young man blurted out.

"For years," Anton whined, contorting his face into an expression of unbearable suffering. "Let's do what the doctor says, eh? In this stove, here!"

Samson carried over the logs and fed them into the fire.

"Hey, do you have any kerosene?" Fyodor enquired.

"I do," Samson admitted.

The Red Army men exchanged glances, joy sparkling in their eyes.

By the time Samson had dug the rubber-stoppered bottle of kerosene out of his cupboard and come back into the living room, Anton was shoving in firewood with might and main. The stove was humming. Samson hadn't heard such a hum in a long while, as he always stoked the stoves sparingly, taking care not to provoke the chimney draughts with wild flames.

An hour later, the living room was as hot as a bathhouse changing room. Anton raked the embers out of the soldiers' stove into a metal bucket Samson had provided, and advised his host to feed them into his own.

"No sense in wasting them," he said.

While Samson was shovelling embers into his stove with a cast-iron dustpan, the Red Army men stripped to the buff and put all their clothes inside theirs. Fyodor brought a mug of water from the kitchen and poured that inside too.

"Take yours off and toss 'em in," Anton told Samson.

"No, thanks. I'm clean," the young man answered, but the words made him feel awkward. He felt the soldiers gave him an unkind look.

"Well, then, come here – and get the kerosene."

The next half hour remained in Samson's memory for the rest of his life, but he never spoke of it to anyone.

"Take that rag." Anton indicated the lace that lay on top of the mirrored dressing table. "Soak it in kerosene and rub us down."

The Belgian lace wasn't fit for the purpose, so Samson got his mother's apron, which she had only worn rarely, when she'd wanted to show her guests that she'd baked a cake all by herself. The apron had been reserved for bringing cake to the table. Now, Samson dripped kerosene over it.

"No!" Fyodor stopped him, coming closer and unnerving Samson with the severe asymmetry of his naked frame, not to mention the strange spots that covered his hairy chest – either dirt or lesions. "The rag's got to be sopping wet!"

Samson's face had never shown such disgust as when he wiped Anton and Fyodor's armpits and crotches with the kerosene-soaked apron, rubbed kerosene into their shaved scalps and ran the apron between their toes like a violinist's bow until they panted with pleasure, grinning crookedly at their host.

"You're just not used to it is all," Anton said mockingly, pretending to inhale the nasty aroma with gusto.

Before long, Fyodor pulled his clothes and footwraps out of the stove. After passing his shirt and long underpants from one hand to the other until they'd cooled a bit, he shook them out. In the light of the lamp, Samson saw dead parasites fall to the floor like dandruff.

Anton and Fyodor put on their underwear while it was still hot, moaning, groaning and smiling contentedly.

"Watch and learn, bookworm." Anton exhaled happily, slipping into his shirt.

Cleansed of their parasites by fire and kerosene, the Red Army men retired to bed without another word.

Chapter 18

The embers Samson had transplanted to his stove added no heat
to his bedroom. He got under the covers, where he only managed
to distract himself from the cold by force of will. Straining the
muscles of his legs, arms and neck, he lay motionless.

To his delight, he immediately heard Anton and Fyodor whispering.

"So warm," Fyodor said. "Like in a bathhouse after a bath."

"Yes," Anton responded. "But now that we're nice and healthy,
they'll just put us on patrol or guard duty again ... We've got
to make a run for it quick, otherwise they might throw us into
battle ... They say Denikin's getting close."

"How can we go, dressed like this? We should've grabbed some
peasant clothes somewhere or stripped a couple of cabbies at night.
This fool's duds are too fancy, don't match our faces – someone'll
stop us right away."

"Don't be so sure," Fyodor argued. "He's got a pretty plain suit
in the wardrobe. Roll that thing around in the stove, get it nice
and sooty, and it won't catch anyone's eye."

"You know," Anton whispered, after a pause. "I think he might've
gone through our things. The forks are on top, now. Used to be
at the bottom."

"You think he wants them for himself?"

"Use your brains ... You forget where he's working, now?"

"Damn!" Fyodor burst out in nothing like a whisper, but then
lowered his voice again: "Maybe we oughta croak him in his sleep,
after all."

"Don't want to," Anton replied. "Don't won't to, but maybe

we've got to. No. The police'll come looking for him – they'll start here, for sure. We'd better ask Grishka to wait for the one-eared freak out in the street, hit 'im there. And let's take the sacks and boxes over to Jacobson tomorrow, tell him we agree on his price. We'll get the money for the new stuff and for what we brought earlier – then it's smooth sailing back home. And, if he gives us trouble, we'll tell him we're taking it all to the pharmacist."

"Right," Fyodor whispered firmly. "You can think straight – not like me."

"Well, you weren't a bell-ringer's apprentice. All I've got to do is close my eyes and I hear the echoes in my head."

"So, if it weren't for the war, you'd be ringing bells, eh?" Fyodor asked.

"Why not?" Anton whispered more cheerfully. "Every day, you're up in the tower and it's like the whole world's yours, far as you can see. Understand? And it's your own hand that sets it all ringing. That's power ..."

Reassured by the knowledge that he wouldn't be strangled that night, Samson fell asleep. And, early the next morning, he was first to leave the flat.

He sat at his father's desk without moving a muscle, recalling and pondering everything he'd heard. And then he composed a neat, detailed new statement.

This time, Nayden extended his free right hand and patted Samson on the shoulder, demonstrating his approval of the document.

"We'll pick them up tonight," he said. "We'll send a truck with four agents. Would you like to take part?"

"No," Samson admitted honestly. "I've seen them naked. I'd be too ashamed."

"For their sake?" Nayden asked in surprise.

"For my own. And my late parents."

"That's fine," Nayden assured him. "But you ought to participate in arrests. It tempers your character. You'll understand people better, be able to read them. Oh, I've got something else for you."

He handed Samson a black leather cap.

"Now you're fully in uniform."

Samson put the cap on his head and realised straight away that it failed to cover his bare earhole, but he tried not to dwell on that. He thanked Nayden.

Lunch at the Soviet cafeteria on Stolypin Street was porridge with pork fat and buckwheat soup with onions. This time, for some reason, they decided to add a slice of bread without demanding additional payment.

Samson had worked up a healthy appetite. He ate with pleasure and thought of Nadezhda. These thoughts seemed especially pleasant after the previous evening and the night that had followed. He didn't wish to dwell on it, but the lice and fleas that had rained onto the floor refused to be swept from his mind, and the naked Red Army men themselves, smelling of kerosene, were lodged in his memory like splinters in a tender heel. Only by concentrating on Nadezhda with all his might could Samson forget about them even briefly.

Towards evening, Sergius Kholodny, the large, solidly built defrocked priest, showed up at the station. It turned out that he'd spent the last two days learning methods of interrogation, which he related to Samson with a powerfully clenched fist resting on his knee.

"Now I know how to talk to them," he added, with obvious menace.

They were sitting in Samson's office – with the young man at the desk and Kholodny in a club chair on the other side – drinking tea supplied by Vasyl.

But they didn't finish their tea. Nayden walked briskly into the office, his face showing anger and alarm.

"Hetman Struk's spies have infiltrated the city," he said. "We have orders to step up patrols. Your turn in one hour. Check everyone's papers, even those of other units you come across. If anyone runs, shoot them. Is that clear?"

Both nodded. A noise from below burst in through the open doors. Someone had come rushing into the station. The tense hum of male voices rose to the first floor. One could guess, but only guess, at short words within this hum. It was as if no-one down there had time for longer ones.

Having received instructions to walk along Prozorivska Road to the old tower, then down Prozorivska Street, past the barracks, to the city slaughterhouse, before turning back, Samson and Kholodny set off with revolvers at their belts.

The city met them with a dour mien. Few windows were lit, and, though the street lamps at the crossroads were, there was hardly a soul in sight.

A cab drove out towards them. While Samson was contemplating whether they ought to stop it and check the passengers, it slipped past, but he did manage to glimpse a woman inside.

"It isn't proper," Kholodny muttered discontentedly. "There should be three men in each patrol, but they sent us out without a third."

"Why should there be three?" Samson asked.

"What do you mean, why? To shoot in three directions, in case we're surrounded. You can't do that with two. And, in general, God loves a trinity." Catching Samson's puzzled look in the light of a street lamp, he quickly added, "But I don't love God and don't care what He thinks."

After walking two blocks along an empty street, they saw a man hurrying towards them, who, as he approached, turned out to be quite old. When asked for his papers, he took out a pre-Revolutionary medical licence from a military hospital and explained that he had stayed late at the home of a patient being treated for poisoning by low-quality alcohol.

"Poor fellow," Kholodny sympathised, and let the elderly doctor go on his way.

On Prozorivska Road, they were met by a patrol of Chinese Red Army men – three men, all with rifles. Only one of them spoke Russian. The initial tension between the five men subsided as soon as they examined each other's papers under a street lamp.

"There ought to be three men in each patrol, right?" Kholodny asked the Russian-speaking Chinese soldier.

"True," the soldier answered with a nod.

"How many of you Chinese soldiers are over here?" Samson asked.

"Military secret."

"But you have a separate company?" Samson continued his line of questioning in a completely friendly tone, unable to contain his curiosity.

"Military secret. But, yes, separate company. Many companies," the soldier replied.

"And what is your name?" Samson pressed on, even though Kholodny was already tugging at his sleeve.

"Soldier Li Yin Jun."

"Oh!" the young man exclaimed. "Sounds like 'in June'!"

Li Yin Jun smiled and nodded in farewell. Then he said something to his comrades in Chinese, and they suddenly stood to attention and saluted the police patrol.

"Good people, even if they aren't Orthodox," Kholodny said, under his breath, as he and Samson continued on their route. "Or maybe that's why they're good . . ."

Several shots rang out in the distance. The policemen stopped and looked around. It was impossible to determine which direction they had come from.

Chapter 19

"Hands up!"

The words thundered inside Samson's head and he turned sharply, as if seeking support or even salvation from Kholodny.

Noticing his partner's pivot, the defrocked priest stopped and gazed at him enquiringly.

"You didn't hear anything?" Samson asked.

"Not a thing," Kholodny admitted.

They were on their way back, heading towards the end of Zhylianska Street. The street lamps had just gone out and dawn was about an hour away.

"No-one," Samson sighed, carefully surveying their surroundings.

Kholodny glanced around too. He looked tired, but still firm and self-confident. In the dark, the lower half of his face didn't seem so glaringly white as it did in the light of day.

Once Samson realised who had been ordered to raise their hands, he concentrated on what was going on in his father's study. But these goings-on weren't especially loud or distinct – a general clamour, the stamping of feet, a slammed door, a couple of blows to a naked or nearly naked body with the butt of a rifle. It was clear, in any case, that the two Red Army men had been arrested and were now on the move to the Lybid station, where they would be escorted to the cells in the basement.

Samson wanted to go home, to check on the state of his flat – to shut and lock the door, air out the smell of his erstwhile guests and then sleep. But people want all sorts of things when they're no longer in complete possession of themselves.

On Zhylianska, they were overtaken by a car driven by a man in military uniform. The eastern edge of the sky grew lighter. Kholodny yawned as he walked.

At the station, they climbed up the stairs and stopped by Nayden's office to deliver their patrol report. He was up and dressed, sitting on the couch and trying to decipher a handwritten document in the flickering light of the bulb that hung from the ceiling.

"Your tenants have been apprehended," he said to Samson. "The stolen goods are in your office. Make an inventory in two copies, then ask Vasyl to bring you statements from recent victims and make a comparison. Maybe you'll find the owners." Then, turning to Kholodny, who stood in the doorway: "Pasechny's waiting for you."

The defrocked priest immediately disappeared.

A chill came over Samson when he entered his office, either because it really was cold in there or because of what he saw next to the wall on the right: not only the three military boxes and two sacks that the Red Army men had deposited in his flat, but also his own chest from the bedroom, in which he kept his clean bedclothes and underwear.

"The agents brought in my personal chest by mistake," he complained to Nayden.

"Happens," Nayden responded, again distracted from the document. "Write up a statement of erroneous confiscation. I'll endorse it, and you'll take the damn thing home."

The light bulb in Samson's office shone uncertainly, nervously. Without taking off his jacket – but unfastening his holster belt and lowering it to the floor – he flipped a sheet from a random tsarist case to its clean side and wrote *Inventory* across the top.

He started with one of the sacks, shaking its contents out onto the floor. The last items to fall, with a clang, were several silver knives, but besides them the sack held only patterns and peices of cut fabric. The fabric was thick, warm. It was striped brown and black, and this combination seemed strange to Samson.

He picked up one pattern, which looked to be the side and front of a waistcoat. The lines of the future seam, as well as the dimensions in centimetres, were marked with white chalk.

Samson attempted to arrange the patterns into a whole suit and, to his surprise, did so quickly and easily. The black-and-brown-striped outfit looked stern and arrogant – certainly the wrong fit for the current moment. Where could one go in such a suit these days? The Soviet cafeteria?

Having listed the patterns and cuts of fabric in his inventory under the number *1*, he added the four silver knives and started on the first of the military boxes.

By the time Vasyl brought Samson a mug of tea and a hunk of bread, the inventory had moved on to a second sheet of paper – the obverse of some old memo about political unreliability with a seal displaying the imperial double-headed eagle.

Under the number *14* Samson entered four boot legs and as many as two dozen other shoe components, including three counters and six soles. Under *15* went nineteen items of silver cutlery. Next came a pair of heavy candlesticks, also silver, two cigarette cases and a yellow leather briefcase containing a bundle of imperial bonds and shares in a steam-powered mill.

By lunchtime, Samson had finally finished the inventory – four dense columns of stolen goods. Only now did the material look not like some abstract booty tossed into boxes and sacks by bandits, but like separate sets of objects, partially indicating potential victims, among whom were two artisans: a tailor and a cobbler. The rest of the items could have belonged to any wealthy Kyivan.

Turning his attention away from the plunder, Samson wrote up a statement requesting the return of his chest. He took it to Nayden for his endorsement, but the latter demanded an inventory of the chest's contents. And so Samson returned to his office, his face concealing neither his fatigue nor his bitter disappointment.

The act of compiling an inventory of his own belongings brought Samson little joy. To make matters worse, at the bottom of the chest he found a bundle of letters from his first love, Polina, whose family had emigrated to Serbia in 1917. He kept this packet out of the inventory, placing it instead in the top drawer of his father's desk, with the family passport.

Merely glancing over the completed statement, Nayden wrote *Return* diagonally across the top, in a sweeping hand, and signed it. Looking up, he noticed how pale the young man was and instructed him to go first to the Soviet cafeteria for lunch, then home for a brief nap.

The late lunch on Stolypin Street breathed new strength into Samson, but this strength added vigour only to his thoughts, not to his body.

As he slurped his potato soup, Samson considered the arrested Red Army men and their spoils. This simple peasant pair's goals and plans were now much clearer to him than they had been the day before. Both had wanted to return home in time for the sowing season. To do so, both had needed to find non-military attire – hence the raids on the tailor and the shoe shop. But these crimes could safely be described as failures. At the tailor's they only got hold of fabric and a pattern, and at the shoe shop they nabbed disparate components that only the cobbler himself could have fashioned into boots. They hadn't obtained what they needed in order to desert without attracting notice. Of course, among the loot, there were also a couple of curtains, a fringed tablecloth and even a lady's fur coat – but these were only suitable for sale or exchange. The only true valuables in the boxes and sacks were a few items of silver – no gold, no precious stones.

Samson was so deep in thought that he didn't even notice himself shoving aside his empty bowl of soup and replacing it with a plate of millet porridge covered with meat sauce.

They probably took it all while the owners were out, Samson deduced, otherwise he would have come across wallets, gold rings, earrings. Then he remembered the yellow leather briefcase full of stocks and bonds. That too they must have found in some hiding place or other, maybe on top of a wardrobe. Just two years ago, the contents would have been worth a lot of money, but now? They must have had no idea – just peeked inside, saw stacks of papers that looked like money and imagined they'd struck it rich.

This time, the compote wasn't sweet. Samson said goodbye to the cook as he walked past her to the door, but she only nodded in response. There was no-one else in the place.

A spring breeze promising the approach of warmth brushed his face.

Chapter 20

In the evening, back in his office, Samson pored over the thick folder of victims' statements he'd received from Vasyl. They were composed arbitrarily, in no set form, and this immediately told the young man what kind of person might be behind this or that sheet of paper. Most of the victims reported robberies – fur coats or overcoats, purses and gold coins surrendered at gunpoint. Samson put aside the six that mentioned silverware. He also came across, almost back to back, two statements from cobblers, one of whom had a workshop not far from Samson's home. One shop had been robbed of ready-made boots and three pairs of repaired women's shoes, while the other lost everything, including components of cowhide and calfskin boots, as well as a box of copper shoenails. Samson added these two to the pile he'd put aside. Then came statements about stolen carriages, a Franz Sodia Ferlach hunting rifle and an assortment of brass instruments – but not a single one from a tailor.

Vasyl brought the young man a mug of tea, eyed him sympathetically and yawned.

"Comrade Nayden asked to see you," he said, and disappeared through the door.

Samson staggered as he rose from the desk and recalled that he had not fulfilled Nayden's order concerning a brief nap. Coming home after his late lunch, he had aired out the flat and had even scrubbed the floor in his father's study with kerosene. The study looked odd without the desk. Thankfully, the abacuses were still on the walls. The smell of kerosene, which evoked such unpleasant memories, lingered in his nostrils, but at least he could rest easy, knowing that the precious room had been disinfected. Now he just needed to fill that strange void left behind by the unlawful requisition ...

"Have you already interrogated your prisoners?" Nayden enquired.

"No, I was studying victims' statements."

"One task does not preclude the other. Especially since the prisoners may remember whom they robbed where."

"So, should I have them brought up to my office?" Samson asked, struggling to comprehend how all this was supposed to happen.

"No. There's an interrogation room on the ground floor. Vasyl will take you. He'll also assign a soldier to escort the prisoners and stand guard. You'll question them one at a time. Take down everything they say, then have them sign or place their right thumb-print underneath. Which of the two is the brains?"

"Anton."

"Then start with the other one. Understood?"

Samson nodded.

Grabbing a pen and some sheets of paper, he followed Vasyl down to the ground floor. The interrogation room resembled a prison cell. There were no windows, and the iron doors were double bolted from the inside. The table in the centre had obviously stood there for ages and looked like a desk in a bad school, deeply scratched with knives or other sharp objects and painted time and time again, most recently a dirty green. On one side of the table stood an uncomfortable chair with a black square of leather on the seat, which contributed no softness whatsoever. On the other side was a stool with surprisingly thick legs. A large iron chain secured the underside of its seat to a ring embedded in the stone floor. Out of curiosity, Samson tried to move the stool, but the chain barely let him budge it an inch.

A Red Army soldier with a youthful face knocked on the door and immediately entered.

"They told me to come here," he reported.

"What is your surname, soldier?" Samson asked.

"No need for surnames, Comrade Policeman," the soldier responded in an unusually soft, musical voice. "I'm Semyon, from Kaluga."

"Alright, Comrade Semyon," Samson assented. "Please bring up Fyodor Bravada for questioning."

"Yes, Comrade!" the Red Army man said with a nod, and left.

Samson prepared for an angry exchange. He straightened the papers in front of him and deliberated for a long time as to where to place the blue glass inkwell, calculating the exact spot that would allow him to dip his pen and return it to the page as effortlessly as possible.

When Semyon led Fyodor into the room, Samson found the prisoner unrecognisable. His face was covered in bruises, his lips were thick and one eye was swollen shut.

"Sit," the young policeman ordered, indicating the stool.

The prisoner sat down.

"Well, tell me all about it."

"What's to tell?"

Samson picked up the inventory.

"Where and from whom did you take these items?"

"What items?" Fyodor asked, gazing at the policeman in front of him with the expression of an exhausted village dullard.

"Patterns for a man's suit and cuts of fabric," Samson read out. "Four silver table knives, two large silver candlesticks—"

"How do I know where we got them?" Fyodor interrupted with a vigorous shrug of his shoulders that made his overcoat bulge. "I'm not from Kyiv. I don't know the streets around here . . ."

"So you just went into random houses and robbed them?" Samson asked.

"That's about the size of it."

The pause that followed gave Samson the chance to recall his first meeting with these Red Army men. When the yard-sweeper's widow had brought them to his door, she'd mentioned that they were looking for a sewing machine.

"Say, why did you need a sewing machine?" he asked, looking Fyodor in the eye. "They weren't being requisitioned then."

"You know, to make us some clothes – trousers, shirts."

"And which of you knows how to sew?"

"Not me," Fyodor admitted. "Maybe Anton."

Samson gave a heavy sigh and his pen began to squeak its way across a sheet of paper, reframing in writing his questions and the prisoner's answers. Soon, he looked up at Fyodor again.

"Wouldn't it have been easier just to take someone's boots, coat and trousers? Why take separate components?"

"Sure it would've," Fyodor agreed. "But that's not what happened . . ."

"Strange," Samson said. "And how is it that you only came across silver in the flats you entered? No gold or stones."

"Anton said we should only take silver, nothing else. He . . ." And here Fyodor fell silent, as if realising that he'd said too much.

"He what?"

"Nothing . . . That's just how it happened, all silver. Didn't see anything else."

"What about the briefcase of stocks and bonds?"

"That was just me being stupid – thought it was money," Fyodor responded, a foolish grin flickering across his thin face.

"What was it Anton said about silver?" Samson returned to his previous question.

"Nothing. He didn't say nothing. I got it wrong."

Samson took down the questions and answers, then sank into thought. He looked at Semyon, who stood motionless near the door with his hand on his rifle, the butt of which rested on the stone floor.

"Alright," Samson spoke again. "You wanted to ask a certain 'Grishka' to kill me. Who is he?"

The prisoner shuddered and cried, "That ain't true!"

"It is indeed true," Samson calmly objected. "I have special walls in my flat. They tell me everything."

"Another soldier," Fyodor mumbled.

"Did he participate in your robberies?"

The prisoner shook his head. "No, he didn't want to. But he's got serious class hatred, Grishka – he's already run a few fat cats through with his bayonet."

"Is that what I am to you? A fat cat?" Samson asked.

"I wouldn't say that," Fyodor responded, looking at the young policeman disdainfully, as if he had miles to go before he attained the status of fat cat.

"What is Grishka's surname?"

"Fertichny."

"His regiment? Company?"

"Nizhyn Regiment. Cook."

"Grishka's a cook?" Samson asked, somewhat surprised.

"Yep."

Samson continued his cunning line of questioning. "My walls also reported that you and Anton discussed a certain 'Jacobson'."

Fyodor froze, tightening his thick lips. He actually looked ice cold.

"Well, who is he?"

"I have no idea," Fyodor whispered, a note of horror in his voice. "That definitely didn't happen."

"What didn't happen?"

"We didn't talk about that."

"And the pharmacist?"

"Which pharmacist?"

"You said that you'd sell the stolen goods either to the pharmacist or to Jacobson."

"I never heard of no Jacobson!"

"Fine," Samson said, suddenly growing anxious. "No Jacobson. Then who's the pharmacist?"

"Don't know; that's all Anton," Fyodor muttered. "Can I go to the latrine?"

"Wait till I take this down," Samson said, then dipped his pen and returned to his transcript. When he finished, he made Fyodor bring his bound hands up to the table, stick his right thumb in the inkwell and place a print at the bottom of the document.

"Now can I go?" Fyodor asked.

"Take him away," Samson commanded Semyon.

"Should I then bring him back?" the soldier asked.

"No, no need. Bring in Anton Tsvigun."

Chapter 21

The bottom step of the wooden staircase creaked under Samson's foot at around midnight. He managed to climb another six steps before the door of the yard-sweeper's flat swung open behind him and the widow, dressed all in black, stuck out her head.

"Samson," she called. "What's the big hurry? There's no-one up there waiting! Your guests were arrested!"

The last thing the sleepy young man wanted at that moment was to talk to the yard-sweeper's widow, but he was cornered and there was no getting out of it. He turned around.

"I know," he said, hoping to climb further – there was one flight of stairs to go.

"Come down, I've got a letter for you," the widow shouted.

"Mail?" Samson wondered aloud.

"No, from Nadezhda."

At that, his legs took off on their own. Overcome by happiness, he didn't even try to skip the first step, which again creaked sharply, bringing a pained grimace to the widow's face.

"Come in," she said, although he was already inside, making his way towards the kitchen.

The electric light was on that night. That meant the power plant had sufficient firewood. Taking a seat at the table, which was littered with dirty plates and cups, Samson glanced up at the modest little lampshade suspended from the ceiling – yellow fabric stretched over a round wire frame.

"I won't heat up any tea." The widow sighed, sitting down beside him. "I can pour you a drop of spiced vodka."

"Please do!" Samson eagerly assented.

A bottle of reddish vodka already graced the table. In front of the widow stood a stemmed shot glass. She filled it, then reached for another – Samson couldn't tell whether it was clean or not – filled that one too, and placed it in front of her guest.

"You're looking awful pale – hollow-cheeked," she said sympathetically.

Samson took a sip. The vodka was strong and bitter, but what he really wanted was something sweet. He recalled his difficult, fruitless interrogation of Anton, who had stared at him with hatred in his eyes, vowing that next time he wouldn't think twice before strangling him with his own hands. The prisoner had shouted with special fury when Samson asked him about Jacobson. If his hands hadn't been bound, he would certainly have wrapped his fingers around Samson's neck. But the rope wouldn't give, and when the prisoner lost all control, soldier Semyon crashed the butt of his rifle into his cheek. Anton immediately quietened down after that, but remained sullen. The transcript of questions and answers didn't come together at all, because Samson couldn't record silence and had no desire to take down insults and threats. It would be clear from the start that the interrogation had failed. Semyon took Anton away to the basement, while Samson went back to his office, left the papers on his desk and decided to report to Nayden the following morning. The case could soon be closed. The stolen goods would be returned to the victims, the failed deserters and partly successful robbers would receive their punishment, while he would turn to other cases. Amid these other cases there would certainly be time for Nadezhda. But then, unexpectedly, she had shown up herself and left a letter.

"So, you're with the police, now?" the widow asked, inspecting the young man thoughtfully.

"Well, yes."

"And you can track down all kinds of killers?"

"I can," Samson responded with excessive self-confidence and looked at his empty glass.

The widow refilled it straight away, and didn't neglect her own, either.

They drank.

"If you find who killed my Peter, I'll pay you in gold," she suddenly declared.

Samson recalled her husband, the yard-sweeper – a large, bearded, loud and affable fellow, who had always unlocked the front door for the young man whenever he came home late from a party, back in his schooldays. The fellow had strong hands. Once, he quarrelled with a drayman and chopped his wagon in half with three blows of an axe. The draymen got together and gave him quite a beating for that, but, after spending two days in bed, he was up and about again, as cheerful, loud and quarrelsome as ever. They found him dead in 1918. It appeared that someone had been pounding at the front door in the middle of the night and the yard-sweeper had opened it. Why, no-one can know.

"Here's your letter," the widow said, handing Samson a note folded in four.

The young man took the note, abandoning his recollections of the murdered yard-sweeper. But then the widow's promise to pay him in gold echoed in his head. He wondered where she might have got her hands on gold. And, in response to this thought, Fyodor's interrogation came to mind. The would-be deserter had explained the absence of gold from their loot by saying he'd been told to take only silver. Samson also remembered the name Jacobson, the mention of which had so frightened Fyodor.

The young man's head began to hurt and buzz, pleading for sleep and rest. He read the note:

Dear Samson,
Where have you disappeared to? I thought our meetings

brought you pleasure, but now I haven't seen your face or heard you voice for several days! Maybe you're bored with me? If so, be honest and tell me!

Nadezhda

"Oh Lord!" Samson burst out.

"What's happened?" the widow asked, alarmed.

"Nearly happened," he responded, and withdrew into himself, trying to figure out when he might be able to see Nadezhda tomorrow. When and where.

"Now that you've arrested those Reds, Nadezhda can move right in!" the widow said. "That'll be good for her, since she works just round the corner. And good for you too – goes without saying . . ."

That last phrase almost angered Samson. What did this old widow mean, good for him? Yet she was right about Nadezhda moving in, and he was glad she'd reminded him. He just needed to think it over after a good night's rest, with a fresh mind. But, then again, he could write a note to Nadezhda before going to bed and leave it with the Red Army soldier guarding the entrance to her place of work. That way, she'd learn first thing in the morning that all her fears were unfounded and that he thought of her and her alone every free minute of the day. It's just that he hadn't had any free minutes in the past three days.

Samson's flat still smelled of kerosene. There was still cold in the air, too, but it wasn't as bad as it had been a week ago. After feeding four birch logs into the stove that heated his bedroom, he climbed under the covers and was immediately carried off down the current of fatigue towards Morpheus. He recalled his plan to write a note to Nadezhda, but his eyes were already closed, his body filling with a heavy, tinny warmth that wouldn't allow him to move or in any other way draw himself from deep sleep.

As soon as he awoke, his mind turned to Nadezhda and the note. In his message, he asked her to forgive him in advance for the hour at which he might appear at her door, promising to try to keep this visit, late though it may be, within the bounds of decency. He explained that he now belonged completely to his job, and said that she, Nadezhda, herself a Soviet employee, should understand him well.

The Red Army soldier on guard took the note without batting an eye, as if he worked at the post office. Apparently, this method of communication was quite common at the Bureau of Statistics.

The first thing Samson did when he arrived at the station was to report to Nayden on the previous day's interrogations and his conclusions. He didn't neglect to mention that he had identified a number of victims.

"Listen," Nayden cautioned, sitting on his couch and kneading the fingers of his left hand, which was suspended by a belt from his neck, with the fingers of his healthy hand. "Don't waste your time. We won't return the silverware – it'll go to the treasury. You can return the fabric and leather if the victims show up on their own and present detailed inventories. Forget everything else. These peasants have committed two crimes: robbery and planned desertion. Desertion is washed away with blood at the front, while robbery ... If there were no war – three years in prison. With the war on – firing squad."

"But I think they were acting on instructions," Samson cut in. "And they're terrified of this person. Jacobson, his name was. He was the one who ordered them to take only silver."

"Nonsense!" Nayden dismissed the suggestion with a wave of his healthy hand. "Maybe someone did tip them off. But we won't waste resources looking for him. I'll discuss it with the higher-ups tomorrow. Most likely, we'll offer them the chance to wash away their crimes with blood – after all, the front is getting closer and closer."

"You mean they may capture Kyiv again?" Samson asked cautiously.

Nayden sighed. "No, no, they will not," he said, after a pause, sounding confident. "They don't have the guts."

"Comrade Nayden, may I ask another question?"

"Well?"

"Why would someone ask them to steal only silver – no gold, no diamonds?" Sincere curiosity sparkled in Samson's eyes, and Nayden couldn't fail to notice it.

He shrugged. "Maybe that someone needs to pour silver ingots . . . or bullets."

"Silver bullets?"

"An unlikely scenario, I admit." Nayden chuckled. "Superstitious people believe silver bullets kill vampires."

"And you believe in vampires?" the young man asked timidly.

Nayden shook his head. "You'd better ask Kholodny," he advised. "Maybe the Church books have something to say about vampires and silver bullets. I haven't read them and I have no intention of doing so. The books I read don't waste words on such claptrap."

Chapter 22

When Samson approached the corner of Zhylianska Street and Dyakov Lane, he grew confused, as there was no residential building in sight. However, what the victimised cobbler had indicated in his statement was not his home address, but the address of his workshop – a small, squat wooden construction, painted blue. By means of this very colouration, it emphasised its rank, its essential difference from the ordinary wooden sheds that enterprising residents had built in every nook and cranny of Halych Square and the adjacent streets and lanes as soon as they sensed the suspension of habitual law and order with the onset of war and revolution. Whereas those unpainted sheds contained firewood and other things for sale, here, in this decent workshop, one's eye was struck by signs of that long-vanished order, and one's nose by the aroma of cobbler's wax, varnish, polish and various types of treated and untreated leather.

"I'm touched," the cobbler said, tears welling up in his eyes. He stared at the components Samson had tipped out of a sack onto the worktable and kept feeling them with his hands, as if it were they that had missed the stolen items most of all. "I'd lost faith ... My wife told me not to bring any complaints to the police. 'They'll make you out to be the guilty one,' she said. 'Don't you see,' she said, 'they don't even remove dead bodies from the streets right away?' But I remember how it was under the tsar. I'd been robbed six times before."

"Six times?" Samson asked, somewhat surprised. "It seemed to me that thefts weren't so common in the old days."

"Oh, young man ... There have always been robberies and

thefts around Halych. I'm not even counting the pickpockets. But I'm touched by this . . . May I at least offer you some money?"

"No, absolutely not," Samson answered, a bit frightened by the offer. "My job is to return stolen goods – that's all. Sign here for receipt, please." He handed the cobbler an inventory of the items.

The cobbler took out a pencil and placed a squiggle at the bottom of the document.

"The thieves did not possess the copper nails you listed in your statement."

"They spilled them out in the street," the cobbler explained. "I later gathered up as many as I could find. I missed a few, of course – they're small, probably fell between the cobblestones. Listen, why don't you come home with me? The wife'll warm up some borscht – what do you say?"

"No, I take my lunches at the cafeteria," Samson said resolutely.

Yet an unprecedented warmth spread across his heart at the realisation that he had made a simple – one might say the simplest – man happy just by performing his official duty. Nayden was right: the people whose silverware had been taken were unlikely to express such gratitude if all or some of their forks and spoons were returned.

From behind, one might easily mistake the cobbler Golikov for a youth of sixteen. Slender, undersized, round-shouldered – even when he stood, his forehead hung over the toes of his shoes as if he was intently interested in those toes and nothing else. But everything fell into place when he sat down in front of the shoe last in his workshop. Then, the cause of his head's constant inclination became clear. The black apron he wore over his sheepskin jacket, which peeked out at the neckline, endowed him with an air of solidity and self-respect.

"If your boots wear out, come see me right away," the owner of the workshop said at parting. "I'm in your debt – keep that in mind!"

Out in the street, in the fresh springtime breeze, Samson stuffed the empty sack into a sizeable canvas bag Vasyl had loaned him from the evidence room. The bag held the suit patterns, but there was more than enough space for the sack.

The young policeman then proceeded along his planned route, taking the number 9 tram to the corner of Mariinsko-Blagovishchenska and Kuznechna streets, and from there going on foot to his late father's tailor on Nimetska. He wanted to hear the man's thoughts about his unidentified colleague, who had suffered a loss by robbery or theft, but did not report it.

Tailors, of course, were of a higher class than cobblers. One could drink tea with them and discuss politics, which his late father's tailor had already proved twice. Besides, Samson thought as he walked, there weren't so many of them in the city, and they probably all knew each other – just like the cobblers, of whom there were probably more, in view of the earthiness and absolute necessity of their work for all residents of Kyiv, not just for those possessed of wealth and taste.

Sivokon, specialist in tailcoats and waistcoats, was delighted to see Samson. He welcomed him cordially into his world, seating him in a soft chair and shouting to his wife to put on the tea kettle.

"The bandage has come off," he said sympathetically, eyeing the healing earhole, which barely showed beneath the young man's leather cap.

"It has," Samson responded with a nod.

"You've changed somehow," Sivokon noted, wrinkling his forehead. "Your face – it's as if you've matured . . ."

"Yes, I feel that way," Samson admitted. Then he opened the square throat of the canvas bag, placed the empty sack on the floor and began to lay the neatly folded suit patterns out on the table.

At this, the tailor's gaze sharpened. He rose from his Viennese chair and came up to the table, smoothed out one pattern with his palm, put on his glasses and leaned closer to examine the numbers chalked on the fabric.

"What is this?" he asked, looking up at the young man. "What have you brought me?"

"These," Samson said, lowering the last piece of chalk-marked black-and-brown-striped fabric onto the table, "are stolen goods . . . But we have no statement from any tailor that matches these items. Perhaps you know if any of your colleagues have recently been robbed?"

"That would be everyone," Sivokon replied with a shrug, then turned his gaze back to the fabric. "But this is Yorkshire wool . . . Would you look at that?" He rubbed the edge of the fabric between his thumb and forefinger. "Expensive – must be from old stock," he concluded. Lifting a piece up to his face with both hands, he added, "Aha, the side, front . . . numbers . . . handwriting looks like Balzer's. He loves to mark them at an angle, rising up."

"Where can I find him?"

"On Baseina, near the old school for foremen. Almost on the corner, across from the covered market. But don't get your hopes up – I heard he was going to Brussels."

"I'll check anyway," Samson said. "If he hasn't left, he'll be glad to have his goods back."

"True," agreed Sivokon, and he again shifted his gaze to the patterns. He lifted another one to his face, shook his head and declared, "A funny size – a husky boy's, by the looks of it. But who'd order his underage son a suit of Yorkshire wool, especially one so formal? There aren't any more imperial or stock-exchange receptions these days, and you wouldn't head out to a weekend work day wearing anything like this . . . Some Red Army man might see it as class warfare and stick his bayonet clean through the suit and its owner . . ."

"Well, maybe he meant to make it for his own son," Samson

suggested. "For his twenty-first birthday, for instance. No-one has cancelled those."

"Not yet," said the tailor.

Samson spotted no shop window that would indicate Balzer's establishment on the segment of Baseina Street where Sivokon had directed him. A confectioner's window, pasted over with newspapers, stared glumly and longingly at the world. Beside this, a door to a shop below street level bore the word DRYSALTER in yellow paint. The ground-floor windows of the two-storey building third from the corner were also half-plastered, but life seemed to be going on as usual on the first floor. The front door was open. Inside, on the wall to the right of the stairs, there was a drawing of a hand pointing up, above the caption CLOTHING REPAIR.

Canvas bag in hand, Samson climbed the wooden steps and knocked on the only door he saw – a tall one.

The bald-headed man with a toothbrush moustache who opened the door examined his visitor intently and angrily through the thick lenses of his spectacles.

"What needs repairing?" he asked, looking down at the bag.

"I'm looking for a tailor named Balzer," Samson responded.

"I don't take major orders anymore," the man replied. "Only minor repairs."

"Does that mean you're him?"

"Yes, I'm Balzer," the man confirmed. "Come inside."

The room behind the door was at once a workshop – apparently temporary – and a thoroughfare, beyond which, it would seem, lay Balzer's flat. A treadle sewing machine stood in one corner on the right. It was draped with a sheet, but this sheet failed to cover the wide pedal used to set the mechanism in motion. An extremely broad table occupied almost half the room. In the far left corner, on a stand, sat five sad irons of different sizes, and to the left, next to the wall, stood a narrow ironing table. Several wooden boxes beneath the windows were likely used to store fabric or tools. The gold-embossed seals of foreign diplomas gleamed in glass-fronted frames on the wall above the irons.

"Well, what have you got there?" Balzer asked impatiently, pointing to the canvas bag. "Go on, I don't have all day."

Samson wasn't irritated by his host's inhospitality. On the contrary, he imagined how Balzer's face would change when he saw the items he had resigned himself to having lost. Surely, if he'd held out any hope, he would have filed a statement.

"I have good news for you," Samson announced. He placed the bag on the table, opened it and began to lay out the pattern.

Balzer turned pale. He looked at the fabric with horror and then, with equal horror, looked up at Samson.

"What is that?" he asked.

"I believe these things were stolen from you. I've come to return them."

Balzer shook his head in denial.

"They aren't mine. Nothing of mine was stolen. There's nothing left to steal," he said. Then he glanced around the room and asked, "Where are you from?"

"The police," Samson admitted. "But I was told this was your speciality – expensive wool."

"Expensive, yes," Balzer confirmed, glancing at the pattern. "But not mine. Take it away!"

Puzzled, Samson began to put the pieces back into the bag, but then suddenly stopped. "Maybe you know who else might have had such fabric?" he suggested, gazing into the tailor's eyes.

Balzer again shook his head before answering. "No idea. Impossible to say. Before the war, there were at least five German tailors in Kyiv. There were more customers here than in Vienna. Maybe one of them . . ."

"Perhaps you recognise the handwriting," Samson said, his finger indicating the numbers chalked above the lines.

"What handwriting? Those are the sizes!" Balzer shot back, clearly nervous.

"May I see one of your own patterns?" Samson asked, his gaze pinning the tailor to the wall.

"I'm not taking any orders, these days ... I have no patterns. Please go."

"Alright, but, if you hear that a tailor's been robbed, you'll come and report it, yes? You know where the Lybid station is?"

"Yes, yes," Balzer said, taking a sudden step forward, nearly pushing Samson away with his chest. "Now go!"

"Quite the character," Samson said under his breath on the bottom step of the wooden staircase.

He stood for a moment, contemplating the meeting that had just occurred. Then, with a shrug, he walked out onto Baseina.

A crow flapped its wings overhead and a feather fell to the road beside him.

Chapter 23

Samson knocked on the closed front door of Nadezhda's home until his hand hurt. Only when he stopped did he hear a woman's frightened voice from within.

"Who do you want?"

"Nadezhda!" he shouted in response, and immediately added, "And Trofim Sigismundovich!"

"They're asleep! Lights are off!"

"Lights are off all across the city," Samson said, looking back at the darkened crossroads. "The power plant must have run out of firewood."

"Alright, wait here. I'll ask," the woman's voice said.

Samson heard shuffling footsteps approaching from the crossroads. This put a fright into him. The solid darkness all but forced him to cling to the closed door, to become part of it, a panel of wood. His right hand rested on his holster, and a finger unfastened its leather strap from the little copper knob. The holster's lid rose.

Just then, when the invisible someone's footsteps seemed to reach the corner of the building, a bolt creaked heavily on the other side of the door and the flame of a candle swayed in the opening. In the flickering glow, Samson saw Nadezhda's face – kind, tender, alarmed.

"Quick, come in," she urged.

Samson pulled the door shut behind him with all his might, and the bolt made it impregnable again.

"My dear Mila is already in bed," said Trofim Sigismundovich, who sat at the table with a warm bathrobe draped over his ordinary clothes – not for the sake of mere cosiness, but for necessary warmth.

Three candles burned in a five-light candelabra at the centre of the table, and the room smelled of kerosene. Samson immediately identified the source of the odour: about two yards from the table, on a rough kitchen stool, stood a Triumph kerosene stove, on which a copper kettle sat boiling, contributing a warm dampness to the living room's atmosphere.

"We've already replaced the water twice," Nadezhda's father announced in a perfectly placid tone, after following his guest's gaze. "My poor Mila wanted to stay up and see you, but she was laid low by a migraine. Please, have a seat – tell us what awaits us."

Samson removed his belt, refastening the holster's cover by hooking the strap over the copper knob, and hung it on the back of his chair. He waited for Nadezhda to finish pouring the tea.

"One hears various things," he said sadly and authoritatively. "The whole country is at war. And we have our own front, of course . . . But, yes, it's looking worse, not better."

Trofim Sigismundovich nodded. "The street lamps are out all over town, now," he added.

"That's temporary . . . But we do have a problem with people stealing state-owned firewood . . ."

"I know. The main thing is to wait out the cold."

"Oh, it's already getting warmer!" Nadezhda cut in joyfully. "In just a little while, we'll start planting flower beds – that should cheer everyone up!"

The conversation turned smoothly towards spring motifs and Samson really did sense a surge of warmth – at least in his heart. He even smiled inwardly. But then he realised that the warmth was actually wafting from the kerosene stove.

Nadezhda's father again followed his guest's gaze, then quickly rose from his chair and went over to put out the stove. Returning to his place at the table, he yawned, which made Samson remember the time.

"Trofim Sigismundovich," the young man began, "my flat is free of its former residents. What I mean is, there is too much space for one person. I would like to offer Nadezhda a room. The flat is right around the corner from her place of work, so she wouldn't need to walk all this way in the dark every evening."

Trofim Sigismundovich sank into thought.

"I don't know how we'll get along without her," he said, after a moment. "Though you're as right as can be. It's a terrifying time – the trams stop running without notice, street lamps go dark and people have grown so ugly inside that they'd slit your throat for an old rouble ... I'd consult with Mila, but she's already asleep. Migraine ..."

He looked at his daughter. She also seemed to be deep in thought, glancing at Samson questioningly, penetratingly, as though she were searching his face, and especially his eyes, for some confirmation of her thoughts and surmises.

"I'd ... probably ... love to," she finally breathed out. "And our chief, Valerian Sergeyevich, would write an order to that effect, to make it official."

"But we've never even paid you a visit," her father said, evidently feeling a bit lost. "It's embarrassing to ask, but what ... amenities do you have for a young woman?"

"Well, you know, I had a sister ... Her room is free. I've never let anyone in there."

"Yes, I know about your sister," Trofim Sigismundovich said, nodding and sighing heavily. "How did you manage to safeguard her room from the new regime?"

"They don't even know about it. I hid my parents' bedroom as well. Blocked one door with a sideboard, the other with a wardrobe."

"How about a little glass of tsarist vodka?" Nadezhda's father suggested unexpectedly.

138

"Papa, what's got into you?" his daughter exclaimed.

"Darling, why don't you go on and get some rest? You have work in the morning. The young man and I will have a little chat, and then I'll walk him down and let him out."

Nadezhda acceded, gave Samson a nod of farewell, smiled and left. Her father brought a decanter and two shot glasses from the sideboard, then moved his chair closer to Samson.

"I understand that you care for her as deeply as we do," he whispered, lifting his glass with two fingers and bringing it to his mouth. "And so I feel well disposed towards you . . ." He drained the glass and waited for Samson to follow his example. "But I wouldn't want you and Nadezhda to . . . irresponsibly . . . indecently . . . you understand?"

Samson nodded.

"Do you believe in God?"

"No, but I have respect," Samson answered.

"Respect for God?"

"Respect for faith as a tradition, though I'm not a believer."

"Well, I'm thinking along the lines of tradition myself," Trofim Sigismundovich said. "If something more than neighbourly should arise in your flat, it may do so only through matrimony . . ."

"Of course," Samson assured him. "I offer only living quarters, protection and care."

"Yes, I see that," Trofim Sigismundovich said, smiling tensely and pouring himself another half-glass.

In order to pull out the bolt, Samson again yanked the bronze handle with all his might. The bolt slid out almost soundlessly. The door opened and let in the smell of smoke. The silence was interrupted by fragmentary echoes of either a late tram or the slap of horseshoes against cobblestones.

"Go with God," Nadezhda's father said in parting and closed the door.

The suddenly interrupted rattle of the bolt revealed to Samson that Trofim Sigismundovich lacked the strength to shut the door tightly. The young man leaned against it with his shoulder.

"Pull again!" he shouted.

"Ah, thank you!" he heard from behind the door when the bolt clanged lightly, having slid all the way into the iron bracket.

Samson didn't much like being invisible yet clearly audible as he walked in total darkness through Podil. Though he lowered his feet to the ground as gently as possible, the metal heel taps on the soles of his boots still gave him away. He had already tried walking on his toes, but this method proved too tiring.

He stopped to rest beside the Fountain of Samson. The city's night-time silence seemed louder there, as if indeterminate noises were rolling down from the hills above. Once in a while, the echo of someone's footsteps would fly into his earless earhole, making him feel uneasy, vulnerable.

Samson pulled his cap down over his right temple, hoping to protect himself from these unhelpful sounds. With the cap askew on his head, he looked just like a regular Podil hoodlum.

Somewhat reassured, he proceeded towards Andrew's Descent.

But then the silhouette of a man stepped out towards him from the shadow of Pyrohoshcha Church and a shot rang out. Against the background of its deafening echo, an errant bullet buzzed like a tiny mosquito past Samson's right temple. The young policeman dropped to the ground, unfastened the strap of his holster, drew the revolver and emptied its cylinder into the silhouette that had fired at him, filling the already shattered silence with seven more strikes of thunder and lightning. Amid these explosive sounds of unexpected battle, something else collapsed onto the road, followed by a groan. Then someone whistled and cried out frantically – but those sounds came from behind the nearby houses, having perhaps bounced more than once between their cold walls.

Quickly jumping to his feet, Samson ran up to the man lying in front of Pyrohoshcha Church. He couldn't see him at all clearly, and he hadn't brought any matches. The man groaned. Samson easily removed the Mauser from his hand, then reached into the pockets of his short overcoat. The sight of the coat gave Samson confidence in the righteousness of his actions and his bravery, since only a bandit would be walking around Kyiv at night dressed like that, with a Mauser.

Samson pulled out some thick papers from the inner pocket and stowed them away in his. In the side pocket, he found a handful of cartridges.

Another shout sounded nearby, followed by the clatter of hobnailed boots.

Not knowing who else might be nearing, Samson rushed up Frolivska Street, leaving behind both the wounded attacker and the strangers hurrying towards the noise of sudden battle. There was no-one he could trust in the lampless darkness of the city.

Chapter 24

In the morning, Samson lay on his side on the very edge of the bed and examined, in the scattered light of dawn, his boots, his holstered revolver and the unholstered Mauser he had left on the floor after coming home. His leather jacket had been treated with somewhat greater respect, ending up draped over the back of the chair at the dressing table.

His head buzzed a little. The young man could as easily ascribe that to the two glasses of vodka he'd downed at Nadezhda's as he could to the shoot-out, from which he'd miraculously emerged victorious.

He remembered his brief conversation with the yard-sweeper's widow, whom he'd had to wake up in order to go upstairs. The front door, which usually remained open late into the night, had this time met him firmly shut, bolted as tightly as Nadezhda's had been. And so Samson again had to knock for a minute, maybe two, before he'd heard the door of the yard-sweeper's flat creak open.

"Who's there?" the widow had called sleepily, only admitting him having digested the response.

"Why'd you lock yourself up?" Samson asked in a tired voice, while inwardly approving her caution.

"Why, he asks," she muttered irritably. "You know plenty well . . . Petliura's men . . ."

"Are they already in town?" the young man joked.

"If not yet, then tomorrow or the day after."

"And who told you that?"

"Heard it at the market."

"Sure, what don't they know at the market?" Samson responded.

"They know a lot, my dear lad," the widow suddenly declared, and her voice no longer sounded sleepy. Quite the contrary. "They know so much, you can't even imagine. The market isn't just for trade, for swapping and lying – it's big politics! People aren't held responsible for their words over there, so they throw the whole honest truth in your face."

Samson had neither the strength nor the desire to discuss news from the market. He'd wanted to help the widow slide the bolt back in place, but she did it herself, easily, because doors constructed responsibly, with heart, remain commensurate with their locks and bolts, don't swell, bend or warp due to rain, snow and wind.

Samson shone a candle on the darkened rectangle of wooden floor between the headboard and the wide windowsill. Until recently, that had been the home of his chest, from which he could have now drawn clean underwear, or even bed linen. But, despite Nayden's endorsement of his statement of erroneous confiscation and return, it remained in Samson's office. If it were here, the jacket would now be lying on top of it, rather than hanging on the back of a chair. He found it convenient to toss his clothes there, on top of the chest, which had always been covered with a tablecloth of white Belgian lace that his mother would wash twice a year.

After lowering his feet to the floor, Samson sat on the bed for a couple of minutes longer, then got up and pulled from his jacket pocket the papers he'd taken from the unknown assailant.

The very first paper he unfolded and read set Samson shivering.

The bearer of this document, Comrade Leonty Adamovich Martens, is an assistant to the head of the Active Department of the Special Branch of the All-Russian Extraordinary Committee (Cheka) attached to the Third Army. All institutions, both civil and military, are obliged to provide him with all possible aid in the performance of his official duties, up to and including: to arrest persons indicated by him, to

conduct searches and seizures immediately at his request, to
check personal documents as he deems necessary. Comrade
Martens is allowed to carry and store all manner of weapons
and must be given unhindered passage.

The photograph glued to the left of the text was additionally stitched with thread, the ends of which were fused into the red wax seal of the institution that had issued the document.

Samson's head was abuzz. The thought that he might have shot a Chekist filled him with horror.

Then, replaying the events of the previous night as if it were a film, he remembered that the Chekist had shot at him first. Why had he done that? Had he been lying in ambush and mistaken Samson for his actual foe?

First the young man's fingers went cold, then his palms. He rubbed them together. His gaze fell on the left side of the bed, where the Chekist's other papers lay. After lowering the identification document, Samson raised the next one to his eyes.

Mandate. This identity card is given to Comrade Mikhail
Vladimirovich Kirillov, member of the Kyiv Provincial
Military Revolutionary Committee and of the Kyiv Provincial
Extraordinary Committee (Cheka), and is certified by signa-
tures and a seal.

The next cardboard document turned out to be some kind of Polish identification card, in the name of a certain Cyprian Budrzewski, without a photograph. The last document, which did have a photograph, certified the identity of Pyotr Filimonovich Kochevykh, assistant to the head of the Kyiv Railway Workshops.

Samson's thoughts were muddled. He picked up the first certificate, with the red seal, and the last. The photographs were indeed the same: a square-faced middle-aged man with blond hair and a slightly contemptuous look in his light-coloured eyes. On one document he was named as the Chekist Martens, on the other as Pyotr Kochevykh, assistant to the head of the Railway Workshops.

The weight on his chest grew heavier. It occurred to him that he had, without the slightest intention, due only to the lack of firewood at the power plant, disrupted some significant Cheka operation. He had heard all about their raids, but, until last night, fate had somehow saved him from witnessing one or, much worse, becoming a target. Now, quite unexpectedly, he had become far more than a witness to an incredible, tragic mistake . . .

Samson decided that he had to report this to Nayden. And he immediately grew calmer.

Honesty is the best means of maintaining self-control and self-respect. That's what Samson's father used to say whenever he sensed his little boy's reluctance to confess to some petty offence. Back then, these words had seemed strange and ponderous to Samson. He knew that people ought to be respected by others, but he couldn't understand why they should also respect themselves. Now, the meaning was clearer, but unfortunately he could no longer share this with his father – except perhaps at the cemetery on Shchekavytsia Hill.

After gathering up the documents and placing them, along with the Mauser and the handful of cartridges, in his briefcase, Samson went down to the station, giving no thought to breakfast or tea. Tea was never a concern, of course – Vasyl always kept everyone on the first floor supplied. He might do the same for those below as well, but Samson wasn't especially interested in the life of the ground floor, with its clerks and interrogation room.

The young policeman turned up at Nayden's small office at an inopportune moment, when the latter was busily writing something at his desk. He asked Samson to come back in half an hour. During that half-hour, Samson lost his burning desire to apprise his senior colleague of the shoot-out near the church. Perhaps this was why, when the time came, he relayed the incident in a confused, halting manner. Nevertheless, he left out no details and laid the Mauser and cartridges, as well as all the documents, on Nayden's table.

"Would you like me to write it all up?" he asked, at the end.

"Hold on," Nayden stopped him.

He studied the documents and turned the Mauser in his hands. His left arm was out of its sling, which presumably meant that his wound no longer troubled him.

"Don't put anything down on paper. I'll hold on to this little lot and do some digging. Then we'll give it some thought," he said, making no attempt to hide his concern.

Before lunch, Samson read through a few dozen victims' statements reporting recent robberies and thefts. No relevant details leapt out, but he observed that they were all written quite competently, which suggested that the victims were all well educated.

"It feels like only the literate are being robbed, these days," he confided to Vasyl as he returned the files.

Vasyl gave the young man a sly look and said, "Only the literate can write. The others just wipe away their tears and move on."

"Perhaps the illiterate don't have anything worth stealing," Samson commented.

"Oh, I wouldn't say that," the chief of tea supplies responded in a significant tone as he left the office.

As he watched him go, Samson noticed the near soundlessness of his boots. They did creak a bit, yes, but the footfalls themselves were quiet. That meant he didn't have metal heel taps.

Shutting and locking his door, Samson pulled off his boots and, with the help of the custom screwdriver used for assembling and disassembling his revolver, freed the soles of their loud metal attachments. Now, he thought, no-one would hear him at night.

He asked Kholodny to keep him company over lunch, and the two walked over to the Soviet cafeteria. In exchange for their vouchers, they each received a bowl of pea soup, a plate of maize porridge with a piece of herring and a glass of fruit compote.

As he slurped his soup, Samson told the former priest about the strange behaviour of the German tailor, who wanted nothing to do with the patterns that had been stolen from him.

"Maybe the fabric he used had been stolen too," Kholodny speculated, rubbing the delicate pale skin of his clean-shaven cheeks. "Could have assumed you'd come to arrest him – probably has his hand buried in the jam pot."

"I wanted to ask something else," Samson mused aloud, looking up at his colleague. And then, despite himself, an entirely different question passed his lips: "Is it possible to get married outside of a church, these days?"

Kholodny nearly choked on his soup. He cleared his throat and a smile of satisfaction spread across his face.

"Of course," he said, sipping his compote. "I know this one atheist priest, name of Artemy. He built himself a chapel on the Dog Path, just past the flophouse and the mortuary. He stops people heading to the Monastery of the Caves and explains all about God and prayers."

"What exactly does he explain?"

"Well, you know, gives sermons against God – explains that they're wasting their time, that prayers won't make their hopes come true."

"But, if he performs the ceremony, it would still be in a church, wouldn't it?" Samson asked, failing to follow Kholodny's reasoning.

"The chapel of a priest who doesn't believe in God is no church. It's practically a Soviet institution."

"If it's an institution, then it must have a seal, to make a union official?"

"I don't know about a seal," Kholodny admitted. "But we passed right by it when we were out on patrol. You can go and ask. Just watch out for those dogs – there's no end of them . . . Remember, the name's Father Artemy."

"I'll remember." Samson nodded, and then the main question he had for Kholodny again flashed through his mind. "I was wondering . . . Why would anyone need a cache of stolen silver?"

"Stolen?" Kholodny asked. "If not stolen, then I would say monasteries. They can always use it – for icon revetments, crosses . . . But stolen – that I don't know. Maybe to cleanse the water in a well? Unlikely. That's how they did it in the old days."

"But say someone believes in vampires – enough to be afraid of them," Samson continued. "Might such a person make silver bullets?"

Kholodny took a deep breath.

"Can't say," he said uncertainly. "They've been finding people drained of blood for centuries. Maybe vampires do exist. Who knows? And, as for silver bullets, I even read about that in the paper once, a long time ago. A fellow killed his neighbour – silver bullet to the heart. Said the poor man was a vampire. But they didn't find any evidence."

"That the neighbour was a vampire?"

"That's right," Kholodny answered. "I'll say this: if vampires do exist, then they've got to be charming – nice, smart people – to lure their victims. They don't go around drinking blood in other people's houses."

"How do you know that?" Samson asked, surprised at his colleague's knowledge.

"That's what they say. I don't believe in it myself. It's darkness that drives these thoughts into people's heads."

Before the sun set, Vasyl came to Samson without tea and announced that Samson and Kholodny would again go on patrol at midnight. This time, they'd be accompanied by an armed Red Army soldier. Until then, Samson could go home and rest.

Samson decided not to walk home, but take a cab – along with his confiscated chest. He found a cart without difficulty and paid the cabby in advance. And, when he and Vasyl were taking the chest out into the street, Samson heard, amid the general uproar pouring from the open doors on the ground floor, the following words: "Look at that ... The one-eared wonder's requisitioned himself a whole chest of stolen goods ..."

These words stuck in Samson's head until midnight. They troubled him so much that, when he was about to go on patrol, he ordered the young Red Army man, Semyon, to head downstairs, where the seconded soldiers were awaiting their assignments, and proclaim loudly, for everyone to hear, that the chest Samson had taken from the station was his own and had only been confiscated by mistake, a fact acknowledged and endorsed by Comrade Nayden.

Chapter 25

Samson was easily awakened by a polite knock at the door. After a night of patrolling, his sleep wasn't particularly deep. His body demanded rest, of course, but his mind was reluctant to switch off. Thoughts swarmed through his head, together with fresh memories from the night, during which they had encountered three other patrols, including another Chinese one. And, of course, at each encounter the patrols checked each other's documents. But all these certificates and confirmations of identity no longer inspired full confidence in Samson's heart. The papers of Martens-Kochevykh – a man with two surnames, one face and one Mauser – would float up before his eyes. If one could even attach multiple names to a photograph, then documents without photos would appear to be totally useless. How could they be trusted? Simply because they bore seals and signatures? There were hundreds of seals and signatures, these days – thousands. For some reason, the only papers Samson didn't suspect were those of the Chinese Red Army men. In general, Chinese names written in Cyrillic somehow aroused his respect, even admiration. The sound of running feet, which still echoed in his right earhole, also contributed to his wakefulness. He and his comrades had heard that sound several times, but they had never gone in pursuit, because it wasn't clear where the feet were running to or from in the Kyiv darkness. The last occasion turned out to be the loudest, and, in that case, in fact, it seemed obvious which direction they should take. Nevertheless, they made no attempt to follow the unknown runner. Had he fired a shot and then taken off, maybe ... But he hadn't. There were other shots, further off, either from the direction of the Dnipro or from Pechersk. These only emphasised what the three on patrol already understood – that, along with the melting snow and ice, scum that had lain frozen all winter long was now thawing out. And this scum had resumed stealing, robbing and killing, only with more frequency than before. There were more thieves around, and it just so happened that their thefts of state-owned firewood deprived the city of street lighting, making the dirty work of robbery that much easier.

The wooden floor pricked Samson's bare feet with fine needles of cold. He had slept in his clothes, having only removed his boots, and this was why he was able to stagger out into the hallway immediately and open the front door.

"Nadezhda's here to see you, with a young gentleman," the yard-sweeper's widow announced. She pushed him aside and stepped into the hallway, followed by the aforementioned pair.

Nadezhda, in her unbuttoned sheepskin coat, smiled at Samson. The young man, who wore a brown leather cap and an unusual black cloth jacket cut like an ordinary leather jacket, nodded in greeting to his host, who immediately extended his hand.

"Valerian Poddomov," the young man introduced himself. "I'm Nadezhda's chief. She said that she might move in here. I thought I'd come and see the place for myself, make sure everything was in order."

"Everything's in order," Samson assured him and yawned.

They entered the living room, and Valerian Poddomov immediately looked through the open door into the bedroom, where his host's boots lay by the bed. Samson closed the door.

"Here, you see, two stoves," he said, drawing the attention of Nadezhda's chief to the flat's sources of heat.

"Is the latrine operational?" Poddomov asked, turning back to the hallway.

"Of course," Samson responded, leading everyone into the kitchen, where he first opened the door to the lavatory, then showed them the bathroom. "Water, as you know, isn't always available."

"And where do you plan to accommodate Nadezhda? In which room?"

The widow roamed the corners of the flat with her eyes – and this irritated Samson. She'd visited him before and had never shown any curiosity about the flat, so why were her eyes prowling about now?

Back in the living room, Samson glanced at the sideboard, which concealed the door to his deceased sister's room. Then his gaze turned to the wardrobe blocking the door to his parents' room.

"You don't have much space here," Poddomov said doubtfully.

Samson's gaze again lingered on the man's strange jacket, which appeared to be home-made. It seemed to him that he discerned some sort of pattern in the fabric, black on black. It looked like a series of crosses . . .

"Give me a hand," he said to Poddomov, and he went over to the left side of the wardrobe. "Let's move it over there."

"You should have emptied it first." Poddomov exhaled heavily after they had transferred the wardrobe to the right wall, where it now stood between the two windows facing the street, partially blocking the right one.

Samson opened the door that the wardrobe had previously concealed. There, in the middle of his parents' spacious bedroom, stood a wide bed. To its left was a mirrored dressing table, two chairs and an étagère with glass perfume bottles and powder boxes.

"Oh, how lovely!" Nadezhda exclaimed, clasping her hands. "Isn't it?" she asked, turning to her chief.

"No doubt," Poddomov agreed. "My wife and I moved in with a confectioner and his family, not far from here. But our quarters aren't as nice as this . . . So, Nadezhda Trofimovna? Will you take it?"

"I will!"

"Well, then – thank you," Valerian said, extending his hand to Samson. "I'll write out an order for relocation, with seal and signature, and Nadezhda Trofimovna will bring it along with her."

"If you don't mind my asking," Samson said, eying the visitor's jacket for the third time, "did you make that yourself?"

"Not a chance!" Poddomov laughed. "They brought us requisitioned cassocks from the Vydubychi Monastery, two per employee. I took mine to the tailor and had him make me a jacket. He padded it with cotton wadding to make it warm."

"Ah, I see," Samson said with a nod. Then he remembered the German tailor, as well as the suit patterns, which still lay in the canvas bag.

Returning to the station before lunch, Samson reported to Nayden and, after asking soldier Semyon to bring up Fyodor Bravada for another round of questioning, went into the windowless room with its chair, table and shackled stool.

Fyodor looked better this time. Either the bruises had faded, or he'd been allowed to scrub his face with soap. He sat down on the stool and frowned at Samson. The young policeman didn't like that. He called Semyon to the door and told him, in a whisper, to ask Vasyl for some tea.

They sat silently in the gloomy room, he and Fyodor, until the soldier brought a tin cup of tea. Samson handed the cup to Fyodor, whose face registered surprise. The prisoner raised his hands, which were bound at the wrists with rope, grabbed the hot cup and lowered it to his knees.

"Tell me," Samson began. "How many tailors did you rob?"

"Don't remember," Fyodor replied. "I already told you, we broke into two shops, but we couldn't find anything to wear."

"Did you get a look at the tailor from whom you took the patterns and the fabric? Was he there in person?"

"Yes, but he was hiding behind a chair."

"And he didn't say anything?"

"Just swore at us."

"In what language?"

"You think I was listening? He swore when Anton nailed him with the butt of his rifle. At first, he jumped out and started shouting."

"What was he shouting? Was it in a foreign language? Or did he have an accent?"

"Called us trash, something else . . . There was one word I didn't get – *schweisse*?"

"Maybe *schwein* or *scheisse*?" Samson asked.

"Yeah, that's it – *scheisse*!"

Samson nodded in satisfaction as he wrote down his questions and Fyodor's answers on a sheet of paper. Then he decided to change the subject and again asked about Jacobson and the silver. But here Fyodor clammed up, turning his face away from the interrogator and towards Semyon. He stared at the soldier and his rifle, which stood like a column, its bayonet pointing up at the gloomy grey ceiling.

"Alright, drink your tea," Samson said, resigning himself to the fact that the conversation would go no further.

After lunch, there was a riot in the basement. The deserters beat a horse thief to a fine pulp. It took Nayden himself to break up the fight. He raced downstairs and fired a revolver over the rioters' heads. They retreated to the far wall, frightened at the fierce gleam in his eyes. Two Red Army men managed to drag the horse thief to the stairs. The other prisoners were locked up, and Nayden leaned over the beaten man, asking, "Got you good, didn't they?"

The horse thief nodded and tried to spit, but instead the bloody saliva dripped from the corner of his mouth.

"I'll tell you what," Nayden said. "Rest up here, then get the hell out. We don't have space for you, anyway. If we catch you again, I'll beat you myself. Understood?"

The horse thief lifted his head slightly, trying to nod again, and mumbled something.

"Prop him up against the wall," Nayden ordered the sentry. "When he's able to walk, let him walk – don't detain him."

In the evening, the deserters were taken away, Anton and Fyodor among them. They were taken in a truck, with guards.

"Close the case on these two," Nayden told Samson, as he stepped into his office and flopped into a club chair. "Write down that they agreed to atone with blood."

"Yes, Comrade," Samson replied obediently.

The file, all twelve of sheets of it, lay on his desk: the interrogation transcripts, along with the inventories of stolen goods.

"You'll stitch that up and put it in a box," Nayden added. Then he looked up at the ceiling, where a single bulb glowed dimly in a green lampshade, and sank into thought. "Those documents you brought present an interesting story," he said with a grin, lowering his gaze to Samson's face. "All fake. There's no Chekist named Martens, no Pole named Budrzewski, no Kirillov and no Kochevykh in the natural world. That is, such creatures might exist in nature, but in some other nature, not in ours. So, no-one knows who it was you killed."

"Killed?" Samson asked, tensing up. "I didn't kill him, I only wounded him."

"Wounded? With three bullets to the heart and four to the stomach?" Nayden laughed. "Pasechny won't believe it . . . He thinks he's the best shot in our precinct, but it turns out he's wrong."

"But he was moaning when I left him! They found him dead?"

"They did. And even snapped a photograph. No-one came to claim the corpse, so they gave it to medical students, at least for now. Took him over to the surgical theatre on Fundukleev Street."

"Would you allow me to conduct one last interrogation?" Samson asked, after a moment. "Not of the deserters themselves, but the tailor they robbed. He was terribly scared when I showed him the patterns . . . And he's German, you know."

"He's just scared that our side is in charge. Half of Kyiv feels the same way," Nayden responded.

"Kholodny suggested that what the soldiers took may have been stolen in the first place, by or for the tailor," Samson said.

"So, you want to spook him and solve another case of theft? Is that what Kholodny's thinking?" Nayden asked, lowering his gaze to the floor and twisting his lips, as if pondering something unpleasant. A moment or two later, he spoke again. "Alright, take a Red Army soldier and lock this German up for a day. He'll reveal all his fears. But don't go after any more thieves, or we'll end up packing the whole basement with rabble again and they'll slit each other's throats."

At around nine o'clock in the evening, Samson found himself stitching together the case documents with coarse grey thread. He was about to cut off the needle with a knife when he remembered his plan to interrogate the German tailor. Maybe the fellow would have something interesting to say – then he'd have to stitch another transcript into the file.

He slid the case, with needle dangling, into the top drawer of his desk, then rolled out a strip of soft mastic, stuck it to the edge of the drawer and pressed in his seal.

The lampless dark again enveloped Kyiv in an atmosphere of fear and danger. The occasional military vehicle drove through the deserted streets, the yellow rays of their headlights trembling. Samson, with wooden holster hanging menacingly from his belt, and soldier Semyon, rifle slung over his shoulder, were walking towards Baseina Street. The soles of Samson's boots landed on the cobblestones with a thud, but without a metallic ring, which pleased the young policeman. He was pleased, too, that the soles of Semyon's boots were similarly discreet. The sounds of their official presence did not rupture the city's humming quiet, but rather blended into it.

Samson found the right entrance at once, and the two almost groped their way up the wooden stairs to the first floor. The young policeman knocked – first politely, then forcefully. It seemed to him that he heard something on the other side, either footsteps or a chair scraping softly across the floor. But no-one opened the door. Samson began to pound on it with both hands.

"Who is there?" the familiar voice finally sounded.

"The police!" Samson shouted. "I brought you those patterns, remember? Open up!"

"I was already asleep," the tailor responded.

"Open the door," Samson insisted. "I have two questions for you."

Once again, there was the sound of a chair moving across a wooden floor, and then came the light rattle of a key unlocking the door. Samson took a step back, as he didn't remember which way the door opened.

It opened outwards. A hand holding a glowing kerosene lamp appeared in the gap, followed by a frightened face.

Samson grabbed the tailor by the wrist and snatched the lamp, causing its glass chimney to fly off and shatter at their feet.

"You're under arrest," Samson said.

It was as if someone had shoved the tailor in the back. He fell on Samson with all his weight. A shot rang out and the tailor's eyes froze in place, while his body became even more unbearably heavy. Samson began to sink to the floor. A man in a coat jumped out from behind the tailor, and Samson lurched back in surprise, bumping his back against the railing and barely keeping his footing on the top step. He couldn't make out the coated man's face in the light of the kerosene flame, which danced wildly in the absence of its glass chimney – only his silhouette and his extended hand, which held a revolver or pistol, its muzzle staring directly at Samson's chest. The young policeman let go of the tailor, whose body slid down and spread out across nearly the entire landing. Samson had maybe a second or two to live, but at that moment soldier Semyon, who had been standing against the wall on the right, grabbed the hand that held the weapon, initiating a struggle – a very short one. The unidentifiable man somehow wriggled free, fired at Semyon and thundered down the stairs. The front door flew open.

A gust of wind from the street blew out the kerosene lamp. It was now dark and quiet. Samson sank to his haunches and felt the prone bodies with his hands. The soldier had hit and smashed the tailor's face with the butt of his rifle as he fell. Both were dead.

Chapter 26

The warm rays of the sun reached down and tinted with gold the mounds of black earth dug out to make ample space for the fraternal Red Army grave on the far left fringes of Oleksandrivsky Park, a good distance from the Church of Alexander Nevsky and the old graves scattered around it. A brass band was playing. The musicians, with their flabby non-military faces, wore army great-coats and boots. Their heads, however, were uncovered, so they couldn't help but feel the radiant touch of the sun on their scalps, just as they couldn't help but feel the light breeze ruffling their hair. This day in early April could have remained in the memory as the initial moment of spring, if not for the chill blowing from the direction of the vast pit, at least seven yards deep, at the bottom of which living Red Army men were packing in the dead, laying their rough-hewn pine coffins shoulder to shoulder.

Samson didn't wish to count the coffins, but he couldn't stop himself. Twenty-two on the far side of the long pit, and therefore twenty-two on the near side, too, where his view was obscured.

Beside him stood Nadezhda, wearing an old dark grey coat – apparently her mother's – and a red kerchief on her head. The tears glistening in her eyes began to roll down her cheeks as soon as the brass band struck up the revolutionary funeral march, "You Fell Victim to a Fateful Struggle".

When they were through with that number, the musicians struck up another, less intelligible, but still tragic melody, reminiscent of a tearful ballad.

A crow cawed and unexpectedly leapt to the ground from one of the branches above Samson's head. The young man watched it waddle through the crowd in the direction of the grave. No-one else seemed to pay attention to the black bird. The music stopped. A commissar jumped onto a small platform cobbled together from wooden boards.

"Dear comrades," he said. "War takes away the best we have. The enemy has not yet been defeated. He hides and shoots from around the corner. But we won't take it any longer. Last year, we declared that the enemies of the revolution would face Red Terror – that it would chew them up and spit them out, and that no-one will so much as remember their existence. But we will not forget you, our fallen heroes. We will elevate you to the rank of Red saints – of those who were unafraid to make the ultimate sacrifice for their faith in a brighter future. You fell victim to a fateful struggle. And the battle continues. New recruits are ready to take your place. We are inexhaustible! We are invincible! We are destined to win, no matter the cost! Hurrah!"

After his "hurrah", the band struck up again, and the Red Army soldiers and officers removed their caps. The blades of a dozen shovels flashed in the sun, and earth drummed on the coffin lids as it was returned to the pit.

A heavy hand descended on Samson's shoulder. The young man shuddered and turned around. Nayden stood on his right. He had already removed his hand, but, catching Samson's gaze, gave him a respectful, almost imperceptible nod.

"This will be a graveyard of heroes," he said softly. "A nice place to remember them. Overlooking the Dnipro."

"He was trying to save me," Samson said sadly, recalling Semyon.

"He did save you," Nayden corrected him. "Simple human heroism. And would you have saved him, had the situation been reversed?"

Samson was stricken by a sudden paralysis of thought. What he had heard in Nayden's question wasn't a question, but an unpleasant statement.

"I don't know," he admitted, after a brief pause.

"I was just asking," Nayden said, shaking his head. "I've tried to put myself in his place, too. He did what he did because he wasn't thinking. The only way to be heroic, to save someone, is to act without thinking ahead. If you're used to thinking and can't help but think ahead, it won't work . . ."

Samson nodded. He couldn't argue with what Nayden had said. Thoughts did sometimes get in the way – namely, when something important can be accomplished only without thinking.

"Come back to our place for a minute," Samson suggested to Nayden, checking with a glance that Nadezhda had heard his invitation.

She had, and now leaned forward a little, looking into Nayden's face. "Yes, yes, do come."

Nayden consented. "Pasechny is running the show at the station, working with fresh recruits," he said, justifying to himself, more than to them, the short-term deviation from official duty to which, in view of the present mournful circumstances, he had agreed.

He entered Samson's flat without so much as a look around, as if he had been there a hundred times already. He spotted the table in the living room and sat down.

Each of them downed a shot glass of medicinal alcohol, which Nadezhda's father had sent over with his daughter. They didn't eat and sat in silence.

"Kyiv will be hard to defend," Nayden said suddenly. "We're surrounded by bandits. From Boryspil, from Sviatoshyn . . . Sometimes they're on our side, sometimes not . . . They launch attacks on the outskirts, loot and steal. We need to strengthen the army."

Samson sighed heavily.

"Did Semyon have a wife?" Nadezhda asked.

Samson rose without answering, went into his room and retrieved from the windowsill the papers he had pulled from the murdered soldier's overcoat. In addition to his identity card and a pass authorising him to walk the streets of Kyiv at any time of night, Semyon also kept in his pocket a photograph of his wife – a simple, thin-faced woman with a slightly upturned nose. Samson lowered the papers onto the table. Nadezhda immediately reached for the photo.

"To my dear husband, Semyon, from his eternally longing wife, Xenia," she read in a trembling voice. And again tears rolled down her cheeks. "I'll never marry," she said. "It's just asking for grief . . ."

Samson looked at her, his eyes widening.

"Nadezhda, what are you talking about?"

"I don't want to end up like that, trapped in eternal grief," she explained in a barely audible voice.

Nayden glanced at her in a critical manner, then rose to his feet and shifted his gaze to Samson.

"We should go. We've paid our respects, now back to the battle."

"Perhaps I ought to visit the scene," Samson said, also rising, but less decisively. "Conduct a search of the tailor's workshop. Might find something important."

"Back to the station, then. I'll write out a search warrant."

"What if someone gets there first?"

"It's sealed."

"But there's no sentry on guard."

"No sentry, true," Nayden agreed. "Alright, go. I'll write the warrant in the evening. Don't forget to stitch it into the case file."

"This is the same case? The deserters?" Samson asked.

"What's the matter with you?" Nayden responded crossly. "Want to toss everything into one pile? No, this is a new case – murder. Double homicide. Understood?"

Samson nodded.

The sun continued to warm the cobblestones and the walls of houses. The people in the street were all poorly dressed, although the faces of some betrayed them as participants in a masquerade where no-one wished to be caught in the wrong costume. Only the soldiers and officers didn't pretend to be anything other than soldiers and officers. They walked with habitual quickness, as if always on duty, and maintained an air of busyness and preoccupation even when sitting in cars and cabs.

The number 7 tram came ringing past, skirting the indoor Besarabsky Market, and some woman peered at Samson from the window as if he were an old acquaintance. The tram turned onto Hora Kruhla.

No-one had broken the seal over the door of Balzer's workshop. Quite possibly no-one had even climbed the steps in the last two days. Samson opened the door and entered. The dead silence within put him in mind of the tailor's and Semyon's tragic end, impelling him to commemorate them with a moment of mournful thought.

Samson looked through every box and drawer, examining two dozen large pieces of fabric. Then he removed the sheet from the treadle sewing machine and discovered beneath its needle three cuts of the familiar black-and-brown-striped Yorkshire wool, chalked with numbers, lines and arrows. These patterns definitely seemed related to those Balzer had so bluntly refused to accept. Samson rolled them up and wedged them in the pocket of his leather jacket. From the side drawer of the sewing table, he drew two notepads and a stack of papers covered with pencilled writing. Then he went into the living quarters, which comprised a room with an iron bed, a kitchenette with an expensive two-tiered kerosene stove, and a toilet with a pitcher and washbasin. Two plywood suitcases lay under the bed – the first fastened with a clasp, the second with a strap. In the one with the clasp, Samson found not only a significant number of Kerenskys, Dumkas and coupons, but also German marks, as well as a small lady's pistol and a dagger with the words *Gott mit uns* engraved on its blade. There was nothing in the other suitcase apart from clothes, which seemed too plain for a man in

Balzer's line of work. At that point, Samson remembered that he hadn't checked the murdered tailor's pockets. Though perhaps it was more surprising that he'd managed – in complete darkness, stunned by the sound of the shot – to feel through the pockets of Semyon's overcoat and pull out the papers. The young policeman placed everything that was of interest to him in one suitcase and carried it out of the flat, sealing the door behind him.

Back at the station, he pulled the old patterns out of the canvas bag and placed the newly acquired pieces on top of them. Looking closely at the chalk marks, he realised that he had found what were to become a pair of jacket pockets. He couldn't quite imagine what these pockets would look like, but he had no doubt that was what they were.

He suddenly recalled the words of Sivokon the tailor, who had examined the stolen set of patterns. What had he said about their size?

Samson strained his memory and called up Balzer's face as the German had opened the door with a kerosene lamp in his hand. Not without difficulty, he replayed the moment when, after the shot, Balzer began to collapse onto him and the figure of the shooter appeared from behind the tailor's back. The figure was tall, strong, stout. Just think how easily he had wriggled free when Semyon had grabbed him – wriggled free, fired and thundered down the stairs.

Samson replayed those thundering footfalls on the wooden steps. The figure must have been huge.

A sudden insight startled Samson's mind. The person who had killed the tailor and Semyon would have worn the Yorkshire wool suit had Anton and Fyodor, who needed civilian clothes in order to desert, not intervened. That had to be the answer.

Samson leaned back in his chair, unbuckling his holster belt and lowering it to the floor. He sat in silence for some five minutes. Then he placed the cut but unsewn suit back in the canvas bag and took

Balzer's notebooks and papers out of the suitcase. He laid them on the desk just to the left of the leather inlay. On the inlay, he placed an old tsarist circular, clean side up, and wrote in pencil: *The case of the murder of Red Army soldier Semyon Glukhov and the tailor Friedrich Balzer, a German national. Begun 3 April 1919.*

Chapter 27

On Friday evening, tired and worried, Samson received guests. Nadezhda's parents arrived on a cart with a suitcase and a chest of her possessions.

The yard-sweeper's widow rushed out into the street to get a better look at the items before they were taken up to Samson's flat.

Trofim Sigismundovich greeted her respectfully, but when he learned from Samson who she was, his gaze in her direction no longer evinced respect.

The widow also got in everyone's way on the stairs, acting as if she expected Samson to invite her up, too. But he was preoccupied with more serious matters, so her tactics merely annoyed him.

He and Nadezhda hadn't managed to prepare dinner, as both had been too busy at work. But, on the way home, Samson had had his cabby pull over at the Soviet cafeteria on Khreshchatyk, where he persuaded the young cook to load four vouchers' worth of pearl-barley porridge with crackling into his state-issued pot. Realising that before her stood a representative of official power and order, she gave him what was likely six vouchers' worth. Needless to say, she didn't offer him any soup or compote. Even if she had, he wouldn't have been able to transport the liquid without significant losses.

While heating the porridge and crackling on his kitchen stove, Samson fretted feverishly over the fact that he didn't have any vodka in the house. There was still half a bottle of his father's beloved hazelnut liqueur left, but it was impolite to put a half-empty bottle on the table. At first, he considered going down to ask the widow, but she preferred moonshine and bitter home-made liqueurs to shop-bought vodka – they were both cheaper and more to a commoner's taste. In the end, he opened the sideboard and spotted a decanter, and the problem resolved itself. Leaving its pulp in the bottle, the hazelnut tincture streamed into its new home, acquiring a dignified appearance.

Nadezhda had taken her mother and father into her room – once the bedroom of Samson's late parents. Trofim Sigismundovich emerged a few minutes later and explained that his daughter was changing for dinner.

Samson imagined Nadezhda going through the dresses and skirts in the newly arrived chest, trying them on and leaning over to the mirror on the dressing table. She would probably ask her mother's opinion every time.

Soon, they were all seated at the table – Nadezhda in a white blouse and dark blue skirt that fell below the knees; her mother, Lyudmila, in a black skirt and warm green jersey; and, of course, Trofim Sigismundovich, with a handkerchief sticking out of the breast pocket of his suit.

They happily ate their porridge and crackling. Nadezhda and her mother abstained from drinking the liqueur, leaving it to Samson and Trofim Sigismundovich.

"You can sleep well here," said Nadezhda. "The windows overlook the courtyard, which is always quiet. The gate is locked, to keep the yard-sweeper's and neighbour's sheds safe."

"Two sheds! Neither of them robbed!" the young woman's father exclaimed, raising the index finger of his right hand. "That's what I call order! We have cellars in the yard – all empty, locks torn off."

"Trofim, dear, what did you expect?" his wife asked, giving him a kindly look. "We're down in Podil, but this is uptown, where they look after things properly."

"Yes," Trofim Sigismundovich responded with a nod. "While we were riding over in the cart, we counted five patrols, three of them

Chinese. By the way, I spoke with a Chinese soldier when I went out for bread. It turns out they're railway builders. They were granted a concession to lay rails to Murmansk under the tsar. Then came the war and revolution. That's how they got to Kyiv. They like it here, but they'd still like to go home."

"We can't let them go now!" Samson chuckled. "On the contrary, I'd like to make them all policemen."

"Well, there are already Chinese in the local Cheka," Trofim Sigismundovich confirmed. "A neighbour told me of a conversation she'd overheard between two Chekists at Zhytniy Market. They were arguing about who shoots the proletariat's enemies better, Red Army soldiers or the Chinese. One said it was the Chinese – their hands never tremble, and they keep their facial muscles so firm that it's as if each of them were Themis herself."

"Oh, Nadezhda, have you told Samson about your extraordinary work?" Lyudmila said, her eyes flashing enthusiastically at her daughter. Then, shooting a disapproving look at her husband, she added, "We've heard enough about executions, wouldn't you say?"

"No, I haven't told him," Nadezhda admitted. "Samson and I don't talk about work. As soon as we start, he gets gloomy and pensive." She gazed tenderly at the young man. "His job is so unpredictable."

"Well, so is yours," her father put in.

"Why would you say that?" the young woman asked. "Our work is extremely predictable! Everything's based on mathematics."

"So, tell me, have you already counted all of Kyiv?" her mother intervened again.

"We've recorded it all, but it will still take some time to add it up," Nadezhda said, nodding. "This isn't a simple census of the population, like under the tsar. We've also measured every home and factory, every flat, every public building . . . Comrades Bisk and Dvinyaninov have successfully organised a gigantic undertaking."

"So how many of us are there in Kyiv, in total?" Trofim

Sigismundovich asked. "I believe you've already told me, but I forget."

"Over five hundred thousand!" Nadezhda responded.

"Including the Red Army?" Samson asked, his face showing surprise.

"No, without the Red Army."

"And without the Chinese?" her father asked.

"Without the Chinese serving in the Red Army," the young woman answered. "We have, of course, counted those who just live here."

"Who makes up the largest share, by nationality?" her mother asked.

"Russians. Then Ukrainians. And the Jewish population is about twenty per cent."

"Are there many Germans?" Samson asked thoughtfully.

"How could she possibly remember it all?" asked Nadezhda's mother, standing up for her daughter, who hesitated over her answer.

"She remembers everything perfectly! If she didn't, they wouldn't have hired her," Trofim Sigismundovich pointed out.

"Three thousand four hundred," Nadezhda finally pronounced. "The smaller groups are easier to count," she added with a smile.

"And what are their professions, these Germans?" Samson asked, his gaze suddenly growing concentrated.

"We didn't ask about professions. Only nationality, age and literacy."

"Well, then, how literate are Kyiv's Germans?" Samson, who had developed a sudden interest in the census, persisted.

"Oh, that's a hard one." Nadezhda sighed. "According to the cards, half of them are illiterate. But that's in Russian – in their own language, they're perfectly literate. The same with the French."

"You mean we have French people here in Kyiv?" her father asked, taken aback.

"Yes, but not many. Just over three hundred."

"I never would have thought!" exclaimed Trofim Sigismundovich. "Maybe they just called themselves French, to set themselves apart, when in fact they're Little Russians or Crimean Karaites?"

"Papa, if we had the time, we might even statistically calculate how many liars there are in Kyiv!" Nadezhda laughed. "But, honestly, what surprises me most is that we seem to have smart streets in town as well as stupid streets."

"What do you mean?" asked Samson.

"Just that! For instance, we live on one of the most literate streets. Podil is only a bit less educated. While the least literate place in Kyiv is Priorka."

"I can't say one way or the other. I don't know a soul who lives there," Trofim Sigismundovich said, shrugging.

"And this is precisely why you don't," Nadezhda responded with a smile. "It appears that literate people like to settle near others of their kind, and it's the same with the illiterate. That's how we get educated streets and stupid ones."

"We mustn't be so arrogant," Lyudmila chimed in, disapproving of her daughter's conclusion. "Illiterate people aren't necessarily stupid. One can learn to read and write, but intelligent thinking is another matter."

This conversation about Kyivan statistics could have gone on endlessly, but it came to a close when Trofim Sigismundovich began to yawn uncontrollably. Samson walked Nadezhda's parents down to the street in his service uniform, revolver at his side. They had to walk as far as the corner of Stepanivska, near the bathhouses, to find a cab. To Samson's surprise, the baths were open, but perhaps only for the Red Army; as they approached the cab, three soldiers, with faces flushed, came out of the bathhouse in their greatcoats, but without weapons.

When the cabby realised that he would be driving the respectable couple, not the man with a revolver, he nodded obligingly, seated

Trofim Sigismundovich and Lyudmila, and covered their knees with warm sackcloth.

The cab took off, its wheels rattling along the cobblestones towards Halych Square. The horses' shoes, too, hammered metallically, contributing a noisy liveliness to the evening darkness. Samson looked around. The soldiers from the bathhouse had already vanished. Nearby, on Stepanivska, the street lamps were lit. Halych Square also shone bright with electricity, but its light only reached Samson from around the corners, as its street lamps didn't fall within his field of vision.

Chapter 28

In the morning, Samson remembered how he had once woken up as a child in the same room in which he now slept – woken up in a panic. He had gone out into the living room to ask his parents to let him into their room, but had stopped in front of their closed door, daring neither to knock nor to open it without knocking.

He remembered this because, towards morning, he had dreamed of Semyon – of how the murdered soldier had told him, on their joint patrol, about Chernihiv and about his dog. The dog was a stray, ownerless, but expensive: a black poodle. She was wearing a dirty leather collar when she came to them, wandering into their courtyard through the hole left in place of the stolen gate. Back then, in Chernihiv, there was no end of trouble with gates. At first, everyone thought that some gang had started snatching the most beautiful exemplars in town so as to sell them in another province. This was a year ago, in 1918. Only later did everyone realise that they were going missing for another purpose – to keep people warm in lieu of firewood, which had suddenly shot up in price. At that point, certain residents started taking their gates off their hinges and hiding them in sheds and cellars. The more prosperous ones began to feed their dogs better, so that they'd have enough bite in their bark to drive away thieves. But the poodle Semyon had adopted didn't bark at all. It was useless, but you don't chase away a little beastie simply on account of that. So they kept on feeding him until spring came. By that time, Semyon had cobbled together a plain gate from old fence planks. You had to lift it to get inside, as it didn't hang clear of the ground, but it was still there to this day, doing its job. That's what Semyon had told Samson. The poodle, though, had run away, either because she'd recalled where her former owner lived, or thanks to the wandering spirit that awakens, just like that, in many people and animals in the springtime.

Remembering Semyon's story had moved Samson so deeply that he went out into the living room without getting dressed and stopped in front of the door to his parents' bedroom, just as he had done when he was a child. His hand reached for the bronze handle all on its own. But then he came to his senses, recalling that Nadezhda now lay in his parents' bed, still asleep. It was early, after all – dawn was only just breaking outside. And she must have been very tired. When he thought of what she'd told them the previous evening, he found it hard even to imagine how she'd managed to record Kyiv's entire population. But, of course, she hadn't done it alone. She herself had said that at least three hundred workers had gone around interviewing the people of Kyiv and writing down all the important details. He had been interviewed by one young woman back in March, which meant there was also a trace of Samson Theophilovich Kolechko in this census.

Then Samson remembered the Germans, of whom there were more than three thousand in Kyiv, only half of whom could read and write in Russian. From the Germans, Samson's thoughts migrated to Balzer the tailor. That's when it clicked. Samson realised that, although the census had not yet been fully analysed, it was already inaccurate, because, in all likelihood, Balzer was still alive by its lights. While Semyon wasn't even in it. So they aren't that important, these statistics. But he wouldn't say that to Nadezhda – she wouldn't understand.

Samson returned to his room and dressed. He wanted just retribution for Semyon and understood that he and he alone could deliver it. Nayden's head was filled with too many other troubles and concerns for his heart to be touched either by Balzer's or Semyon's murder. But the case had touched Samson's heart. And it hurt like a wound.

His fingers reached up to his bare earhole and stroked the scars. That wound had healed, but it would never disappear.

Never? Samson repeated the unpleasant word in his mind. No, he needed to come up with something. He felt too ugly without an ear.

He went into his father's study and retrieved the Montpensier tin from the bookcase. He wanted to open it, but changed his mind. He was afraid – afraid to see part of him dead and shrivelled like an autumn leaf. Instead, he tapped the tin with his finger and listened. His severed ear hadn't lost its astonishing gift – the gift of hearing whatever happened around it and transmitting the sounds to his brain.

This brought a smile to Samson's face – a good-natured, restrained smile.

Later, he took the canvas bag with Balzer's patterns and caught a cab to Sivokon's, on Nimetska.

His father's tailor opened the door in his apron and greeted him cordially.

Once inside the workshop, Samson realised that Sivokon had an order. The tailor's dummy wore an unfinished jacket of so small a size that it couldn't possibly be fastened across the mannequin's torso.

"You have work?" Samson asked.

"Yes," the tailor responded with a nod. "Thank God. Although, I'll be paid in firewood and food rather than money. So, what brings you here? Did you go and see Balzer?"

"I did," the young man answered. "I went. Twice. The second time I saw him, he was killed – before my very eyes. It's a miracle I survived."

Sivokon heaved a heavy sigh. "I'm making this jacket for a Red commissar. Chinese."

"Ah, that makes sense," Samson said. "They're all terribly thin – don't eat enough . . ."

"He explained that to me. It's cultural. For endurance, and for getting out of difficult situations."

"I wanted to offer you some work, too."

"You'd like me to alter your father's suit, maybe?" the tailor guessed.

"No. I'd like to know if you'd be able to make a suit using Balzer's patterns."

"What would you need that for?" Sivokon asked, dumbfounded.

"I believe the man who commissioned the suit killed Balzer and Semyon, the soldier who accompanied me. If you could finish it, I'd get a better sense of the killer's build. You yourself said that it was out of the ordinary. So, you see, the suit may serve as an important piece of evidence."

"Alright, then, get them out."

They laid out the patterns on the large sewing table. Sivokon quickly and skilfully assembled all three parts of the suit. He turned Samson's most recent finds over in his hands, curiously, and shook his head. Then he looked over everything again.

"Yes, extremely peculiar. In fact, I've never seen anything like it in all my days. No more than five feet tall, but a chest like a beer keg. The legs aren't as thick, though," he added, walking over to the trouser patterns. "A strange figure – fractured – as if he were made of two different people: one down below, another up top."

"That's fantasy," Samson said, shaking his head.

"Why fantasy?" Sivokon retorted in a serious tone. "Maybe the trousers were intended for someone else."

Samson carefully examined the waistcoat, jacket and trouser patterns. "But it's the same fabric."

"Yes, the fabric is the same," Sivokon agreed. "Now, how do you propose to pay me?"

"I'll petition my commanding officer. After all, this is part of the investigation. We're looking for a murderer."

"Alright," Sivokon pronounced heavily. "But there's something else – you can't exactly bring in the customer."

"So what?" Samson asked, failing to grasp the point.

"I'll need to order a new tailor's dummy for these dimensions," he said, indicating the torso draped with the Chinese commissar's service jacket.

"Will it be expensive?"

"Not cheap."

"Put in the order. If we run out of official money, I'll make up the difference personally."

When Nayden learned of Samson's plan to nab the killer with the help of a new suit, it took him a long while to regain his composure.

"Who does that?" he almost shouted in his small, cramped office. "You need to be dusting for fingerprints, not commissioning clothes! Are you that pig-ignorant?"

"I've never worked as an investigator before and I don't know how to look for prints," Samson said, spreading his hands in confusion. "The only course I've taken is in marksmanship!"

"Vasyl has several boxes of tsarist criminal cases. Read and learn!"

"I will," Samson agreed. "But will you allocate the money for the tailor? I need enough to pay for both the suit and the mannequin."

"What mannequin?" Nayden asked, boiling over once more.

"Tailors use mannequins. Didn't you know?" Samson asked, genuinely surprised.

"I've never commissioned a suit!" the commander shot back. "A tailor at the market made my jacket – no mannequin, no fitting. A good tailor has as keen an eye as a seasoned artilleryman: bullseye, straight off. And why should I waste my time with your killers, anyway, when we're besieged by gangs on all sides? Any day now we'll get the order to join the city's defences with the Chekists!"

"But I'm looking for the man who murdered Semyon," Samson

said, looking piercingly into Nayden's eyes. "We saw him buried together. How could we just forget all about him?"

"No-one's forgetting anyone," Nayden said, his tone growing more conciliatory. "We'll allocate the money, if we have it. But less than he's asking for."

"He hasn't said how much he wants yet."

"And don't you go asking. Let him finish it first, then we'll see."

Chapter 29

It turned out old Vasyl had spent nearly his entire working life in the building on Tarasivska, largely behind a clerk's desk. But Samson only learned of this when he and Vasyl had tea together, at his suggestion. Vasyl obligingly brought two mugs and the two of them sat down in the soft "superfluous" requisitioned club chairs, although it was quite uncomfortable to drink in them – they had to lean forward to avoid accidentally spilling the liquid down their necks.

As soon as they were seated, Samson asked who was responsible for fingerprints at the station.

"No-one's responsible," Vasyl said, grinning and throwing a sly, narrow-eyed glance at Samson. "Do you consider this real work? What we're doing now?" Apparently forgetting about his mug of tea, Vasyl jerked his hand, but restrained himself in time, although a drop did slosh over the edge and onto the floor. "It's revolutionary cacophony! People are armed to the teeth, there's no order and we've got a hundred times more bandits and robbers running around than ever before. And, of course, the experienced policemen and detectives have all been dismissed – all that's left of them are signatures on old cases—"

"Do you yourself know how to take fingerprints?" Samson cut him off.

"Why should I? I'm just a pencil pusher. My job is to know all there is to know about full stops and commas and stamps. I have no cause to touch fingerprint powder or any of that equipment."

Samson perked up. "Do we have such equipment?"

"Not anymore. When the station was raided for the first time, Nestor Ivanovich ran off with it."

"Nestor Ivanovich?"

"He was our fingerprint expert – the fellow in charge of criminal fingertips."

"Is he still alive?"

"Who knows? Maybe so, but where to find him is another matter."

"You wouldn't happen to have his address?"

"I certainly do. The little grey cells haven't dried up quite yet," Vasyl said, tapping himself on the temple. "He lives at 5 Dionisiev Lane, Flat 3. There were times I was sent to fetch him at night, but that hasn't happened in a couple of years."

"Let's check!" Samson suggested, his eyes sparkling with excitement. "This may be our lucky day."

"Do you need the equipment or Nestor Ivanovich himself?" Vasyl asked, his tone growing more serious.

"Both!" Samson responded.

An hour later, having overtaken the number 4 tram by cab, they turned onto Dionisiev Lane and stopped in front of Nestor Ivanovich's old address. The overcast sky promised rain, but it had been promising it since early morning and people had long stopped looking up, realising that, these days, promises – even the promises of nature – meant nothing.

A flight of wooden steps, emitting generous creaks beneath their feet, led them up to a shabby door on the first floor. The door bore no number, but Vasyl's actions showed that he'd been here before. His hand reached up to the right, just above the jamb, where a little hole gaped in the centre of a round piece of metal resembling a dessert saucer that was neatly embedded in the wall.

Samson realised that Vasyl wanted to pull the bell-cord, but it was gone.

Perplexed, Vasyl pursed his lips, grunted and thumped on the door three times with the edge of his fist.

"They've torn out everything they could," he muttered. "Young hooligans, I bet, still wet behind the ears."

The shuffling of feet sounded on the other side of the door.

"Who is it?" a hoarse voice asked.

"It's me, Vasyl, from the station."

The door opened. Samson, who had expected to see an ancient old fellow, was surprised: before him stood a short black-haired man with a thoroughly youthful face. He wore loose warm trousers – dull grey, like felt boots – and a black cardigan with large buttons. This Nestor Ivanovich looked younger than Vasyl.

"Come in, come in," he said, glancing with curiosity at the young man who had accompanied his old colleague from the station. "Step into the kitchen. It's a poky little flat – just a bed and a kitchen."

As their host ushered them in, Samson noticed he was limping.

Vasyl looked around in surprise. "But where did the living room go?"

"They cut it off," the host said with a sigh. "Cut it off from me – put up boards and grafted it onto what used to be Krivoshchekov's place. It's now a hostel for officers in training."

"Have they at least left you the WC?" Vasyl asked with a note of pity in his voice.

"They have," Nestor Ivanovich responded, indicating with a nod the narrow door to the lavatory. "I haven't seen you in some time."

"You know how it is, these days," Vasyl said, sitting down on a stool. "What are you waiting for? Have a seat," he added, glancing at Samson and pointing to a bentwood chair beside the table. Then he looked back at their host. "This is our new investigator, so to speak – name of Samson. He asked about you."

"About me?" Nestor Ivanovich responded with some surprise. Noticing a large bobble of wool on his cardigan, he plucked it off and flicked it to the floor.

"About your work, your little case of equipment."

Nestor Ivanovich perked up. The conversation that followed was quiet but lively.

"You mean to tell me that you have no-one collecting and analysing papillary ridges at the station?" he asked, disbelieving Vasyl's words.

"Not entirely." Vasyl shook his head. "We sometimes get help from the Cheka. But we haven't had a permanent expert since you left."

"And you were sent to ask me to return to work?" the host enquired with hope in his voice.

Both visitors shook their heads.

"I needed to have a murder scene on Baseina dusted for prints, but no-one told me ... I myself actually specialise in electricity, not in murders, but here we are," Samson offered apologetically.

"And who was killed on Baseina?" Nestor Ivanovich asked, his little grey eyes lighting up.

"Two men," Samson explained. "A German tailor and a Red Army soldier from Chernihiv. The latter was with me."

"So you yourself could have been killed?"

"That's right. But the soldier grappled with him – with the killer. An unequal fight."

"I see," Nestor Ivanovich responded. "Well, what can I do for you?"

"If I asked you to accompany me to the scene and look for prints," Samson said, looking ingratiatingly into his host's eyes, "what would you say?"

"If you pay for the cab ride there and back, why not? It's a shame to lead a senseless existence when the sense of your existence can bring some good to the world."

When they arrived at the Baseina Street address, the driver, whom Samson had promised to pay in money, swore and stared in bewilderment at the embarrassed young policeman and the odd little fellow with a case in his hand.

"For God's sake, take it and eat! It's as good as money," repeated Samson, who was indeed ashamed that what he'd found in his pocket wasn't his ordinary wallet, in which Kerensky roubles fitted best, but meal vouchers with purple police stamps.

"Who's gonna take those from me?" the driver roared again, breaking off his stream of profanity. But now he peered at the little papers more closely, bringing them up to his very nose.

"They'll take them, I promise – both at the Soviet cafeteria on Khreshchatyk, which is right nearby, and at the one on Stolypin Street! These aren't receipts!"

The driver shook his head, struck his horse with his whip and took off without looking back.

"Forgive me, I've never left my money at home before," Samson said to Nestor Ivanovich.

"It's nothing. He'll stuff his belly with joy. They love bread, like a cow loves hay."

Samson gave another sigh. "They don't give out bread for those vouchers. You need to buy it separately."

They walked up to the door, behind which, on the wall to the right, a pointing finger above the words CLOTHING REPAIR suggested going up to the first floor.

To Samson's horror, his mastic seal had been torn off the door and lay by the wall.

"Someone's been here," Samson pronounced despairingly, turning his grief-stricken eyes to his companion.

"So much the better," Nestor Ivanovich responded with a smile. "Makes things interesting!"

Nothing seemed to have changed in the workshop. Without putting down his case, the fingerprint expert pulled out a magnifying glass and used it to examine the edge of the sewing table. Then he lowered his case onto that table and opened it.

"You go ahead and do your work here. I'll take a look at his living quarters," Samson told him.

The first thing that caught Samson's eye was a dark stain near the German tailor's bed, which had itself remained untouched. He squatted down and pressed the tip of his finger against the stain, which felt sticky, like dried blood. And then something else caught his eye: a crude medical stretcher leaning against the wall in the corner of the room. He was sure it hadn't been there on his last visit.

Samson approached, took hold of the upper ends of its two poles and spread them apart, stretching the thick canvas between them. He was surprised to see that the handles had an unusual shape, uncomfortable to grip. He checked the lower ends of the poles, and there, too, the last two inches were carved into a square, the edges of which would dig into the palms of anyone bearing a sick or wounded person on the canvas.

Puzzled, Samson looked around the room and immediately spotted two pieces of wood that looked like the sides of a box, only with holes cut into them. Lifting one from the floor, he grasped their purpose: the stretcher could also be used as a camp bed. The two-inch square ends of the poles fitted the holes in the pieces of wood, which served as the head- and footboard of the camp bed.

Someone had spent the night here, Samson concluded. He decided to take a closer look at the other rooms in Balzer's flat.

Firmly established in the air of the little kitchen was the stench of tobacco, which also hadn't been there the last time. On the table, which was decorated with black circles left behind by hot pots and pans, lay onion skins and a knife with a scuffed metal handle.

Samson lowered his hand to the tabletop and felt the dried breadcrumbs that were by now nearly embedded in it.

His thoughts returned to the stain. If someone had spent the night here, it was on the camp bed, but the stain was near the German's bed. Why? Whoever had spent the night had also had a snack, but had left nothing else behind. Would he come back? Or was he killed here?

The questions kept piling up. It all felt particularly odd because, according to Samson's initial observations, the German had lived alone.

Smacking his lips in annoyance, Samson returned to the workshop and found Nestor Ivanovich going over the surfaces of the treadle sewing machine. Passion shone in the fingerprint expert's tensely grinning face.

"Well, what have you found?" Samson asked.

"Extremely interesting," he answered, without taking his eyes off the black enamel platform on the left side of which rested the presser foot. "Here we find, preserved, all ten fingers of Mr Tailor, making it easy to tell the host's prints from the guest's," he added, his lips tightening into another tense, fervent smile.

Chapter 30

That evening, as Samson sat at his father's desk and looked through Balzer's papers for the third time, his thoughts kept returning to the door on Baseina Street, which he had resealed. The seal was largely pointless, serving only as a warning that the police occasionally checked on the door. Indeed, the warning itself could have the opposite effect on anyone accustomed to changes in power and the absence of law and order. Why was the door sealed? they'd wonder. Maybe there was something valuable in there, something that the police hadn't yet had the chance to carry away due to overabundant criminal activity in the vicinity.

Of course, Samson kept driving these speculations from his mind, trying instead to concentrate, to sharpen his eyes and to identify something important in the tailor's notes and accounts, written in both Russian and German.

But, as soon as he'd dismissed his fears about the seal, other questions crept into his head – questions about the camp-bed stretcher and about the bloodstain. Nor was Nestor Ivanovich far from his mind. After their examination was completed, Samson had invited him to the station, but the fingerprint expert refused. He went back to Dionisiev Lane on foot, saying that he could execute all the necessary analyses at home. He added that they'd need to meet to discuss the results, but also not at the station – somewhere else. Samson could visit him at home, but not before the following evening.

The following evening seemed both far away and rather close. Time flew a little slower these days because, a little over a month earlier, the sun had begun to linger in the sky. And, even if one couldn't see the sun, darkness still settled a little later each evening, and life on the street persisted a little longer – although that life depended less on the sun than on people themselves, on their courage or foolhardiness.

"Cup of tea, Samson Theophilovich?" asked Vasyl, entering the office with mug in hand.

Samson nodded.

"Were you satisfied with Nestor Ivanovich's work?" the old man asked stealthily, as he was leaving, his hand already on the door handle.

"I don't know," Samson responded, lifting his eyes from a piece of paper. "But thank you, anyway. I might pay him a visit tomorrow. He didn't want to come here."

"Yes." Vasyl nodded. "He was a quarrelsome employee, so he wasn't especially well liked around here, either. Not liked, but appreciated."

"What made him so quarrelsome?"

"He's got a keen eye and he was always telling the investigators how to do their jobs. That rubbed them the wrong way. The chief in particular."

"But we have a whole new staff here."

"For now . . . But what if the old ones come back?" Vasyl asked, widening his eyes and raising his thick grey eyebrows with an air of significance.

"Why would they come back?" Samson responded, failing to understand. "New government means new police . . ."

"God willing, God willing," Vasyl whispered on his way out, carefully closing the door behind him.

Samson shrugged. He glanced at the floor to the left, at his wooden holster, and thought that, should something happen, he might not be able to get to his revolver in time. He was surprised at this thought, until he realised that it had arisen as a result of Vasyl's chatter. Waving it away, he took up another piece of paper, which turned out to be a receipt: *Lavrenty Govda, 8 Kuznechna Street, received a relined green frock coat*. It was signed, and in the lower right corner were two German words: *vollständig bezahlt –* paid in full.

It occurred to Samson that Kuznechna was just two blocks away. And he could ask the yard-sweeper at number 8 for the number of Lavrenty's flat.

At about nine, when it was already dark, Samson set off for home by way of Kuznechna. He found the right house quickly. A bearded yard-sweeper opened the front door after the first thump of the young policeman's fist. Samson informed him that he was there to see Laventry Govda on official business.

"High time!" responded the yard-sweeper, looking delighted. "How long can that man be allowed to drink the blood of the working people? Third floor, on the left."

Samson climbed the stone steps slowly. He was used to the creak of wooden stairs and unaccustomed to this stony silence. The yard-sweeper's mention of blood-drinking had brought to mind his recent conversation with Kholodny about silver bullets and vampires. Although the former priest had claimed not to believe in all that supernatural nonsense, just as he didn't believe in God, he had refused to accept that God didn't exist.

The young policeman stopped in front of a tall set of doors. To the right, in the corner, stood an iron umbrella stand, and beside it was a mud-scraper of the sort that used to be installed at main entrances, as well as a boot-scrubber. It seemed it had become normal to climb the stairs in dirty boots and clean them only before entering a flat.

Samson grunted. All the same, he did insert his boots between the twin brushes of the scrubber, running them back and forth – first the left, then the right. Only then did his hand reach for and twist the doorbell embedded in a round, concave brass plate. He heard a ring on the other side of the door.

Quick nervous footsteps approached and the door swung open, revealing a tall man in black trousers and a green frock coat. He looked displeased. Three playing cards were held fanned between the thumb and forefinger of his right hand.

The first thing the man did was to glance at his visitor's boots, then at his cleaning apparatus. His gaze rose to the wooden holster, where it lingered.

"What do you want?" he asked impatiently.

"I'm with the police," Samson informed him, staring in turn at the man's green frock coat. "Did you have that mended at Balzer's?"

"You've come at an extremely inopportune time," the owner of the flat said. "Yes, I did. And so what? I'm terribly busy."

He obviously had no intention of letting Samson in.

"I have only two questions," Samson announced politely. "I'm sorry to say that your tailor was murdered."

"The German? Murdered?" the man asked in surprise. He seemed to lean back, as if the news had genuinely upset him.

"May I ask a couple of questions?" Samson went on.

"Alright, but make it quick," Lavrenty Govda responded, twisting his mouth. "You can see that I'm busy."

"Of course," Samson said, licking his lips nervously. "What can you tell me about Balzer?"

"He's a tailor!" the owner said, again leaning back and twisting his lips, as if preparing to snort. "What else is there to say?"

"Well, what kind of man was he? Friendly? Secretive?"

"You're positively obsessed with him, aren't you? Friendly for a German, not like the others. When I paid him in full for the coat, he treated me to a Rhine wine. Went down to the cellar to get it. Our tailors don't treat their clients to good wine. It you're lucky, they'll bring you a cup of watery tea."

"To the cellar?" Samson asked. "But he lived on the first floor. He received you on Baseina Street, didn't he? On the first floor?"

"Yes. Then he went down to the cellar and returned with a bottle. He uncorked it and we drank it quickly – I was in a hurry. That was all. I've only met him twice – brought the coat, picked it up."

Samson didn't even have time to say goodbye before the door slammed shut in his face, followed by the sound of a chain slipping into its hook and the clang of a bolt.

He remembered the yard-sweeper's words about this character, and sympathised.

As he was going down the stone steps, another realisation caught up with him: this Lavrenty Govda had not been at all afraid of his revolver and leather jacket. Nor did he seem to notice his bare earhole. In general, he had behaved as few people could afford to behave these days – coolly and arrogantly.

Samson pulled out the deadbolt from the inside of the front door and heard another door creak open. The yard-sweeper emerged again.

"Well," he asked, "did you show him who's boss?"

"Why do you feel he needs to be shown who's boss?"

"Whaddaya mean? He's running a bourgeois den up there! They play cards all night, have scantily clad girls brought by cab. Is that what we fought for, facing down the tsar's guns?"

"Did you fight?" Samson asked doubtfully, examining the yard-sweeper's round, jowly, bearded face.

"Hell, I'm talking about our people," the man snarled. "You know, those who applied their strength."

"I came to deal with another matter, for now," Samson said, having decided to reassure the yard-sweeper, as he didn't quite know what to expect from the fellow. "I needed to tell him that his tailor was murdered . . ."

"You don't say?" the yard-sweeper responded, his face growing friendly again, as if the news had perked him up. "Was there a good reason?"

"I don't know yet," Samson admitted, and went out into the street.

The deadbolt clanged behind him. Cool damp air hit his face. And from somewhere above came the thin, importunate barking of a small dog.

Surprised by the sound, Samson raised his eyes and surveyed all six balconies on the façade of 8 Kuznechna Street. He noticed no movement whatsoever.

Chapter 31

The yard-sweeper's widow opened the front door quickly, at the first knock. In her hand, she held a kerosene lamp with the wick turned down as low as it would go. She glanced at the tenant's face in the lamplight.

"You look out of sorts," she said. "Nadezhda came home two hours ago, also tired."

Samson didn't answer. Silently, he went up to the first floor, skipping the squeaky step. The flat was quiet. The power was out, but the moon was shining. It laid its blue quadrangles on the floor under the windows.

Leaving his boots in the hallway, Samson walked up to the door of his parents' bedroom. He listened close, his right earhole up against the door, as if he wanted to hear everything: both random noises and those sounds that might tell him whether Nadezhda was already asleep or still awake, staring up at the ceiling.

He lit a candle and scooped up a glass of water from the copper basin in the kitchen. It tasted normal. Nadezhda must have filled it when she'd come home, to use for tea and food. The city usually turned off the water by eight in the evening.

Samson had neither the strength nor the desire to boil water for tea. There was kerosene in the stove, but to fuss about and wait half an hour for the water to boil? No, it wasn't worth the bother. He felt bad enough already. Bad and ashamed. Why hadn't they assigned him to a course in criminal investigation straight away? Why only a course in marksmanship? Why hadn't this Lavrenty Govda been afraid of him? Never mind afraid – why hadn't he shown him the least respect? What right did he have to keep him on the threshold and then slam the door in his face? And why hadn't Samson himself thought of dusting the crime scene for fingerprints? Why hadn't he thoroughly examined the house on Baseina, checking whether anyone else lived there? Why hadn't he thought of going down to the cellar, from which Balzer had fetched a bottle of Rhine wine?

Samson sat down at the table in the living room with a mug of water. He moved the burning candle a little further away from himself, at arm's length. When he took a sip, the water seemed to catch in his throat, like a piece of ice. He felt his neck, as if he could find the lodged gulp by touch and push it down.

And now his thoughts grew confused. The taste of Rhine wine appeared on his tongue – probably the very wine to which Balzer had treated his rich client. But was he rich? A rich man would have ordered a new frock coat or jacket, not had an old one relined. Not rich, then. And if he wasn't rich, but was still so frightfully arrogant, then he must be a swindler, a petty crook. Of course, Samson concluded – a gambler. After all, he'd been holding three cards when he opened the door.

Samson's right arm began to ache. He must have placed his elbow awkwardly on the tabletop. And then he dropped his open palm onto the table. The loud clap spooked him, and his eyes darted to his parents' bedroom door.

I have to go to sleep, he ordered himself firmly, but he didn't budge.

And then his parents' bedroom door opened, revealing Nadezhda's angelic half-frightened, half-questioning face.

"Can't sleep?" she asked, pulling the edge of her yellow velvet dressing gown over her chest, having forgotten to tie the belt when she got up and threw it on.

She sat down beside him. "What's the matter?"

"I'm confused," admitted Samson. "I feel like a fool – and I believe others see me as a fool, too ... I need to study. Take courses. Everyone's studying, these days. No-one turns up at a new job without studying and performs perfectly. Everything's slipping through my fingers. And slipping my mind . . . I need to find Semyon's killer. That crime can't be forgiven. And he killed Balzer the tailor, too – he was in the tailor's workshop when Semyon and I arrived. So, I think I can find him through the tailor – even though the tailor's dead. But I've started to doubt myself. I don't know what is the right thing to do."

"You wouldn't do anything that wasn't right."

"No, that's not what I mean. I just feel foolish – like I'm missing something obvious and important, simply not seeing it. I feel I can't think the right way, so that everything becomes clear and I know exactly what to do."

"You have to write it all down," Nadezhda said, gently extending her hand to his face. Her cold fingers brushed his cheek, left ear, temple and neck. "You probably rely on memory and intuition . . . But you need to write things down. Like we did with the census, back in March. Three hundred people with cards and pencils, entering all the information, filling out all the columns. That's the only way to make sure you're right – the only way to be sure of the result, that the count is correct."

Samson sighed. "But the census is easier. Everything is clear: what to ask, where to write down the answer. I don't have cards . . . I do have rules, though, and I can already do a few things according to these rules. I can hold interrogations: question and answer. But how can I work out the answer to a question that I neither perceive nor understand? I don't have cards for that, do you know what I mean?"

"Samson, dear." Nadezhda yawned, letting go of the edge of her dressing gown and covering her mouth with her left palm. "You're just tired. Just think of what you need to do tomorrow, and your mind will start to drift off, so that tomorrow it can be ready for anything."

"Tomorrow?" Samson tried to think. "Tomorrow, I have to go down to the tailor's cellar. And then to see Nestor Ivanovich."

"Tomorrow's just a few hours away. Get some rest, so you wake up as fresh as can be."

Samson slowly shook his head, then looked down mournfully.

Nadezhda took his face in her palms, lifting it and turning it towards her. The reflected candlelight played symmetrically in her eyes.

"Let's go," she pronounced softly. "I'll put you to sleep."

On legs of cotton wool, Samson followed her into his parents' bedroom. She took off his clothes, sat him on the right side of the bed, then gently laid him down with her strong hands, making sure that the back of his head sank into the soft pillow. Then she went to lie down on the other side of the bed, under the same blanket.

A couple of minutes of quiet and darkness revived him somewhat. He turned on his side to study the blurry outline of her profile as she lay on her back. Her even breaths raised and lowered her chest beneath the blanket. She must be asleep.

"Nadezhda," he whispered. "Marry me."

His words didn't disturb her even breathing. Nothing in her profile stirred. She was definitely asleep.

He rolled over onto his stomach. A mosquito whined to the right of him, and Samson pulled out his hand and slapped the healed wound. The echo of the clap resounded in the innermost corners of his brain. And then it occurred to him that it was early in the year for mosquitoes – still too cold. He realised that it might have been his severed ear hearing things in his father's study. But the ear was in a tin, which distorted most sounds. All except human voices. Those it merely imbued with metallic sonority.

"Everything will be fine," he whispered to himself.

As the clap's echoes subsided, quiet and darkness resumed their reign. Nadezhda's even breathing constituted the sweetest part of this quiet, precisely the part that lulled him to sleep.

Chapter 32

Samson froze as he entered his office. At his father's desk, in the gloom of the poorly lit room, sat a man with cards of some kind spread out before him. To the left of these cards a small case lay open.

"Who are you and what are you doing?" asked Samson warily.

"Ah, greetings! Vasyl let me in. He told me to sit here and wait for you," a familiar voice replied.

Samson breathed a sigh of relief.

"Yes, Nestor Ivanovich, by all means, sit. I was planning to come and see you in the evening, but this is better."

Out of habit, Samson removed his holster belt. He carried it to the nearest club chair and sat down. As he lowered the belt at his side, the holster thudded on the wooden floor.

"What have you brought me?" Samson asked, intuiting that such an early visit could signify an important development.

"Well, Samson Theophilovich, here's my report. This card bears the prints of the tailor, while this one features all the fingers, except for the pinkies, of the other fellow." Nestor Ivanovich waved the two cards in the air. "There were a couple of old episodic prints as well, but they don't belong to anyone relevant."

"So, there were two people living in the flat?"

"Yes. The prints found in the kitchen and the bedroom make that clear."

"What about that stretcher-bed I hadn't seen before?"

"The other man's prints were all over it," the fingerprint expert said with a nod.

"Where is he, then? And who is he?"

"That's up to you to find out, Mr Investigator." Nestor Ivanovich chuckled. "I'll leave you the cards. If anything should come up, you know where I live. And do tell your superiors that they shouldn't allow such a stench to linger at the entrance to the station."

"It rises from the cells in the basement," Samson explained.

It sounded like he was defending himself.

"All the same. Do you suppose that fleas and lice can't climb stairs?"

The small case clicked shut. Nestor Ivanovich snatched it up from the desk and, nodding farewell, walked out of the office.

Samson went over to the door and repeatedly flipped the black light switch up and down. His eyes followed the braided wiring that climbed the wall to the ceiling. The bulb barely emitted light. The world beyond the window was still cloudy and grey. As if to hold on to his cheer and freshness of spirit, he brought to mind the previous night, during which he had, for the first time in his life, slept in his parents' bed. And not only that, but he had done so next to Nadezhda. He thought of her with gratitude in his heart – thought of how she had, like a mother, caressed him, lulled him to sleep, reassured him. No, she had reassured him in her own way, like a woman. Had his whisper come to her in a dream? Had it broken through her sleep? She couldn't have not heard him.

He entered Nayden's office with a firm, confident step and reported that he had dealt with the fingerprints, having found an expert who'd previously worked at the station and who was ready to help when needed. He also asked for two Red Army soldiers, preferably Chinese, to accompany him to Baseina Street, where the three of them would search Balzer's cellar.

"They don't send us Chinese soldiers. The Cheka seconded them all for special duty. Vasyl will assign you two of our own men. And you can take a cart with you – recently requisitioned. It's out in the courtyard. See what furniture you can take, since the tailor has no need of it."

"Well, there's a stretcher-bed and an ordinary bed, an iron one, and also a sewing machine."

"We definitely don't need the sewing machine, and not the stretcher either. But take the bed. We'll put it in the storeroom, so the guards can get some shut-eye between shifts."

Samson rode up to Balzer's house around noon, accompanied by two Red Army men and an armed police driver. The skies promised rain, growing gloomier by the minute, but not a drop fell.

The mastic seal had again been torn from the door, but that wasn't what struck Samson most. His eyes were drawn, almost hypnotised, to two words written on the wall in charcoal: *Await death*. The brokenness of the letters was no less frightening than their meaning. And, rather than a dot or an exclamation mark, what punctuated them was a circle containing two points for eyes and a line for a nose. And this entire little circle – that is, this vague human face – was crossed out by a thick diagonal streak of charcoal.

Revolver in hand, Samson went through all the rooms of the tailor's flat. Everything seemed to stand and lie where he'd left it. Neither the presence of anything new nor the absence of anything old caught his eye.

Who should await death, if the flat's owner has already been killed? Samson wondered, returning to the front door, beyond which, on the landing, the two soldiers stood awaiting orders.

Samson came out to speak to them, resolute and angry.

"So, comrade fighters," he said, looking closely at their faces in turn and trying to determine how quick-witted and disciplined they were. "We will now search for the cellar belonging to the victim of the crime. When we find it, I ask you not to touch a thing without my permission."

"Yes, comrade," one of them responded, while the other gave a wordless nod.

The wooden steps creaked beneath three pairs of boots descending from the first floor. In the entryway, with his back to the front door, Samson carefully looked around. The first door on the left led to what appeared to be a shopfront, but it had obviously not been opened for a long time. Further down, along the left wall, he saw a very narrow door, which could not have been the entrance to a flat. And, after that, the little hallway seemed to turn behind the staircase that climbed up to the first floor.

"Check that narrow door," Samson ordered the Red Army men.

One of them rushed towards it.

"It's locked," he announced.

"Break in."

The Red Army soldier removed his rifle from his shoulder, then attached his bayonet and inserted it into the opening between the door and the doorpost. He leaned back, pulling the butt of his rifle towards him. The crack of wood burst into Samson's left ear as an extremely unpleasant sound, and, at the same time, it swam into his right earhole in a completely different manner, not so sharp and irritating.

"Just mops and brooms in here," the soldier reported, throwing his rifle over his shoulder.

"What about down there, under the stairs?"

"Another door, wider, but lower to the ground."

"Break it."

"Ha!" One of the soldiers laughed. "Easy-peasy."

Something metallic dropped resoundingly onto the wooden floor.

"Cellar," one of the men reported.

"Excellent!" Samson exclaimed, drawing matches and three candles from his pocket. He lit the candles, handing one to each of the soldiers.

"Remember, don't touch a thing without my permission," Samson repeated. Stooping, he stepped through the low opening.

The smell of damp hit his nostrils. With burning candle in hand, he went down into the cellar, which turned out to be much deeper than he'd expected. His boots counted no fewer than nine steps before the hard, even plank floor appeared beneath their feet. After two paces, Samson, followed by the soldiers, stopped before two padlocked doors – the kind that, in large flats, usually concealed servants' quarters. Samson ran the light of the candle across the doors, looking for numbers or other signs that might help determine which one they ought to tackle first. The padlock on the left looked rather ancient and somewhat rusty, which immediately indicated either the poverty or long absence of its owner. The one on the right had a body of black metal, and its clean steel shackle reflected the candlelight.

"This one," Samson ordered.

One of the soldiers easily tore the iron ring out of the door frame, after which the door, together with its dangling padlock, swung open.

The space behind it had a completely different, un-cellar-like smell. It smacked of vanilla and coffee. One could discern the corners of the furniture in the darkness.

Samson drew out two more candles and lit them from his own. He handed one each to the Red Army men and ordered them to spread their arms. Then he arranged the soldiers so he could take in the entire room and its contents. In the far corner, a pot-bellied stove stood like a black barrel, its chimney rising up to the ceiling, and next to it he saw a neatly arranged miniature woodpile, about two feet high. To the right were crates and chests, then a cabinet.

One of the soldiers sneezed and the room immediately grew darker. He had covered his mouth with his hand, blowing out the candle.

"Careful!" Samson shouted. "Light it again."

He led the soldiers over to the pot-bellied stove, the crates and the chests. Now it was impossible to see the door through which they had entered.

But Samson had noticed nothing of interest near the entrance.

Everything interesting was here, at the opposite end of the room. And, sure enough, there it was: a crate of wine bottles, their wax-sealed necks poking out. The crate was designed to hold twenty, and three or four were missing.

"Not vodka?" one of the soldiers asked, leaning slightly towards the crate, not daring to leave the spot where Samson had placed him.

"No, wine," Samson replied. "From the Rhine."

"Port wine, you say?" the Red Army man asked.

"No."

Then Samson's eyes fell on a rectangular piece of carpet, lying directly on the plank floor, about a yard from the left wall, next to the stove. He squatted down and brought the candle close. The carpet was trampled, almost worn away in places, and it seemed from the impressions left in the dust that something had, until recently, stood between it and the wall. Two perpendicular strips of two-and-a-half feet each were separated by a distance of seven or seven-and-a-half feet. Samson smiled. He realised what might have stood there a couple of days earlier: a camp bed consisting of a stretcher and head- and footboards – the very one he had noticed the previous evening in the tailor's flat. This meant that the man who had been spending his nights in the tailor's cellar had decided to move upstairs. Actually, the two had already been living up there together, as Nestor Ivanovich had determined. They had lived, dined and bathed in the flat. And yet, one of them had long – or at least for some time – been sleeping or hiding in the cellar. But why had he decided to return upstairs when Balzer was killed? Who was he? Or she? No, a woman would hardly be willing to spend her nights on a camp bed down in the cellar . . . For that, one needed especially strong nerves and a very compelling reason. It could only have been a man.

Samson went over to the nearest chest and opened the lid. He asked one of the soldiers to bring both his candles closer, but not so close that the wax would drip into the chest.

The young policeman saw two bolts of dark fabric. Picking one up with his left hand, he moved it aside. Beneath it was a piece of pigskin. He lifted up its edge, revealing a trove of silver – spoons, chalices, saucers. Samson stuck his hand inside and the silver clinked pleasantly and gently, unobtrusively.

The trove was a foot and a half deep. How much silver could there be? A hundred pounds? No less than that.

Samson shook his head in amazement and glanced at the Red Army men. They too were eyeing the noble metal with curiosity, but their faces were stern and calm.

"Here," Samson said, thrusting his candle at the nearest soldier, who took two in one hand. Then, with his unencumbered hands, he began to place the silver items onto the cloth, trying to reach the bottom of the chest. Soon, he felt pigskin again, only this time it was rolled up and something was hidden inside it.

Samson pulled out the roll. It was heavy. He began to unfurl it, revealing a rather long, smooth object of glinting silver, rounded and knobby at one end, resembling part of a walking stick.

The young policeman pulled it fully out of the pigskin. His hand had never felt silver this smooth and pleasant to the touch. The object's noble form reminded him of something, while its unexpected weight strained his muscles. It seemed to him that what he held in his hands was some important, precious component of a large tower clock – or perhaps of some secret ecclesiastical mechanism. After all, church folk were quite fond of silver.

He turned the object this way and that, still trying to figure out what it reminded him of.

"Looks like a bone," one of the Red Army men declared, leaning forward as far as he could without budging from his designated spot. "An awful lot like a bone. A horse's or a cow's."

That's it, Samson thought, running his fingers along the silver object and around its knobby end. It was a bone made of silver, probably intended for some religious ritual and stolen from a cathedral or monastery.

"Well, men," he said, emerging from his thoughts. "You see how many precious objects there are? Do you think we can safely deliver them to the station?"

"Why not?" the soldier nearest him responded. "We've got bullets. And it's broad daylight – bandits are afraid of us in the daytime, not like at night."

Chapter 33

"What have you done? What are you, a junk dealer?" Nayden said, almost shouting, as he nervously paced the free space remaining on the floor of Samson's office.

He walked over to the three wooden boxes filled with German books, picked up a volume and immediately threw it back as a look of disgust contorted his face.

"You make two whole trips with the cart and don't even bring back the iron bed?" he continued, shaking his head in indignation. "Go over to Kholodny's office – you'll see what a proper place of work ought to look like. Yes, he has a pile of papers on his desk, but everything else is as clean as a whistle! No boxes on the floor, that's for sure. And he's investigating the murder of confectioner Michelson and his daughters! I assure you, there are more things in that flat than in your cellar – did he cart them all here? Of course not – because he thinks with his head, not with his hands. Your hands reach for everything you see!"

"But I've brought in seventy pounds of silver, all stolen. And I couldn't look through the books over there – you can't see much by candlelight," Samson replied, trying to justify his actions while shifting from foot to foot in front of his chair. He didn't dare to sit down in the presence of his angry commander.

"The state bank's already sent someone for your silver. We can't store it here. They'll thank you – but not me. I will never thank you for this disarray!" Nayden pronounced the last word with a strong emphasis on *dis*, as if that was its most significant syllable.

"I can't give them everything," Samson protested. "I need to retain one item for my investigation."

"Which item?"

"That one, there," Samson answered, nodding towards the table, where the silver bone lay wrapped in its pigskin.

"Well, then, go ahead and claim it as material evidence. Keep it for now. But everything else?" Nayden turned furiously towards the boxes of books.

"What's all this noise about?" Vasyl's good-natured voice sounded after a creak of the door. He held two mugs of tea. "A noisy day, this – shouting on the ground floor, shouting up here . . ."

"Who's shouting on the ground floor?" Nayden asked, tearing his eyes away from the irritating boxes.

"They brought in a gypsy from the Jewish bazaar. She filched a gold cigarette case from a commissar of the border regiment and managed to hide it so well that our boys can't find it. Now, she's screaming to high heaven that she didn't do it."

"Another fool!" Nayden exclaimed, angry again. "Why would a commissar need a gold cigarette case? Silver not good enough for him?"

"Maybe he couldn't find one," Vasyl defended the unknown victimised commissar. "Everyone wants a silver case, you know."

"I'll make sure to get the bed," Samson spoke up, sensing that Nayden was growing less irritated and might soon recover his usual even-tempered mood.

"What bed?"

"The iron one. From Balzer. For the guards."

"How do you suppose you'll do that? You think our only cart is forever at your disposal? We're in total disarray! I can't even get statistics on cases. That desk down there is sitting empty. People get hired, then vanish after two days."

"Comrade Nayden," said Samson, suddenly looking livelier and sitting down resolutely at his desk. "I need another document – one requesting the assistance of the Provincial Bureau of Statistics.

They recently conducted a census of Kyiv, from which we could learn who resided in Balzer's household."

Nayden froze for a moment, scratched behind his right ear and peered at Samson. "You mean you weren't given a document requesting the assistance of all official bodies and institutions?" he asked, squinting unkindly at Vasyl.

"You bet he was, like everyone else," Vasyl answered quickly.

"Yes, I was," Samson confirmed, his memory refreshed.

"So take that anywhere you'd like. We don't have enough paper to make out separate requests to each institution." At that point, Nayden again looked at the boxes of books and scrunched up his nose, as if he were sniffing them. "And get these books out of here – today! You want an infestation of mice?"

"Mice don't settle where rats have made their home," Vasyl remarked placidly.

"Who are these rats you have in mind?" Nayden snapped, turning sharply towards him.

"The ones in the cells in the basement. There's a hole in the corner, leads right into the sewer. That's how they get in."

"Then get someone to plug up the hole."

"Get who, exactly?"

"Whichever branch of the Soviet service plugs holes!"

"Except for the trams, the railway and the power plant, the only branches up and running so far do nothing but issue documents."

"In that case, keep quiet. And make yourself useful."

"I'm quiet, I'm quiet ... And useful."

"Really? Who was it that started yapping about rats?"

"Me. But without intent."

"That's just it – you do everything without intent! And what a word you've picked up there ... Intent!"

"Well, it's important. It aggravates the crime. Lack of intent does the opposite."

Footsteps pounded outside. Someone came hurtling up the stairs, as if in pursuit or being pursued.

"Comrade Nayden! Comrade Nayden!" a rasping cry flew in through the half-open door.

"What's the matter now?" Nayden shouted in response, and the door immediately opened. Pasechny stopped on the threshold, out of breath.

"There's a rebellion in Mezhyhirya and Vyshgorod! They're holding soldiers and commissars captive, threatening to shoot them all."

"Who?" asked Nayden. He had clearly been caught off guard – for an instant, he looked helpless, bewildered.

"Local villagers – with Hetman Struk. He told them the Bolsheviks were deceiving them. He's already parcelling out land. The Cheka sent an equestrian detachment."

"Fucking bastards," Nayden burst out, his face growing steely and mean, like the blade of a knife. He spat on the floor.

Samson didn't like that. Hearing the news, he had leapt up from his desk, but now his eyes rested on the floor, where the commander had spat.

"Disapprove, do you?" Nayden sneered, smearing the saliva about with the sole of his boot.

After throwing another unkind glance at Samson, he left the office, and Vasyl ran out after him.

The internal guard at the Provincial Bureau of Statistics carefully read the request for assistance presented by Samson and sent him up to see Comrade Serbsky. But, as soon as he set foot on the first floor's wooden surface, which was coated with a strange yellow paint, he saw a door with a sign: VALERIAN SERGEYEVICH PODDOMOV. DEPARTMENT OF STATISTICAL COUNTING. He immediately recalled the young man who had accompanied Nadezhda on her visit to his flat. He also recalled the young man's unusual jacket, made from requisitioned Church fabric, with its black-on-black crosses. He recalled, too, how the young man had inappropriately called the toilet a "latrine", which most likely indicated that he had grown up or recently lived in lodgings devoid of indoor sanitary facilities.

Samson stopped in front of the door and smiled. After walking through streets unsettled by rumours of rebellion, he felt more comfortable here. On his way over, he had caught a few mean-spirited glances at his jacket and holster – and these had come, to his surprise, from people with clean, seemingly educated faces.

Such rumours always inspired a degree of vague petulance among the people of Kyiv. Servants and the poor, whose faces wore blank expressions, would grow jumpier, more quarrelsome, while more prosperous townsfolk were driven to glare in this piercing, repulsive manner, as if something beastly were pouring out of their bodies through their eyes – some feral mix of fear and fury.

Valerian Sergeyevich didn't immediately recognise Samson. However, as soon as his visitor introduced himself and held out the request for assistance, Nadezhda's chief got up from his desk, which was littered with folders, and waved the document away good-naturedly with both hands.

"Yes, of course, I came to your place with Nadezhda. You live near here," he said.

Learning of his visitor's desire to see the census card of the household at 3 Baseina, he immediately summoned an elderly employee in a blue, very clerkish dress, and ordered her to retrieve the necessary document. While she searched, Poddomov treated Samson to tea and a bagel.

"There's a baker next door. He twists and bakes them at home, then takes them round the institutions. Very reasonable."

Samson liked the bagel and bit into it with restraint, so that the soft, sweetish taste would unfurl slowly over his tongue. By the time he finished his tea, he still held a third of the bagel in his hand.

Just then, the employee returned with a box of cards. She placed the box onto her chief's desk, on top of the folders, and flipped through the cards, noting the indicators of streets and houses.

"Here," she said, plucking one out while making sure that its place in the box remained open, so that the order of data would not be muddled. "Which flat do you need?" she asked, looking up at Samson.

"First floor, above the empty café or confectioner's shop."

"I see." The woman nodded. "Retail and living quarters. It isn't a flat, it's a residential sewing workshop, with two residents: Friedrich Franzevich Balzer, citizen of Germany, born in 1867, literate, and Luc Jeanovich Jacobson, citizen of Belgium, born in 1895, illiterate."

"Can I borrow that card?" Samson pleaded, enkindled by what he'd heard.

"Absolutely not," the employee replied indignantly, fixing him with a cold stare. "This is vital statistical data."

"You can copy out what you need," Poddomov advised him, taking a pencil and a blank sheet of paper from his desk drawer.

Samson began to copy out the information from the card, which the employee held firmly in front of his face, as if she were afraid to let it out of her hands. The young policeman rejoiced at the opportunity to write on a completely blank sheet of paper, pencilling each letter as neatly as he could. Such luxuries were unavailable back at the station, while this bureau was amply supplied – a fact that he found less than encouraging. It indicated that, in the eyes of the highest-ranking commissars, statistics were more important than fighting crime.

"Drop in and say hello to Nadezhda," Poddomov suggested at parting.

Samson entered without knocking. There, at three desks, work was in full swing – papers and cards rustling, pencils and abacuses emitting their particular, quietly significant sounds.

Nadezhda was sitting by the window. When she noticed her visitor, she looked surprised and frowned. Rising briskly to her feet, she approached Samson, pushed him out of the room and shut the door behind her.

"Is something the matter?" she asked sternly.

A very young woman passing them in the corridor slowed down and seemed to prick up her ears.

"I came on official business," Samson answered, showing her the sheet of paper with names and surnames. "Needed to learn who resided at a certain address."

"Ah." Nadezhda relaxed. "Official business is fine. I thought you'd just shown up to distract me."

Chapter 34

Still exhilarated from his visit to the Provincial Bureau of Statistics, Samson decided to walk to the morgue at the Oleksandrivska Clinical Hospital, where, Vasyl had told him, the lifeless bodies of Balzer and Semyon had been taken, and from which the Red Army soldier had been transported to Oleksandrivsky Park for his solemn burial the following day. Semyon had been buried, but Balzer was still at the morgue. Samson recalled once again that, because of the way the soldier's body had fallen on top of the tailor's, he hadn't managed to check Balzer's pockets. This was important, because, nowadays, since people could never be certain whether or not they'd make it home after leaving their flats, they placed the easy-to-carry things they treasured most – photos of loved ones, documents – in their pockets, to keep them close to their hearts, and sometimes even sewed their pockets up, in order to protect those treasured items from the dexterous fingers of thieves.

Samson didn't wish to consider the fact that they might have stripped the late Balzer naked at the morgue. Anything could happen over there, of course, where two hundred dead bodies were overseen by just two orderlies. But the tailor had been shot in the back at point-blank range and must have lost almost all his blood through his terrible wound, which meant that his clothes would be of no use to anyone. In these troubled times, people wouldn't undress a dead body unless they were interested in its clothes, especially when one recalled that the hospital had long been a terminus from which both typhoid patients and the seriously wounded departed with ever greater frequency from earthly life. It was said that the orderlies themselves were constantly being replaced due to infection and death. That is why they tried to spend as little time as possible with the hordes of corpses forced into astoundingly close proximity. The unburied dead seem to call out to the living around them, bidding them to follow in their footsteps.

These thoughts about Balzer refreshed the memory of that horrible evening in Samson's mind. He recalled the figure of the gunman, who had twisted his body with astonishing deftness during the brief skirmish with Semyon and raced down the stairs past the young policeman, who had been rendered mute and motionless by the shots. Samson still couldn't understand why he hadn't noticed the man's face – why all he had seen in its place was an ink stain . . . Why hadn't he caught the glint of his eyes, made out the tip of his nose? True, it was dark. Nevertheless, he'd stood no more than three feet away . . .

Hastily, with measured step, six Red Army men with rifles over their shoulders came round the corner from Mala Vasylkivska Street. Samson kept on walking to the end of Rohnidynska, then turned left onto Prozorivska. In another seven minutes or so, he'd reach the dosshouse, and, soon after that, his destination.

Who was this Luc Jacobson, Samson wondered, and why had he been living with Balzer? Maybe "living" wasn't the word – "hiding" was more like it. But what need did he have to hide if the pair of thieving Red Army men were so afraid of him? That was a proper riddle. Also, if he was hiding, why would he have given his information to the census-takers? Or was it Balzer who'd told them about his housemate – his year of birth, his Belgian citizenship? No, something didn't add up. There was stolen silver hidden in the cellar, and the man had clearly been spending his nights down there . . . So, he must be the very same Jacobson whom Fyodor and Anton had feared. Maybe he'd been renting a corner of Balzer's flat. That could be why Balzer had been so afraid of Samson that first time, refusing to admit that the suit patterns had been stolen from him.

"May I trouble you for a moment?" An elderly woman's voice drew Samson's attention.

He stopped and saw a nun, all in black, a staff and a little knapsack in her hands.

"How can I help you?" he asked.

"How do I get to the Monastery of the Caves?"

"You just follow the Dog Path, over there, to the right and along the bottom of the ravine," he said, pointing. "But do hurry. There aren't many people down there and it can be dangerous. Someone might attack you."

"Oh, young man, who would attack me? The good Lord is my protector. May He bless you!" the old nun chirped, trotting off as Samson had indicated. Yet she did walk quickly, though her steps were shorter than his.

He was heading in the same direction and would hardly have overtaken her at his normal speed, but his pace was especially slow now, restrained by the thoughts and questions he was trying to write down in his mind, as though on some invisible wall.

Many days had passed since Balzer's murder, yet it was only yesterday that Samson had noticed that fresh threat scribbled in charcoal on the wall by the door: *Await death*. This suggested that the threat was intended for the man hiding in the flat – that is, for Jacobson, whom the Red Army men had feared and for whom they had stolen all that silver ... Samson shook his head, as if the action might clear his mind like a thunderstorm clears the sky. Some were afraid of Jacobson, others threatened him. And Samson hadn't found any silver bullets, only a large bone that looked to have been cast from molten silverware ... Maybe this Jacobson was Balzer's son? But Balzer was German and Jacobson Belgian ... That didn't make much sense. What about year of birth? Balzer was fifty-two and Jacobson twenty-four ...

Samson again conjured up the figure who had shot Semyon and the tailor, mentally applying Jacobson's age to its movements. This raised doubts. The murderer had behaved too decisively. Would it have been so easy for a man of twenty-four to shoot someone in the back?

If Balzer was in the morgue, then surely he was still wearing his blood-soaked clothing. And no-one there was likely to have searched him – for fear of contagion or God's wrath. These were simple people, after all – God-fearing people.

The morgue at the Oleksandrivska Clinical Hospital turned out to be the cavernous, deep basement of a three-storey building that also housed an anatomical theatre and classrooms for medical students. From the outside, it looked impressive, although its façade didn't seem to have been repainted for a couple of years, and only in fresh sunlight did it appear to recover its former fresh yellow colour. The wide double doors suggested that things were constantly being brought in and taken out.

"Picking up a corpse?" a man in a white coat – young in appearance, but with a voice coarsened by tobacco and drink – called out to Samson in the gloomy corridor.

"No, not picking up. Only checking on. I'm with the police."

"Police corpses are in the third room on the right. There's a light switch at the entrance. And shut the door behind you – don't let out the cold air."

In the room described, fully dressed corpses lay on a dozen iron tables and on the stone floor between them. The light bulb in its tin cone shone dimly by design, so as not to frighten the living with what it illuminated, nor to wake the dead.

Samson felt chilly. He pulled at his belt and tried to fasten it tighter, but, after the first unsuccessful attempt, returned its little steel tongue to its accustomed hole.

The corpses lay on their backs, their swollen or tautened faces turned towards the ceiling. The young policeman well remembered Balzer, with his trimmed moustache. After wending his way between the bodies and stepping over a peasant whose unbuttoned flannel shirt would never again close over his bloated, blue torso, Samson returned to the door. Balzer wasn't there.

He found the orderly and asked to consult the morgue's records. Together they checked for entries from that ill-fated evening. It turned out that the bodies of Friedrich Balzer and Semyon Glukhov were only brought in the following morning. In the last column of the ruled book, in the entry concerning Semyon Glukhov, Samson read: *Released for burial on 3 April*. In the entry concerning Friedrich Balzer, he read the same words – *Released for burial* – but in a different handwriting, and with no date.

"Who released Balzer?" Samson asked, gazing into the orderly's eyes.

"How do I know?" The man shrugged, and something about the gesture seemed odd to Samson. He took a closer look and only at that moment realised that the orderly had slipped his white medical gown over a thick sheepskin coat.

"Who was working that day?" Samson pressed him, jabbing his finger at the record of Balzer's release.

"But there's no date," the orderly replied, looking at the visitor's finger.

"Such disorder," Samson sighed angrily.

"You bet," the orderly agreed. "Go ahead and spend a few hours in this cold, with this stench in your nostrils – then we'll see how much you care about order. Have you got a cigarette?"

"I don't smoke," Samson replied sharply, sensing that his irritation was about to burst to the surface in ruder ways.

"Suppose I'll have to smoke my own, then." The orderly hiked up the right side of his gown, reached into the pocket of his coat, pulled out a pack of cigarettes and walked off towards the front door.

Samson had no choice but to follow. The visit to the morgue had been fruitless, or so he felt at first. But, as he moved away from the building, warming himself more with the sight than with the rays of the peeping sun, it occurred to him that, since Balzer's body had been claimed for burial, then the tailor must have been dear to someone. And this someone could only have been Luc Jacobson, who had lived in Balzer's residential sewing workshop, as the Kyiv census card had it. None of this fitted, of course, with the fact that Jacobson was a criminal. Then again, even criminals were capable of tender feelings. Balzer's age opened up the possibility that he was Jacobson's father – but why the different surnames and citizenships? It was also hard to get one's mind around the notion that the person who had shot Balzer in the back at point-blank range could then have claimed his body for burial. So perhaps it wasn't Jacobson who had killed Balzer and Semyon . . . But then – who was it?

Samson's feet brought him to 3 Baseina of their own accord. As he approached the building that was, sadly, now familiar to him, deliberating whether or not to enter, behind him resounded the growing clatter of horseshoes striking cobblestones. It was as if this clatter hit his legs from behind – they nearly buckled. Samson staggered to the side. Through his terrified mind flashed the sabre that had killed his father, followed by the one that had severed his ear. He flattened himself against the wall of number 3 and looked from side to side, trying to regain control over his body, which had suddenly gone weak and ungovernable.

A Red Army cavalry detachment galloped past, hurried and tense. With rifles slung over their shoulders, sabres dangling at their sides and angry faces ready for battle, they skirted the right side of the Besarabsky Market and disappeared behind it.

The roar of the horsemen gradually faded from Samson's ears, but the tremor that their sudden appearance had set off in his body still lingered. On top of this, he was now seized by the worrying thought that the Red Army men were galloping to battle – to take on the rebels. And so, with hasty steps, he started out for the station, anxiously scanning the faces of passers-by. It seemed to him that they were also in a hurry, intending either to hide or simply to get as far away as possible from what could not be avoided – because, no matter where you hide, you can't escape a collective misfortune. It will always catch up with you, making sure you get your share.

There was a truck parked in front of the Lybid station, in the back of which two dozen fighters sat on two benches or stood upright. Vasyl and Pasechny were lifting a box of ammunition into place.

"Oh, Samson! Great – get on!" Pasechny shouted. "Nayden says you're a crack shot. Time to prove it!"

Samson obediently approached the truck.

"Get on where?" one of the Red Army soldiers in the back protested. "We'll hit a bump and he'll fall clean off – there ain't no room."

"He's right," another soldier agreed.

"How about the front?" asked Pasechny.

"Kholodny's up in the passenger's seat."

"Alright, then. Get going."

The truck pulled away.

"What's going on?" Samson asked Pasechny nervously.

"What, he asks," Pasechny responded irritably. "The hetmans have gone and captured Priorka and Kurenivka. There's fighting at Podil. We're surrounded. But the border regiment is on the move. We'll crush the bastards – drown them in their own blood."

Samson went up to his office. The chests of silver were where he'd left them, as were the boxes of German books. The silver bone wrapped in pigskin still lay on his desk.

Then shots rang out in the street. Samson pulled his revolver from its holster and raced down the stairs, bounding over several steps at a time. He leapt through the front doors and saw a man lying face down in the middle of the road. Pasechny ran up to the man, Mauser in hand, turned him over on his back, took a closer look at his face and threw open his greatcoat.

"Who is he?" Samson asked as he drew nearer.

"One of our prisoners. Made a run for it," Pasechny responded angrily. "They smell freedom now. They'll be climbing up the walls, just you watch. We've got to break their fever." He marched back into the station.

A minute later, Samson heard further shots. The young policeman ran inside and saw Pasechny, Mauser still in hand, coming up the stairs from the basement, a buzz of voices and a groan rising behind him.

"That ought to calm them down," he announced, heading towards the entrance. "A reminder that death is cheap around here. A lot cheaper than life."

Chapter 35

By one in the morning on 9 April, only Vasyl and Samson remained at the Lybid station. The two of them would either stand on the threshold with revolvers in hand, listening to the echoes of both close and distant gunshots galloping on and on along the roofs of Kyiv, or huddle just inside the front door, so as not to be ambushed.

Nayden and Pasechny had been summoned by telephone to defend the Cheka headquarters on Sadova Street.

"Fight to the death," Nayden had commanded them on leaving. And, in his mouth, "death" sounded perfectly concrete and inevitable.

The electricity had been cut off, and now Samson was tormented by doubts. Did this merely indicate the usual lack of firewood, or had one of the hetmans seized the power plant and plunged Kyiv into darkness on purpose, in the hope of taking it faster?

The basement resounded with rumbling and clanging. Samson could only guess at what the prisoners were up to, and he was reluctant to do so. Pasechny's warning shots had left one or two among the motley crowd dead or wounded. But that seemed unimportant. The prisoner killed while trying to escape was still out there too, lying right in middle of the road, and no-one was about to take him away, or even to move him off to the side. It was up to the authorities to dispose of corpses – and tonight the authorities were fighting for survival. They were busy making corpses, not taking them away. Half the corpses belonged to the authorities, and half the authorities were corpses now.

"What do you think's going on?" Samson asked Vasyl vaguely.

"I don't know," Vasyl admitted. "At times like these, it's best not to think. Better to listen."

And they fell silent again, turning their attention to the shots and echoes, and to the noise in the basement. Suddenly that noise intensified – iron bars hit the ground. The stairs buzzed with wheezing, guttural voices. A wave of prisoners rose up and splashed out into the street. Samson and Vasyl barely managed to leap out of the way. The first prisoner stumbled over the corpse in the middle of the road and tumbled, moaning and groaning, onto the cobblestones, but then he got to his feet and took off uphill, in the direction of the Botanical Garden. The thudding of his feet was drowned out by the general thumping and rumbling of the other runners, though some, perhaps most of them, headed downhill.

Samson raised his revolver and tried to decide, as quickly as possible, at which receding back he ought to aim.

Vasyl stopped him. "Don't. What good would it do?"

The noise of running feet subsided with surprising speed. Gunfire again echoed over the rooftops.

"There's no-one left down there. Let's go inside," Vasyl suggested.

They went in and locked the doors behind them. A groan rose from the basement. Someone was in no state to escape.

They went up to the first floor, to Samson's office. Vasyl lit a candle.

"Some tea?" he asked. "We've got kerosene."

Samson shook his head. "I'm scared," he mumbled.

Vasyl tried to reassure him. "Everyone's scared."

"No, I'm not scared for myself. I have to go home . . . Check on Nadezhda . . ."

"And, what, leave me here alone?"

"I'd be quick – there and back. Just to make sure she's alright."

Vasyl kept quiet and stared at the candle flame, which, thanks to the closed windows and doors, was steady, almost motionless.

"Go, then," he said at last. "But get changed first. Grab a

sheepskin coat from the evidence room and leave the holster here. Those coats have deep pockets."

Samson had great difficulty running through the dark in the thick sheepskin. This was mostly due to the size of the coat – he hadn't realised at first just how huge it was. Only when he began to fasten the buttons out on the street did he feel himself to be a clapper dangling inside an enormous bell. The cold, sharp wind blowing in his face made things worse. Eventually, he pulled the right half of the coat under his left arm and pressed the left side to his chest with his right hand. Then he ran, sticking close to the walls of the houses, hearing nothing of his own footsteps, but catching the sound of distant gunfire. His cap slid to the left, leaving his earless earhole exposed. Samson adjusted it as he ran, and the shooting grew quieter, as if the left ear didn't admit background sounds, while his bare earhole was all-embracing, omnivorous.

When he reached his home, he looked up at the first-floor windows, and was horrified to see them lit, faintly but distinctly.

He knocked on the front door.

"Who is it? What do you want?" the frightened widow's voice asked after a long minute.

She let him in quickly.

"I told you bandits would take the city," she murmured. "That's all anyone was talking about at the market ... And now you've got refugees in your flat."

Samson wasn't listening – he flew right up to the first floor. Only there did her closing remark sink in.

"What refugees?" he called down.

But the widow, who had already returned to her flat, didn't hear him.

In the hallway, he stumbled over a trunk and some sacks.

At the living-room table, visibly frightened and wearing their coats, sat Nadezhda's parents. Their daughter sat beside them.

Three candles were burning. It was their light that Samson had seen from below.

Without saying a word, Samson ran up to the table and blew them out.

"You can't risk it," he said. "They'll see you ... Welcome!"

"We barely made it," Lyudmila gasped. "The cabbies are taking advantage of people's fear and grief, squeezing them dry ..."

"How does Podil look?" Samson asked.

"Robbery, murder," Trofim Sigismundovich said in a deadened voice. "We saw two dead bodies along the way. And bandits with white armbands. They shot at us, too."

"Do try to relax," Samson pleaded. "Go to bed. It might all blow over. They haven't reached this part of town yet."

"I can't," the young woman's mother complained. "What if they kill us in our sleep? What an Easter we'll have this year! Kulich bread, baked with blood ..."

"Mama, don't talk like that!" Nadezhda spoke up. "The main thing is to wait until dawn. The light of day drives fear away – clears everything right up."

"If only someone would win out and take power for good. Otherwise, they'll all just kill each other – and us, too, while they're at it."

"Papa, don't!"

"Do go to bed. You don't have to sleep, but you need to lie down. It will soothe your nerves," Samson insisted.

"Where would we lie down?" the young woman's father asked, looking around in the darkness.

"You can spend the night in there, where Nadezhda sleeps. That bed is wider. And Nadezhda will take my bed."

"What about you?" Lyudmila asked plaintively.

"I'm needed back at the station. To keep watch. There are only two of us left."

*

The corpse still lay in the middle of the road in front of the station. The strange silence, free even of the sounds of distant gunfire, made Samson warier than ever. He knocked on the closed doors, then shouted, "Vasyl! It's me, Samson!"

The doors opened.

"Well?" asked Vasyl.

"Things look bad in Podil, but here . . . all quiet."

Vasyl shook his head. "I don't like it, this silence."

He held a lighted kerosene lamp in his hand.

They went upstairs and sat in Samson's office again.

"Someone was moaning down there in the basement," Samson said, just to break the silence.

"Yes, I went and had a look. He was already dead," Vasyl responded.

"No-one else down there?"

"No-one. We'll have to start from scratch."

Samson sniggered and an odd smile appeared on his face.

"If we live long enough," he whispered.

Chapter 36

Two days later, on 11 April, towards noon, the Kurenivka rebellion was finally crushed. The sun shone down on the city from a perfectly clear blue sky, observing streets on which civilians went about their peaceful affairs and Red Army men pursued their military duties. Both groups exchanged suspicious glances when they came across each other, but the enmity still circulating through the city's air didn't push them into outright conflict. On the contrary, they walked away from one another more quickly than they came together, occasionally creating the impression that people were running in fear. Yet, in reality, their steps only accelerated as they approached their chosen goals, which is the normal way of things.

Nayden and Kholodny had returned to the station the night before – dirty, tired and angry. On learning of the prisoners' escape, Nayden simply spat and remained silent, but his face turned crimson. Eventually he declared that he was off to get some shut-eye in his office, but that they should wake him immediately if anything happened. Kholodny also tucked himself away in some corner or other to catch up on sleep. But they were both up by six, and then Samson finally heard Nayden's brief dramatic chronicle of the preceding three days, during which the hetman-led villagers had seized the state bank and half of Kyiv, including the train station, and surrounded the Red Army garrison in Podil. If it hadn't been for the Chinese detachment, the bandits would have killed every single soldier. But now the bank was back in the right hands, as was the station, and a little later it emerged that plain-clothes Chekists had been shooting anyone who'd forgotten to rip off their white armband. They ended up dispatching about a hundred of these fatally forgetful rebels in different parts of the city.

Two companies of Red Army men arrived by rail from Kharkiv to fortify the outskirts of the city, beyond which it was now dangerous to go, since all the outlying districts and nearby villages had fallen under the complete and cruel control of Hetman Struk, the "Green" Hetman Danylo Terpylo and a few other warlords. Of course, they were unlikely to try to seize the city again so soon after their failed attempt. Kyiv's hackles were up – it was ready for battle. Three armoured trains had returned to their places of deployment, with one of them attracting enthusiastic or frightened attention right beside the station.

On the evening of 11 April, Samson took Nadezhda's parents home to Podil, entering their flat first, revolver in hand, just in case new tenants had moved in without permission. Luckily, the flat had remained untouched by the rebellion, although two corpses with white armbands on the sleeves of their padded jackets, but without boots or weapons, still lay in front of the neighbouring house.

Samson spent that night at the station too, sinking into a soft requisitioned club chair.

Kholodny also spent the night there, as did, it goes without saying, Vasyl and Nayden, who lived there – although Vasyl never stopped complaining that the roof in his hut in Protasiv Yar had been leaking for two years.

"Pasechny's dead," Nayden told Samson, after waking him in the middle of the night. "From his wounds. Just got word. There's a memorial service tomorrow. Many killed . . . We'll say our good-byes to him then."

"Should we go on with our cases?" Samson asked cautiously, in a sleepy voice.

"Go on with the open cases, start new ones, finish them all, send them off to the archive. Back to normal – with a break for the burial."

The ceremony again took place on the far left edge of Oleksandrivsky Park, on the cliff overlooking the Dnipro. Samson stared at the pit, which was slightly smaller than the mass grave in which Semyon lay. He stared, doubting the accuracy of his memory. It seemed to him that this new pit had been dug in the same spot as the old one – that he was standing where he had stood then, with the same trees at the same distance behind his back and to the right of him. But that was impossible. After all, the old grave had also been seven yards deep, which meant that, if they'd dug this one in the same spot, they would have long ago stumbled upon the coffins of already buried heroes.

"Where's the other mass grave?" Samson asked Nayden in a whisper. "The one where they buried Semyon."

Nayden looked around, then pointed to the right. "Over there. Not far."

"Why isn't there a monument?"

"It's early days. Monuments to heroes are erected when victory is complete. We have a long way to go."

This time around, the memorial speeches were brief, the speakers laconic. Everyone in attendance looked worn out, utterly exhausted. There were hardly any women present, and few of the children and adolescents who sometimes came in droves to watch heroes laid to rest.

"We'll pay our respects at the station," Nayden told Samson, indicating with a nod of his head that the young man should follow him. The band was still playing the last mournful tune. Having thrown off their greatcoats, soldiers were shovelling earth into the grave. Far off to the right, ten men in workers' garb were doing the opposite: just beginning to dig a new pit. It must have been for the following day, or just for the future.

They returned to the station on foot. The air felt warm in the sun, but the temperature was probably below ten degrees. From time to time, Nayden would shoot a sharp glance to the side, at a group of passers-by hurrying off somewhere. It seemed to Samson that he was carefully inspecting the sleeves of their coats and jackets, still looking out for white armbands.

"What's that?" Nayden said, nodding at the pigskin-wrapped silver bone on Samson's desk.

Vasyl was placing shot glasses beside it and filling them with store-bought vodka – four of them, cut-glass and stemmed.

"But I told you—" Samson began to explain.

"Ah, yes, I remember," Nayden cut him off. "Did you mark it down as evidence?"

"Yes."

"Good. Where's Kholodny?"

"I'll be right back," Vasyl said, scurrying out.

He returned a couple of minutes later, and behind him, yawning, came the former priest, with three days' stubble on his pale, flabby cheeks.

"He slept through it," Vasyl explained.

"They buried him?" Kholodny enquired.

"Uh-huh," Nayden breathed out, barely moving his lips.

"With the saints give rest, O Christ, to the soul of Thy servant—"

"Knock it off," Nayden interrupted him sternly. "It's Pasechny they buried, not some old biddy from the nunnery."

"Damn," Kholodny said, shaking his head regretfully. "Three nights without sleep and the past sneaks up on you . . . To hell with it!" He raised a glass and brought it to his lips. "To the fallen hero! May he live in Red memory and glory!"

"To the fallen hero!" Nayden, Samson and Vasyl echoed him.

They emptied their glasses.

"Alright." Nayden exhaled. "We can't be wasting time on death. Back to work!" Without looking at anyone, he went out.

Vasyl and Kholodny followed.

Samson sat down at his desk, unrolled the pigskin and hefted the heavy, smooth silver bone.

"Back to work," he whispered, and set about thinking. This time, the heavy bone in his hands pushed his thoughts in a particular direction.

He wrapped the object back up, then found a sackcloth bag in which he could carry it inconspicuously, without attracting the attention of people on the street.

Nikolay Nikolaevich Vatrukhin appeared to be immeasurably glad to see Samson. He himself didn't look too good. His sunken cheeks spoke of a meagre diet, and the absence of Tonya, his servant, aroused the suspicion that no-one was looking after his household and ensuring his comfort.

"It's good to see you're still alive," he offered, instead of a greeting, as he let his visitor inside. "Dr Patlakh's family in Lukyanivka were all killed, robbed . . . No end of trouble, these days . . ."

Samson nodded. "We've had some killed too."

They stepped into the living room.

"I'm keeping house myself now," Vatrukhin announced, spreading his hands. "I couldn't pay Tonya. After I took down the sign, my old patients must have decided that I'd died or emigrated. That was the end of it. No money, no food. Tonya left for Fastiv, to live with her sister, who at least has a cow . . ."

"Perhaps you can hang the sign up again?" Samson suggested.

"No. I'm too afraid. One can endure hunger, but not death."

"Then please accept a couple of vouchers," Samson said, holding out two pieces of paper bearing purple stamps and the typewritten words *One Meal* in the same purple ink. "The food in Soviet cafeterias isn't at all bad. Delicious gravies, especially for porridge."

"Thank you . . . Thank you very much," the eye doctor replied, greatly moved. "Someday I'll repay you, by God. Or treat you for free."

"I've come to get your advice," Samson admitted, and immediately drew the bone wrapped in pigskin from the sackcloth bag. He placed it on the oval table. "You wouldn't happen to know what this is, would you?"

"I certainly would, young man. *Os femoris* – a femur," Vatrukhin declared, then picked up the object and examined it. "Left," he added. "Well made, but for what purpose I can't say. Perhaps someone ordered a silver skeleton from a jeweller?"

The doctor sank into thought. A dreamy smile played on his emaciated face.

"If I were a surgeon celebrating a milestone in my career, I'd be delighted to receive such a gift. A silver skeleton for a surgeon's living room. A marvellous idea, no?"

"So, you think it was intended as a gift?" Samson asked doubtfully.

"Oh, I didn't say that – I was just fantasising . . . Maybe you'd better ask a surgeon? I don't specialise in bones, as you know. Not in ears and not in bones."

"Do you know any surgeons?"

"Yes, of course. There's Princess Vera Gedroits, for one . . ."

"Princess?" Samson asked, even more doubtfully. "Aren't surgeons . . . men?"

"They usually are, yes, but she's different – more skilled and knowledgeable than the rest put together. A walking *Brockhaus and Efron Encyclopedia*."

"Could we go and see her now?"

"She's quite some distance away, but, if you have money for a cab, I don't see why not."

"Money isn't a problem. I can afford the fare there and back,"

Samson promised. "I just hope the cabbies have crawled out of their holes by now. They feared the rebels would take their horses."

"We're sure to find one by the baths across from the People's House," Vatrukhin declared confidently as he hastily pulled a woollen cardigan over his thick linen shirt and buttoned it. "She employs an excellent cook – we might get lucky and arrive in time for lunch." Then, in an apologetic tone, he added, "My head's full of fantasies today . . . It must be the joy of seeing you alive and well. But please don't think that I've became attached to you in some special way . . . As a certain French poet wrote, 'If I see you alive, then I too am alive.' You see, life, especially someone else's life, is transmitted to the brain by means of vision. Nearly everything is transmitted to the brain by means of vision. Now, where are my boots?"

Vatrukhin froze for a moment, then walked resolutely into the hallway.

Chapter 37

As Samson soon learned, this surgeon-princess of Vatrukhin's lived quite near him – at 7 Kruhlouniversytetska. However, the eye doctor measured distance not by miles, but by the strength in his tired legs, which evaporated after just five minutes of walking.

The young policemen wasn't put out. On the contrary, his spirits rose as he realised that the cabby would hardly charge anything for such a short ride.

Vera Ignatyevna Gedroits, it appeared, was not only a woman in a largely male profession, but also one who bore herself in a manly fashion. She was Samson's height, and she greeted them wearing a black trouser suit, although the cut of her jacket had soft, feminine lines. The manner in which she held out her hand to Vatrukhin was rather brusque. Then Samson himself experienced her firm handshake, which convinced him straight away that she had more than enough power and control to perform her job.

"This is my good friend," the eye doctor said, vouching for Samson. "In these times, friends can turn out to be all sorts of things," he added, as if apologetically. "And so Samson found work as a criminal investigator, although all his life he had dreamed of electricity."

"Well, come in, come in," the hostess cut in. She had a deep voice. "I was just about to have some tea with ham. You'll join me. Pelageya, dear, where are you?" she called out, turning around.

"Here," the maid's voice sounded.

"Cut two more pieces," Vera Ignatyevna commanded.

She led them into a room that one might easily have called a hall. The wide chairs on cabriole legs arranged around the table looked like some species of noble spider. The lamp on the table was a porcelain nymph holding aloft a sky-coloured shade.

Pelageya, the servant, whose face did not betray her age, brought in a samovar and placed it beside the nymph. She then left and reappeared with a platter, one side of which was occupied by sliced bread and the other by thick and fragrant pieces of ham.

"It looks like we have everything," Vera Ignatyevna boomed. "But there's no butter, these days. Pelageya, dear, would you pour the tea?"

The maid first half-filled the cups with tea from the teapot on top of the samovar, then added the boiling water.

The ham smelled of sweet woodsmoke. Samson couldn't resist and reached for a piece of it, along with a slice of bread.

"Samson Theophilovich is in possession of a strange object," Vatrukhin began through a mouthful of bread and ham. "Go on, Samson, pick it up off the floor and show Vera Ignatyevna."

Samson bent down, pulled out the silver bone and offered it to their hostess, feeling its weight.

Vera Ignatyevna all but snatched the bone from the young man's hands, easily and confidently. She first cast a quick glance over it, then looked more carefully at one extreme, followed by the other, which seemed less extreme, as it were, as it had what looked like a short rounded extension projecting from it.

"What do you think?" asked Vatrukhin. "I myself have never encountered such an *os femoris* before, but I'm not a bones man . . ."

"Exquisite work," Vera Ignatyevna thought aloud. "More lapidary than a jeweller's. The *collum femoris* is in perfect proportion to the rest. I can't even guess the purpose for such an ideal copy . . ."

"Ah, well, I remember a case when a professor specialising in ocular diseases was presented with a porcelain eye," Vatrukhin spoke up. "I was in attendance. Extremely beautiful object, in its own box. Everyone at the table gasped."

Vera Ignatyevna chuckled. "Nikolay Nikolaevich, as you know, I specialise in maxillofacial surgery. I assure you, if someone were to present me with a silver jaw, they would be in immediate need of my services. Or perhaps yours. Such bad taste . . ."

"*De gustibus non est disputandum*," Vatrukhin murmured thoughtfully with a shrug. "For some, Artsybashev's *Sanin* is the height of literary achievement; for others, it's mere pornography—"

"Well, is the ham to your taste?" the hostess interrupted the eye doctor, her eyes indicating the pink piece of meat left on the platter.

"Of course!" answered Vatrukhin.

Samson also nodded.

"You see, there is a criterion of taste and there are deviations, which can be discussed, but by no means justified."

The intonation of Vera Ignatyevna's pronouncement seemed eerily familiar to Samson. He thought about it and remembered that one of his schoolteachers liked to deliver maxims just as melodiously and was also particularly fond of the phrase "by no means".

"What are you thinking about?" Vera Ignatyevna asked her young guest. "Don't you agree?"

"Oh, yes, I very much agree," Samson said, emerging from his recollections. "Does your interest in maxillofacial surgery only embrace the jaw?" he suddenly asked.

"No, the entire skull." She chuckled and, tilting her head slightly, peered at the scar where Samson's right ear had been. "Have you already been under the scalpel?" she asked sympathetically.

"No, under a sabre," the young man replied, giving a sigh. "I was wondering whether this might be repaired . . . But how would one attach a prosthesis? Sew it on?"

"The wound is healed," Vera Ignatyevna declared definitively. "You won't grow a new ear, while the prostheses some patients order for themselves and wear on strings are unhygienic. If I were you, I wouldn't even consider it."

Then the hostess finally plucked the last slice of bread and last piece of ham from the platter. She chewed with relish, her lower jaw moving decisively up and down, lending her face a masculine expression.

"You know ..." Her face suddenly froze. "There's a chatty surgeon at the Jewish hospital, a bit of a laughing stock. One of my patients told me this fellow's in the habit of saying that, if bones were made of silver, they'd neither hurt nor break."

"And do doctors often receive expensive gifts?" Samson asked, looking into Vera Ignatyevna's eyes. Then he turned to Vatrukhin, recalling his story of the porcelain eye.

"Good doctors? Often," the latter responded.

"This ham was a gift," Vera Ignatyevna admitted. "A patient brought me an entire leg of pork yesterday – a gesture of gratitude."

"Superb ham," the eye doctor drawled and licked his lips, glancing at the empty platter as if ready to ask for more.

"It's hard to survive without such gifts, these days," the hostess said. "A hungry surgeon should not be allowed to operate."

After taking Vatrukhin home by cab, Samson decided to go over to Sivokon's on Nimetska. The tailor was at home, but not working. Neither kerosene nor candles illuminated the ground floor windows, but, almost as soon as he knocked, Samson heard a door open on the first floor and footsteps descending the stairs.

"Ah! The freak-show ringmaster has come for his suit," the tailor joked. "Please, come in, come in."

In the workshop, by the dim light of a kerosene lamp, Samson saw a jacket stretched over a swollen tailor's dummy. The tailor screwed up the wick and the light grew as bright as that of an electric bulb. It was now easier to make out the jacket's strange size and shape.

"If such a client exists," Sivokon pronounced as he approached the dummy and stroked the jacket's shoulder, "then he is most certainly a freak of nature or suffers from some physical ailment ..."

He picked up the suit's trousers from his sewing table and positioned them below the jacket.

"Very thin legs. You can't take a broad step in these trousers. A completely different size, starting with the belt," he said, touching the hem of the jacket. "This person would be absurdly heavy above the waist and puny below. Maybe his legs are gone? That would make sense – he'd always be seated. Because it's really impossible to walk in such trousers. Oh, and another interesting detail . . ."

The tailor beckoned Samson over to the dummy.

"Have a look," he said, opening one of the side pockets and lifting the lamp over it at a slight angle.

Samson had a look, then stuck his hand inside. There was something sewn into the jacket pocket. His fingers seemed to have entered and got stuck in small holes, as if he had slipped his hand into a glove.

"It's the same on the other side," the tailor said. "I thought it was a mistake in the pattern, but no – it appears to be intentional."

"What is it?" Samson asked.

"Customers make odd requests from time to time. Once, I made a tailcoat with a hidden pocket for a dagger! They gave me the dagger for a day, so I could make sure the fit was just right."

"So, what do you make of these holes?" Samson asked, gazing at the experienced tailor as if he were a much-admired schoolteacher.

"Those aren't just any holes," the tailor responded with a sly smile. "It's a hidden bandolier."

"Excuse me?"

"Each pocket can fit fifteen bullets. Pistol-sized ammunition, of course."

Samson briskly turned the pocket inside out and saw a ribbon with loops, into which his fingers had slipped. He pulled two bullets out of his revolver and thrust them into the loops. A perfect fit.

"You see? It's your client, not mine," the tailor declared in an almost cheerful voice. "You can take these back with you. I've already prepared an invoice."

He drew a handwritten sheet of paper from the inside pocket of his jacket.

"Did it amount to a lot?"

"One hundred and fifty roubles – only, they say money will be banned soon. I'd prefer to take it in salt or sugar, which I could later exchange."

"I'll see what I can do," Samson promised uncertainly, thrusting the invoice into his jacket pocket.

"Take the mannequin, too. I ordered it for your suit, so I have no use for it."

"Is it exactly the size of the suit?" Samson asked, examining the dummy, which, if it were fitted with a head, would be about two inches shorter than the young policeman himself.

"Not only the size of the suit, but also of the customer who'd been measured for it."

"Alright, then, I will take it. May I also borrow a dozen or so pins?"

The tailor walked over to his sewing table, picked up a piece of paper, stuck some pins in firmly, so that they'd stay in place, and handed it to the visitor.

Back in his office, Samson buttoned the jacket over the mannequin's torso and pinned the trousers on beneath it. They nearly reached the floor. It occurred to him that it might be useful to find a suitable head and attach it. Then he would have at his disposal an almost exact dummy of the criminal, whom he had to find in order to dot all the i's.

"What is *that*?" Nayden asked unhappily, having come to see Samson with a different question – a question he promptly forgot when he saw the mannequin.

"This is Jacobson," Samson responded. "It seems his figure will be easy to recognise."

"His figure? Not his face?" Nayden followed up, his lips twisting.

"So far. But, from a distance, or from the side, a figure is easier to spot than a face."

"Well, yes, some figures are indeed easier to spot than faces," Nayden agreed, relaxing his smirk. "I came to tell you that the people from the state bank are coming tomorrow, for the silver. It turns out that we'll have new money soon, with silver coins. Maybe our thief knew about that and planned to sell the stolen silver to the state somehow? Only the fool didn't realise that, in times of war, the state doesn't buy metal – it requisitions what it needs—"

"He's no fool," Samson responded. "And I doubt he knew about the new money. I think . . . No, I'd better show you. Come closer."

He pulled open a jacket pocket and positioned it so that the light from the electric bulb would reach inside.

"A fabric bandolier," Samson explained. "And there's one just like it in the other pocket. Fifteen rounds each. Maybe he really was collecting silver for bullets."

"What about the bone?" Nayden asked.

"Maybe for bullets and the bone as well. That could have been a gift for a doctor, like the holy gifts Catholics make to the Church, you know?"

"What would I know about that?" Nayden shot back indignantly. "I'm not a Catholic, or any other sort of believer."

"Ah, well, when some part of a Catholic's body is healed, the person brings a silver copy of that part – a small one – to the Church, as a gift. They hang these silver copies beneath the icons. And this man," Samson added, indicating the mannequin, "has something wrong with his legs. The silver bone is a femur. So, it all adds up. He's Belgian, and so likely a Catholic. Definitely not Orthodox. And the bullets could be silver too. Who knows?"

"If you have ideas, pursue them. And get rid of those German books. Can't you smell that rotting paper?"

Samson nodded. His eyes followed Nayden as the latter departed, then turned to the mannequin.

"Well, Luc Jeanovich Jacobson," he muttered. "When shall we meet?"

Chapter 38

Samson took a tram to Iona Zaitsev's Jewish Surgical Hospital. The tram was overflowing with passengers whose appearance disturbed his stomach. The young policeman constantly imagined he sensed someone slyly pulling at his holster. For a while, he held the canvas bag with the silver bone tightly gripped in his hands, but then he slipped it under his shirt and felt safer.

"Are any surgeons available now?" he asked an elderly man in a greasy grey coat and an inappropriate student cap, who had stepped unsteadily out of the hospital.

"Don't go to Trattner," the man responded, bringing his pock-marked face close to Samson's. "He'll cut you to pieces . . . Reeks of vodka. Go see Schor."

Samson realised that before him stood an expert on local surgeons, and he desperately wanted to learn more. Yet his thoughts were muddled. Finding the right question was no easy task.

"Is Schor . . . German?" Samson asked.

"They're all Germans – Trattner, Schor, Brandman! Who else would cut you for free?"

"Free altogether?" Samson asked with some surprise. "No need for a gift, even?"

"What sort of gift?" the man asked, gazing at the young policeman uncomprehendingly. And then he noticed the holster. "Searching for bribe-takers, eh?" he guessed, baring his small yellow teeth. "Look elsewhere. This is a place for the poor."

"No, I'm searching for a surgeon," Samson responded, trying to sound worried. "My comrade's bones hurt – he can't even walk anymore! An old woman I know told me there was a surgeon here, the best in Kyiv, who talks a lot about silver bones."

"Fellow who says they neither hurt nor break?" The man chuckled. "That would be Trattner! But don't go to him. That old woman never had a run-in with his knife, I promise you that – otherwise she'd be worm food."

"Trattner," Samson repeated.

"That's right. Remember the name. And avoid it like the plague."

When Samson glanced into the waiting room on the ground floor, his gaze encountered three elderly vagrants and a young pregnant gypsy sitting on a bench along the wall. He immediately closed the door and went up to the first floor. The silver bone was in his hands once again.

As soon as he stepped out into the corridor, a short rotund woman in a blue coat ran up to him.

"Where do you think you're going in those dirty boots!" she screeched. "Wait over there!"

"I'm here to speak to Dr Trattner."

"Didn't you see the bucket of water and bleach at the top of the stairs? Clean your boots, then we'll talk."

Samson stepped back out through the doors. An unpleasant but medicinal odour rose from the bucket. He stepped into the liquid, one foot at a time, then picked up a rag from the floor and wiped off the boots. The leather looked, if not entirely clean, then at least wet. When he returned to the corridor, the noisy nurse was gone.

Trattner turned out to be a giant, head and shoulders taller than Samson. Catching sight of the holster, he allowed its bearer to enter his office, the peeling walls of which were plastered with old medical posters depicting skeletons accompanied by explanatory captions.

"I'm with the police," Samson said, introducing himself and sitting down in the chair reserved for patients. "We have a riddle to solve, and Vera Ignatyevna Gedroits suggested you might be able to help."

"Vera Ignatyevna?" Trattner asked, with no trace of admiration in his voice.

But Samson had already extracted the silver bone from the canvas bag and its pigskin. He handed it to the surgeon.

Trattner looked at the bone in bewilderment, then took hold of it.

"*Os femoris*, left," he declared decisively. "Where did you get such a thing?"

"That doesn't matter! The question is: what purpose could it serve? Might it be an offering to a surgeon – a sign of gratitude for a successful operation?"

"Hardly!" Trattner laughed out loud. "At a hospital for the needy?"

"How about at a different hospital? For those less in need?"

"Still nonsense . . ."

"Aren't you yourself in the habit of praising silver bones?" Samson spoke carefully. "Saying that they neither hurt nor break? What inspired these thoughts of yours?"

"I read a fairy tale once, when I was a child, about a silver boy. It made an impression on me."

"How odd . . . This bone belonged to a man from Belgium, with bad legs. He might have trouble walking . . ."

"From Belgium?" Trattner asked, sinking into thought. "A young man?"

"Yes, young," Samson confirmed.

"A bit awkward, too?" the surgeon added. "Wait one moment." He rose to his feet and stepped out, leaving Samson alone within the four peeling walls with their posters of skeletons.

Samson got up from his chair and examined one of the posters.

Then the door opened and the surgeon entered with a cardboard envelope in his hands. He walked over to his desk, pulled a large photographic plate from the envelope and bent his head over it.

"Jacobson?" he asked.

"Yes, Jacobson!" Samson replied ecstatically. "Luc Jeanovich."

"I don't have that information, just the surname, Jacobson – a citizen of Belgium, Jewish. The X-ray was taken for free on Reitarska Street. He left it with me so he wouldn't have to bring it again. Tuberculosis of the left femur. *Os femoris*, just like this one."

He picked up the silver bone, held it next to the photographic plate and shifted his gaze from one to the other and back.

"An exact replica." He exhaled in surprise. "Lapidary precision!"

"What did he want from you?" Samson asked.

"An operation – what else? And for free, of course. Here we do everything for free, but only for a little while longer . . ."

"You mean . . . he wanted you to remove the diseased bone and replace it with this one?"

"No, young man! One can't replace a living bone with a silver one!"

"But silver bones neither hurt nor break," Samson pronounced with a smile.

"Only in fairy tales," the surgeon responded dryly. "I don't recall exactly what I told him. But, judging by this X-ray, an operation would do no good."

"But he left it with you. When did he say he'd be back?"

"I don't remember," Trattner admitted. "We see scores of patients every day. Sometimes they return – we admit them, operate . . . But at least three months have passed since he was last here."

A neat compact truck was parked outside the police station. Men in uniform were carrying small but heavy canvas bags out of the building and placing them in the back of the vehicle.

When he reached the top of the stairs, Samson realised that they were from the state bank, taking away the silver that had been confiscated from the Red Army soldiers and from Balzer's basement. Two men were counting the objects extracted from the chests and sacks, recording them and packing them in the bank's canvas bags, while others carried the full bags down to the truck.

"Well done, you," said a man in dark work clothes, sitting at Samson's desk. He was recording the numbers of knives, forks and spoons in a thick account book. "We're in great need of silver. Soon, we'll be minting Soviet coins."

Samson nodded, tightening his grip on the silver bone wrapped in canvas and pigskin. He walked around the desk, opened the bottom drawer and slipped the item in diagonally. Then he gently shut the drawer, sat down in a club chair and began to observe the process.

An hour later, he was finally alone amid the empty chests and sacks, and the three boxes of German books that so irritated Nayden. If the commander were to enter the office now, his nose would immediately turn towards those boxes, and Samson would have to explain once more why he hadn't got rid of the dusty German books.

Samson walked over to the books and sniffed the air. Yes, they had a cellar-like odour – but not because they were printed in Germany, only because they had been stored in a cellar.

His eyes fell on the empty sacks strewn about the floor. He picked one up and began to transfer books into it. Almost an entire box's worth fitted into that one sack. He tied it up and sniffed it. It smelled of burlap, not of damp paper. He transferred the rest of the books into sacks, then carried the boxes down into the yard, where the station's horse and cart stood waiting.

On his return, he noticed that the air seemed to have grown drier. Maybe the smell had been coming off the boxes the whole time, he thought, not the books.

Right at that moment, Nayden walked into the office. He shot a glance at the wall opposite the door and, spotting no boxes, relaxed and gave a barely perceptible smile.

"The People's Commissar of Finance has asked us to convey his gratitude to you," he said. "When they put it in writing, we'll award you the document and celebrate with a drink. Congratulations!"

"Thank you," Samson responded, approaching the commander to shake his hand. "I'll try to keep it up."

"Do," Nayden said with a nod, and left.

In the evening, when it was already dark, Samson and Nadezhda sat by a kerosene lamp, drinking tea and chewing doughnuts with peas, which the Provincial Bureau of Statistics had given her as a bonus. The doughnuts were a tad too salty, but they were fresh, and, in combination with sweet tea and a leisurely conversation, they made the evening feel special. It was still cold in the flat, and this was probably why Samson and Nadezhda held their cups in their hands both as they sipped and as they set them back on the table.

"A real head-scratcher," Samson went on, after giving his summary of the Jacobson case. "The surgeon said that, in his condition, he shouldn't be able to walk, but he's hiding out . . . He may even be on the run, evading the people who've threatened to kill him. And giving us the slip, too. But how far could he go? When you consider the fact that he returned to Balzer's flat . . ."

"Will you arrest him?" Nadezhda asked.

"Certainly," the young policeman firmly declared. "And then we'll get to the bottom of this. At this point, there's so much I don't understand. More precisely, sometimes everything seems to add up, but the next day it falls to pieces . . ."

There was a polite knock at the door. The yard-sweeper's widow had clearly decided to disturb them.

Samson went out into the hallway and opened the door.

"There's a letter for you," the widow, clutching a small kerosene lamp in her hand, informed him in a somewhat frightened voice. She nodded down the stairs.

"Could you bring it up?"

"I can't. It's written on the wall."

"On the wall?"

"Come down, I'll shine a light on it."

They stepped out of the front door into the darkness of the street. She led him to the corner of the building and held her lamp against the wall. In its light, Samson saw broken letters drawn with a sharp piece of coal, making up two words: *Await death*. And next to them was the same circle, crossed out diagonally, with two points for eyes and a line for a nose.

"What made you think that was for me?" Samson asked coolly.

"Who else would it be for?" the yard-sweeper's widow asked on her way back to the front door.

Chapter 39

Samson didn't sleep a wink that night and kept the door to his bedroom open. Occasionally, he would lie down to calm his body and thoughts, but, as soon as he felt he was about to lapse into the realm of Morpheus, he would immediately apply all his will-power and lower his heels to the cold wooden floor. Only at the first sign of dawn did a thought form in his head, which buzzed from self-imposed sleeplessness – a thought that might not save him, but could at least help. He crept into his father's study on tiptoe and retrieved the tin that held his severed ear. In the hall-way, he inserted the tin into the gap between his front door and its bronze handle, wedging it in with a crumpled piece of newspa-per. Now, if someone should break down the door, the falling tin would – thanks to the ear within, which, though severed, had not abandoned its owner – fill Samson's head with a roar, informing him of the uninvited visitors.

Reassured, he returned to his bedroom and lay down again. All strength left his body. His eyes closed. He now had neither the will nor the fear necessary to stay awake.

"Samson ... Samson dear," a warm, familiar voice sounded nearby. "There's a little box on the door."

With difficulty, he opened his eyes. Nadezhda stood before him, wearing her sheepskin coat and kerchief.

"You were moaning so loudly, I thought you were sick! But your forehead is cool," she added in a gentle, caring tone. "Are you feeling ill?"

"No, no," he said, shaking his head. "I just had a nasty dream, and I was up half the night."

"Was it something you ate?"

"No," Samson answered as consciousness slowly returned to his head. He now understood that he couldn't let Nadezhda go to work without warning her. "Wait, I'll get up."

"I've got to go!"

"Please, wait just one minute! Step out and I'll get dressed."

She smiled and walked out, closing the door behind her.

When he entered the living room, Samson saw Nadezhda standing near the table. He placed his hands on her shoulders, as if he wanted to draw her into his arms. But he didn't – he only looked fixedly into her eyes.

"Can you stay with your parents tonight? Tonight and the night after?"

"Why?" the young woman asked, her eyes widening.

"I've received a threat. It looks like someone's been following me, and now they know where I live."

"And where will you stay?" Nadezhda asked, her face showing sudden concern. "What if they come looking for you?"

"I'll figure it out. But you go straight to your parents after work, alright? And don't come back here until I tell you it's safe."

"Alright." A muscle twitched in her face, betraying her doubts. "Did I do something to offend you?" she said, switching to an alarmed whisper.

"How? Not at all! When you see the corner of the building, you'll understand."

Nadezhda returned to her bedroom, gathered a bagful of things without which a young woman cannot go to sleep and get up in the morning, kissed Samson on the cheek and, without concealing the sadness and anxiety in her eyes, left the flat.

Left alone, Samson wedged the tin into the gap by the door handle with another piece of crumpled newspaper. After that he went down to the street with a wet rag in his hand and tried to wipe the charcoal threat off the wall The inscription diffused into an dark oblong patch, but at least the letters and crossed-out face were gone.

The police station resounded with a loud rumbling. Workers from the arsenal factory were repairing the prison bars and door in the basement. The noise from below seemed to ebb and flow in waves – an echo would rise to the ceiling of the first floor, then descend and collide with a new rising echo.

Samson needed solid, practical advice from a person capable of unusual thinking. He chose Kholodny, but the door to the former priest's office was closed and sealed.

"He'll be back soon," Nayden told Samson. "Your case moving along?"

"Yes, it's moving," Samson answered reluctantly.

"Wrap it up, will you? We're getting additional staff today – two specialists from Kharkiv. But yesterday alone we received more than a hundred reports of crimes and twelve dead bodies."

"Who'll be assigned to all that?" Samson asked, taken aback.

"We dropped the corpses on the Cheka, and the reported thefts – those went into cold storage . . . But you know what's interesting?"

"What?"

"This silver fever seems to have broken," Nayden declared with a smile. "Now the thieves are only interested in gold, diamonds, emeralds . . ."

About forty minutes later, Kholodny stepped into Samson's office himself.

"You were looking for me?" he offered by way of a greeting. And then his eyes fell on the jacketed mannequin. "What the heck is that?"

"Prototype of my criminal," Samson explained. "His figure."

Approaching the mannequin, Kholodny examined it first from the side, then from the front.

"Fascinating," he said. "Never seen that before. Anyhow, what's new?"

Samson outlined the events of recent days, summarising his conversation with Trattner and describing the charcoal inscriptions near Balzer's door and on the corner of his own building.

"You mean they're threatening both him –" Kholodny nodded at the mannequin – "and you?"

"Yes. But who are they?"

"Have you got any paper? A big sheet?" Kholodny asked.

"No, just small ones. I write on the back."

"No need! They brought us a whole load of paper from the printing house on Khreshchatyk – wait here."

Kholodny stepped out into the corridor and shouted, "Vasyl! Where are you?" He then demanded that Vasyl, who seemed to have appeared immediately, bring Samson a new supply of paper.

Five minutes later, a three-pound stack of clean yellow paper lay on Samson's father's desk, along with two half-pound stacks of ruled sheets with words printed on them.

Kholodny took a piece of yellow paper and a pencil, leaned over the desk and, with his head down, looked at Samson.

"In fact, you do the writing," he decided, sliding the sheet over to Samson, who sat in his usual place.

"What will I write?"

"The names of everyone involved in this case."

Samson stared at the paper and sighed. "Columns or rows?"

"Single column, of course. Like debtors for marriage and baptism fees."

Samson wrote, in a graceful hand, *Anton Tsvigun*, and beneath that, *Fyodor Bravada*, then added the names of cobbler Golikov, tailor Balzer, Jacobson . . .

Here, Samson grew pensive. He drew from the top drawer a slim file, sewn on one edge with grey thread, which held the case of the Red Army deserters and a couple of sheets from the new case concerning the silver stolen for Jacobson. After skimming the transcripts of Fyodor's interrogations, he added *Red Army soldier Grigory, called Grishka* to the column.

"Is that everyone?" Kholodny asked incredulously. "Why didn't you list yourself?"

"But I'm the investigator."

Kholodny pulled the file towards him and opened it to the first page. "You made the initial complaint." He pointed to Samson's signature at the bottom.

"Right." Samson added his name to the column.

"That's it?"

"If we don't count those I've interviewed."

"We won't, for the time being. Now write out the charcoal threat next to those who were threatened," Kholodny suggested. "You can skip the little face."

Samson reluctantly traced, in his lovely handwriting, those two nasty words next to his own and Jacobson's names.

"So, who's left among the unthreatened?" Kholodny straightened his back and peered at the list. "The cobbler is a victim. His goods were returned, so we can forget about him. The soldiers, however, are criminals. Which one was the ringleader?"

"Anton Tsvigun, a bell-ringer's apprentice," Samson answered. "I never met Grishka, but Fyodor is a simple peasant, only dreamed of sowing his fields."

"Bell-ringers are cunning people ... Sometimes dangerous," Kholodny pronounced. "Might not be pious at all. They like to sit up above everyone in their bell tower, but hardly set foot in the church. A fellow climbs up to the tower and rings the bell often enough, well, he starts thinking he's important, acting high and mighty. So, you say Anton's the ringleader? That makes sense. Now, which of them was most afraid of Jacobson?"

"Fyodor. Anton simply refused to speak about him, but Fyodor started – then stopped, out of fear."

"Maybe Anton put the fear of Jacobson into Fyodor the way priests put the fear of hell into parishioners at church?" Kholodny ventured.

"Maybe so," Samson agreed. And then he remembered the census card from 3 Baseina Street. "You know," he said, his eyes suddenly aglow and his severed ear, or rather the scar in its place, itching, "in the census, Balzer was recorded as literate, while Jacobson –" Samson looked back at the jacketed mannequin – "Jacobson was listed as illiterate. But how could a Belgian be illiterate?"

"Well, maybe he can't read or write in Russian. He could be new to Kyiv, right?"

"Yes, could be," Samson answered, growing pensive again. "But, if he's new to Kyiv and doesn't really know the language, how could he become an important criminal? Why should anyone be afraid of him?"

"Remember how much silver you found at his place," Kholodny said, pursing his lips and looking intently at Samson, who took this look to mean that his interlocutor disagreed with his thoughts. Or partly disagreed.

"Maybe his line was storing stolen goods?" Kholodny offered. "Like you!"

"What do you mean, like me?" Samson cried, stunned by the accusation.

"Well, how long did the patterns and the silver remain in your flat before you reported the crime?"

Samson bowed his head, sighing heavily. Kholodny was right, and he didn't seem to be accusing him of anything especially serious. After all, back then, he still had no idea what Red Army soldiers were allowed, or not allowed, to do.

"We must get them back and interrogate them again," the young policeman declared, trying to sound decisive. "Anton and Fyodor. And force them to give up Grishka."

"They're probably still locked up at Lukyanivska Prison. That's where they're keeping the deserters they've rounded up, putting them in a special unit. I'll send for Anton and Fyodor. But let me tell you what I really think. I think that, after they began to suspect you, they hid their next haul at Jacobson's place. When you yourself got everything out of Jacobson's, and when their spoils were taken from your flat, they got angry at you both. That's why they're leaving you those threats in charcoal."

"But if they're in prison . . ."

"Anton and Fyodor are in prison, but Grishka's on the loose. And you think there are only three of them?" Kholodny smirked sarcastically. "Alright, I'll send someone to fetch Anton and Fyodor. We were just assigned a new detachment of soldiers, to replace the ones killed in Podil. As soon as they bring the two fellows back, we'll interrogate them."

Chapter 40

The news from Lukyanivska Prison was bleak. All the deserters had fled during the Kurenivka rebellion. Five guards were killed in the escape and eight wounded – two of them severely and cruelly. In an act of revenge – or pure malice – their eyes had been gouged out.

Kholodny was no less saddened by this than Samson.

"I bet they're long gone," he muttered. "Some ran home, others joined up with the hetmans."

"So, the threats ... aren't coming from Anton and Fyodor?" Samson asked doubtfully.

Kholodny considered this. "Maybe they stayed. You haven't got under anyone else's skin lately, have you?"

Samson shook his head.

"Here's what we'll do," Kholodny declared. "I'll spend a few nights at your place. If they show their faces, we'll give them hell. I don't see how we can track them down ourselves. Who knows where in Kyiv they're holed up?"

Suddenly Samson realised that, having spent all morning and afternoon trying to get his mind around the new dangers he was facing, he hadn't had breakfast or lunch. And now it was nearly five o'clock. The light outside was turning grey, foreshadowing the sharp onset first of dusk, then of night.

He proposed that he and Kholodny have dinner together, and so they went off to the Soviet cafeteria on Stolypin Street. On the way, the two policemen stopped at the very bottom of Stolypin Street, where it intersected with Bibikovsky Boulevard. A café on that corner glowed from within, bright as a circus. And this despite the fact that the electricity was weak tonight, as feeble as an ailing kitten. The lamps at the station had emitted only a dim glow.

"How do they manage to keep it so bright?" Kholodny asked.

"My guess is they have a generator. Let's have a listen," Samson advised.

However, in that part of town, due to the arrangement of the buildings around Halych Square, the noise of the city was instantly burdened by an echo. It was all but impossible to make out individual sounds in that double din.

Kholodny shook his head sadly, indicating that he couldn't hear anything in particular. Turning his left ear to the café, Samson too heard nothing discernible. But when he turned his right side to the building, he detected the rhythmic noise of an engine. Its volume held steady, which meant it wasn't a passing car.

"I bet it's out in the courtyard," Samson told Kholodny, and they continued up Stolypin Street.

They stopped again in front of the building after next, but this time not due to any bright lights inside. Here, Kholodny's attention was drawn to an open barbershop, within which, in rather dim light, he made out the figure of a man seated in a barber's chair.

Kholodny's palm passed over his own cheeks, which were overgrown with stubble.

"Let's duck in," he suggested. "I don't feel comfortable with this hair on my face ... My razor's dull and my neighbours stole my strop. They're drunks – work down at the sewerage station ... Always reek either of yesterday's booze or ... their job."

They stepped into the shop and the barber leapt to his feet, delighted to see them. He seated Kholodny in the chair and Samson on a bench, placing a pre-revolutionary English fashion magazine in the young policeman's hands. Then he began to work up a lather in a blue enamel mug.

Samson leafed through the magazine mindlessly, unable to put aside his weighty thoughts and fears. But, when he reached a certain page, his hand stopped and his gaze grew sharper. There, in a photograph reproduced far more clearly than it would have been in a newspaper, a man was wearing exactly the same suit in which the surgeon-princess Vera Ignatyevna Gedroits had met him and Vatrukhin the other day.

So she wears men's clothes, Samson thought, somewhat bemused. But then he came up with a solid explanation. She was, after all, a surgeon, and that was a largely male profession. In order for her colleagues to treat her as if she were on an equal footing with them, she had to dress the part.

The hand that had been leafing through the magazine came back to life. Other pictures flashed before Samson's eyes, but these no longer drew his attention. His thoughts returned to the charcoal threats and to the uncertainty of the coming evening.

At around eight, the two policemen approached Samson's home, and a shiver ran down his limbs and spine. On the corner of the building, he saw a new inscription in charcoal, in the same handwriting, just above the dark oblong patch left from the previous threat. Someone had rewritten what Samson had erased that morning, word for word.

Kholodny struck a match and brought it up to the inscription.

"Parochial schooling, maybe two years," he said, pointing out the *w* with his left hand. "Only two words: *Await death*. They say criminals like to express themselves more floridly than that. And this fellow has trouble making out the letters – look."

"Could it just be the fact that he's writing in charcoal?"

"Charcoal, chalk – what's the difference?"

"Still, no mistakes," Samson countered, wanting to argue against his colleague's logical analysis out of fear or perhaps for some other reason.

"What kind of mistake could he make?" Kholodny asked with a shrug. "There's not much to get wrong."

The yard-sweeper's widow didn't open the front door straight away. She apologised, saying that she was cooking broth.

"Where did you get the meat?" Kholodny asked her sternly, and she, surprisingly, took fright, seemed to choke a bit, and scurried back into her flat, bolting the door behind her.

"Quite a mansion," Kholodny proclaimed as he looked around Samson's living room. There was a touch of jealousy in his voice.

"I'm not alone here," Samson hastened to explain. "The flat has been shared a long time. First with the Red Army men, as you know, and then . . . it also housed some refugees from Podil, who just left."

For the next two hours, they lingered over a pot of tea – sitting in the dark, listening to the silence. The city provided electricity that evening, if only feebly, but Samson didn't turn on the light.

"Say, if everyone turns to atheism," Samson asked unexpectedly, "do you think we'll forget God altogether?"

"Of course," Kholodny responded. "Just think of how many gods we've had in the past. All forgotten, save the last one. Last ones, I should say, since the Easterners still have Allah."

"But, if people forget God, what will they believe in?"

The former priest grew meditative. "In themselves, in the future, in the power of nature."

At that moment, there was a knock. A polite one. Samson recognised it as the widow's and jumped up to open the door.

"I see people walking around down there," she whispered fearfully. "They come close, then slink away. Spotted them from my window."

"How many are there?" Samson asked.

"Two, in leather jackets and caps. Look like Chekists."

Samson grew cold – cold in the legs and hot in the head, as if he felt a simultaneous infusion of fear and courage.

"Open the front door a crack," he whispered hastily to the widow, "then hide in the furthest corner of your flat and don't move."

"But what about Nadezhda? What if they kill her?"

"She's with her parents, don't worry about her," Samson reassured the woman.

He stood listening until he heard the widow carry out his instructions and unbolt the front door. Then he locked his own door, making sure that the Montpensier tin was firmly inserted behind the handle, and returned to the living room.

"They'll attack before long," he informed Kholodny.

His colleague immediately drew his Mauser pistol and placed it on the table, then dug out a handful of bullets from his jacket pocket and started loading the gun.

Samson also pulled his revolver from his holster, but he placed it on his knees, not letting it out of his grip.

"It would be better to wound them, not kill them," he whispered. "That way, we could interrogate them."

"Let's try it," Kholodny agreed. "Killing's no good, anyway. Unchristian."

Samson gave his colleague a quizzical look, but Kholodny didn't notice. He kept on loading the Mauser, slowly and carefully.

"How many rounds can that take?" Samson asked.

"Ten," Kholodny answered. "They say some Mausers can fit twenty, but I haven't come across any like that. Maybe we'll get lucky and snag one from these fellows?" He chuckled.

Samson heard a distant noise – footsteps – and immediately guessed its source.

Three shots rang out and the tin fell from its perch, clanging loudly against the wooden floor and rolling away.

It was as if a tram's iron wheel were rolling through Samson's head. He covered his earhole with his right hand, trying to protect it, but the revolver began to slip from his knees. He grabbed it and squatted next to the table.

The door swung open with great force and someone stormed into the flat, boots pounding the floor. There were shots. Kholodny huddled against the wall on the right and opened fire. Samson pulled his trigger three times, aiming in the direction of the hallway, then saw a spark struck from the copper kettle on the table by an intruder's bullet. He rolled away, stopping before reaching the wardrobe between the windows, and emptied his revolver into the darkness. Reloading feverishly, he dropped a bullet to the floor, felt for it and inserted it into the drum.

"Hey," Kholodny whispered. "Listen – it's quiet."

Samson, his head still full of noise, heard his colleague's whisper against the background of that noise and grew confused. He froze. Since the whisper was audible, he reasoned, the noise must be entirely in his head. The whisper had reached him from the outer quiet.

"I didn't hear them fall," Kholodny whispered again. "Maybe they took cover? You've got a kitchen and bathroom out there."

After listening close for a moment, Samson answered, "Yes, they might have."

"Let's crawl over there," Kholodny suggested.

The floor seemed surprisingly cold to Samson. Trying not to make unnecessary noise, he crawled as worms do, first pulling his legs up two inches, then pushing his body forward. He heard himself crawling – heard it all too well – and so slowed his progress towards the hallway door even further.

And suddenly the warm smell of blood hit his nostrils. His palm landed in a sticky puddle a foot from his face.

"Blood," he whispered.

"Son of a bitch!" cried Kholodny, and several shots rang out.

In the flashes from the muzzle, Samson saw two motionless bodies lying prone in front of himself and Kholodny. They wore leather jackets and had pistols in their hands. The leg of the one closest to Kholodny was tucked up under his body.

"We killed them?" Samson asked, no longer whispering.

"Maybe there's someone else out there?" Kholodny said as he

got up on one knee, then rose to his feet. "Hey, get in here!" he shouted towards the open door.

Pointing his Mauser, he stepped over the corpse and stopped at the door jamb. There, he bent his knees and leaned over to the other side, almost lying down.

"Quiet," he whispered. "No-one there."

Then he took a deep breath and – shouting "Hands up!" – leapt to his feet and burst into the kitchen.

Samson heard the doors to the lavatory and the bathroom swing open. Lights went on in the kitchen. Kholodny returned to the living room and flipped the light switch there, too.

They turned the bodies onto their backs.

"That's Anton," Samson confirmed quietly, nodding towards one of them.

Anton lay with his angry eyes open. His forehead was smeared with blood. The second man was still bleeding from a wound in his neck. He too was dead.

"It's impossible to shoot to wound in the dark." Kholodny sighed regretfully. "I couldn't see where I was aiming."

"Neither could I," Samson commiserated.

He searched the pockets of Anton's leather jacket, trousers and cloth tunic. There was nothing but loose bullets on one side, and, on the other, just a dozen large Duma-issued thousand-rouble notes, folded several times, and a pack of small grey Soviet-issued thirty-rouble notes. In the second man's inner pocket, he found papers in the name of Grigory Sheburshin, a Red Army soldier assigned to the reserve battalion of the Kyiv Provincial Extraordinary Committee (Cheka), certified by signatures and a number of round and triangular stamps. Grigory Sheburshin was to be given unhindered passage through Kyiv at all hours, and all institutions, both civil and military, were obliged to provide him with all possible aid. He had twice completed the Red marksmanship course, and two weeks ago he'd received two changes of underwear, a leather jacket and cap, calfskin boots and three pairs of footwraps from the military clothing warehouse, along with a tsarist officer's belt, the buckle of which had been mechanically smoothed.

"To erase the double-headed eagle," Samson muttered, refolding that last piece of paper from the dead man's pocket. "But Fyodor said Grishka was a cook . . ."

"We've got to hand them over to the Chekists," Kholodny declared.

"Why would they need corpses?"

"Well, one of them has their documents. And the other's an accomplice. Maybe they'll take their fingerprints, find something else on them."

"Yes," Samson agreed, as the face of Nestor Ivanovich and the fingerprint expert's little case floated up in his memory. "You're right. We have to hand them over."

"Have you got anyone to help scrub the floor?" Kholodny asked sympathetically, looking down at the pools of blood.

"Don't worry, I'll take care of it."

"We shouldn't be tramping around here. Let's go back to the station. We'll call up the Chekists and send them over. Let them figure it out – we'll catch some sleep in your cushy chairs."

Samson liked the idea. As they were leaving, he bent down, picked up the Montpensier tin and thrust it into his jacket pocket.

"Sweet tooth, eh?" asked the former priest, looking back.

Samson nodded and smiled slyly. But Kholodny, who led the way down the stairs, did not notice.

Chapter 41

Having covered both sides of a clean sheet of yellow paper with a detailed account of all that had transpired during the night, Samson stuck the report into the case file. Then he remembered the tin, transferred it to the top drawer of his desk, to which it was no stranger, and went back to his soft club chair, with its broad, excessively reclined back. He dozed off, thinking about the Chekists operating in his flat at that very moment. It's true that thoughts about the night's activities accompanied him even in his half-slumber, but they seemed to play out on the fringes of his mind, and not, as usual, at its very centre.

Earlier, when he and Kholodny had just returned to the station, they'd woken Nayden and told him everything. The commander had put in the call to Sadova Street himself, and the Cheka had dispatched its agents. He'd also labelled Samson and Kholodny "fools" for not informing him in advance of their plans to enter into a night-time shoot-out with an unknown number of criminals. He wouldn't have allowed it, he said – but he wasn't sufficiently awake to get angry in earnest. After his call to the Cheka, he had relayed the order to describe the night's events in detail. As broken-down and confused as Samson had felt at that point, he'd still managed to make a sensible decision: Kholodny would write the account for the Cheka, while he himself would write one for the Jacobson case file, making a copy for the file on the Red Army deserters, one of whom already lay, deservedly, among the police corpses in the morgue by the Dog Path – unless the Chekists stored their corpses elsewhere.

The lovely image of Nadezhda, whom Samson hadn't seen in

over twenty-four hours, suddenly appeared in his half-dream. He fondly recalled their "untouchable night", when she'd laid him down in her bed and soothed him to sleep. They had lain quietly there, in the bed on which his dear parents had slept for two decades. There had been something magical about it, that unhurried flow of kindness and bliss, the memory of which now swam up before him like a sort of medieval engraving. And for some reason, in his partial slumber, he saw beneath the image the name of the engraver, who was clearly German, because he had called his work *Sorge – Care*. On this engraving conjured by his half-dreaming mind, an exhausted hero lay sleeping, his head tilted back. Turned on her side and resting on her elbow, a half-naked nymph watched him with gentle concern. She supported the hero's head with the palm of her hand, while her long hair poured down along her arm onto the bed.

Someone peeked into the office, but chose not to disturb the slumbering policeman. Trying to retreat as quietly as possible, however, this someone failed to close the door properly. Now, Samson half-heard the patter of footsteps, along with snippets of brief conversations. But suddenly a loud rumble burst through the crack. There was thumping downstairs, on the ground floor. And a few times doors were slammed too loudly.

Samson opened his eyes and looked at the other club chair. Where was Kholodny?

Then he remembered that, after a couple of hours of napping, his colleague had gone back to his own office. He calmed down and focused on the noise coming from below. Rising to his feet, he went out to the stairs and took a few steps down. Then he froze, staring at the thick white sacks that lay along the walls, at the foot of the stairs and right up to the entrance on both sides. Seconded Red Army soldiers were bringing in new sacks, bent under their weight, and dumping them wherever they could, while trying to keep a path open.

"Stay out of the basement," Nayden's voice sounded.

Curiosity led Samson downstairs.

"Confiscated salt from a thieves' storehouse," Nayden declared, without waiting for the young policeman's questions. "Called in the agents from the Provincial Food Committee, but they're delayed."

"So much salt?" Samson said, surprised, having counted twenty sacks just beside the stairs and at the entrance.

"What do you expect? It's as valuable as gold, these days. Has there ever been a time when salt was more valuable than sugar?"

Samson recalled that the food at the Soviet cafeteria had indeed seemed terribly under-salted recently.

"Perhaps they steal it from the cafeterias?" he pondered aloud.

"You'd only get small amounts from cafeterias, but here we have sackfuls. These were taken off trains. I tell you, it's sheer *dis*array," Nayden said. He again emphasised the *dis*, his courageous face expressing significant horror.

"Who's in charge of keeping order, over there?"

"Who, he asks! The Cheka, of course. But the railway is like its own empire – each branch a province with its own governor and army."

"So why don't they defend their goods from thieves?" Samson objected.

"And who said they don't have their own thieves?" Nayden responded, his condescending look cutting off Samson's further attempts to express his thoughts. But then the young policeman remembered the tailor Sivokon's request, and the debt for the suit and the mannequin.

"Do you suppose we can keep one sack, for investigative purposes?" he asked carefully.

"What do we need a whole sack of salt for? Vasyl has already poured out three pounds for our needs."

"We have to pay the tailor for finishing the criminal's suit."

"You mean he won't accept money?"

"He asked for goods."

"How much do you think we should give him?"

"He made out an invoice for one hundred and fifty roubles. That's with the mannequin."

Nayden considered this for a moment, then waved his hand and said, "Write out a formal request to compensate your tailor for his assistance in the investigation – to pay him in salt to the value of one hundred and fifty roubles. How much salt that comes out to . . . I'll determine later."

Wakefulness slowly returned to Samson's body and mind, especially after he finished his second mug of tea, which the solicitous Vasyl had brought him with a piece of fresh white bread.

"Where did the bread come from?" Samson asked. He had long grown accustomed to drinking tea on an empty stomach, or one reinforced, on rare occasions, by a bagel or a tooth-crackingly dry biscuit.

"Our boys rescued a baker on Halych Square yesterday. Recovered twenty pounds of bread after a shoot-out. Still warm! Happened by chance," Vasyl explained.

"What do you mean, by chance?"

"The boys were driving by at just the right moment. Some bandits came scurrying out of the bakery like cockroaches, all holding bags of bread. So they shot them. Well, today he brought us some fresh bread. You see? We're appreciated," Vasyl added, with pride in his voice.

Sipping his tea, Samson reread what he had written before his nap. It occurred to him that he now had nothing to fear, no-one from whom to "await death". And that meant Jacobson too had nothing to fear – only he didn't know it. Perhaps it would be possible to inform him, so that he could emerge from his hiding place? But wouldn't he then be afraid of the one who'd informed him?

Samson sighed and thought harder still, trying to reason tactically, step by step. Say he went over to Baseina Street. He might not encounter Jacobson, but he might detect traces of a recent visit, since the Belgian had returned previously, after Balzer's murder – indeed, he had even moved his camp bed upstairs. Perhaps Samson could leave a message somewhere on the wall, saying that the danger had passed? But, if Jacobson had been sufficiently intimidated by the original death threat, he might decide that this was a trap and go deeper into hiding. How to coax him out, then? Not to mention the fact that he was likely armed . . . Otherwise, why would he have ordered bandoliers for his pockets? A shoot-out was all but inevitable. On the bright side, Jacobson was probably operating alone. He was a foreigner, and, for reasons unknown, had fallen out with his Red Army gang.

Samson looked up at the ceiling, then at the window. His eyes drifted down to the sacks of books – sacks that had replaced the boxes and eliminated all objections.

Why did people look more kindly on sacks than on boxes? he wondered. Because you couldn't see what was inside, if they were tied? Or because of their shape?

The soft white bread melted in his mouth, completely dissolving in the tea and adding to it a satisfying sweetness.

Jacobson had to eat somewhere, the young policeman thought. He had to use the toilet. There had been no smell of food or kerosene in the cellar. A certain culinary odour had lingered in Balzer's kitchen, but it seemed to be quite old. Samson decided to go and check the place again.

Chapter 42

The leftmost front door on Baseina was lower than the other two front doors of the same building. That is, it wasn't a proper main entrance.

Before going up the stairs, Samson walked along the façade, examining the half-plastered windows.

An air of war and devastation wafted from the filthy, vacant display windows beneath the sewing workshop.

It was harder to open the front door than it had been previously. Looking closely, Samson noticed that a wooden block had been inserted in place of the broken lock.

He also noticed the heads of two-inch steel nails in the door to the abandoned confectioner's shop. The nails had been driven in along the edges – with great force, it seemed, because the heads were rounded in places and sunk deep into the wood.

Samson took hold of the simple handle and pulled at the door. A wasted effort, as he had suspected it would be: the door was tightly nailed to its frame. On the first floor, he spotted no charcoal threat on the wall. Instead, he saw a dark smeared spot similar to the one he had left on the corner of his own building. Jacobson had been back.

His eyes wandered over to Balzer's door. The mastic seal he had stuck over it was also gone. But the door was shut. Samson leaned close to the lock and saw beside it the head of the same type of two-inch steel nail as he'd found below, which had been hammered in at an angle that would land it as deep as possible in the doorpost.

Samson tried the door. It didn't give, but it did emit a plaintive creak – which meant it wasn't as tightly nailed as the one below.

The young policeman tugged at the handle, straining. The nail came out of the post and the door opened. He stood perfectly still, listening. The silence lent him confidence. Calmly, without so much as unfastening the cover of his holster, he stepped inside.

In the sewing workshop, all things stood and lay where Samson had left them. He made his way into the residential part of the flat. The dismantled camp bed was missing. Nothing else drew his attention – except the wall above Balzer's bed. There, hanging on a nail, was an unusual photograph, the size of an engraving, in a glass-fronted wooden frame.

The young policeman removed it from the wall and went over to the window to get a better look. It was a beach scene: a couple in bathing suits, about forty years old, with six children, three on each side – two boys in sailor blouses and short trousers, and four girls. All the children looked about eight or ten years old: too close in age to all be siblings.

Samson pulled the photo out of its frame. On the cardboard below the image, embossed in gold, were the words *Fotostudio Zellner*. On the back, handwritten in ink, was the following inscription: *Den Haag, zoet augustus 1907*.

Samson recognised the man as Balzer, twelve years younger. His face beamed with joy and optimism. Although he and his wife weren't embracing, they were holding hands, bonded by their lightly touching palms. The children gazed into the camera with fascinated eyes, as if they were expecting some rare bird to come flying out of it.

Peering closely at the two boys, Samson noticed nothing special about their faces or appearance. Ordinary children.

Could he have overlooked the photo last time? Yes, he could have. He didn't remember the wall above the bed. He had been more concerned with the floor and the stretcher-bed in the corner.

Entering the kitchen, he froze. There were two buckets of water under the washbasin, and the table and cabinet looked to have been freshly cleaned. There were no dirty dishes anywhere to be seen, but there were spotless plates and cups on the middle tier of the cupboard to the left of the washbasin.

Nervously, Samson checked the lavatory and the bathroom. No-one.

All thoughts vanished from his mind, clearing the way for wordless confusion – a sense of imminent danger.

The index finger of his right hand unfastened the cover of his holster. He listened intently once again. Not the slightest noise. Only the hum of the street below.

Returning from the bathroom, he stopped in the middle of the kitchen.

His legs felt numb and he was afraid to move. He just kept turning his head and trying to think, to distract himself from the animal fear that so embarrassed him – though there was no-one but him to cast judgement.

At last, the numbness in his legs subsided. Revolver in hand, he opened the lower doors of the cupboard, revealing the blue gleam of Meissen porcelain.

He looked back at the door to the lavatory, from which his eyes wandered along the right wall, towards the bathroom. They paused on a narrow door, about two feet wide, of the sort that usually concealed a broom cupboard. Why hadn't he opened it before?

Swallowing nervously, barely lifting the soles of his boots from the wooden floor, Samson approached the narrow door.

For a moment, as he looked at the doorknob, which resembled the knob at the top of an old man's cane, he wondered whether he shouldn't shoot first.

His imagination conjured up that old man with a cane, wrapping the fellow in a warm striped dressing gown.

Samson's trigger finger itched, but his left hand reached for the doorknob. He jerked the door towards himself and thrust his revolver forward, ready to fire at once.

The tension did not leave his body, even after he realised the cupboard was empty. It was larger than he'd expected, and Samson noticed that what should have been its back wall was in fact another door – a bit wider than the outer door. The standard iron door handle indicated that behind it might lie a different room or the building's back stairs, to which kitchens often have access.

Having calmed down, Samson stepped into the cupboard, stared inquisitively at the door handle and sighed heavily. He had no desire to repeat the fruitless attack he had just launched, but there was no other way to find out what lay behind the door.

Choosing the moment of greatest concentration, he jerked this second door towards himself and thrust his revolver forward. The door swung open easily, soundlessly, as if it were made of air. Samson now saw a strange device: a large iron wheel with a thick rope rounding its rim and hanging down on either side.

The first thing that occurred to the young policeman was that the wheel resembled the wheel of the treadle sewing machine that sat in Balzer's workshop, draped with a sheet. Only it seemed far thicker and heavier.

The ensuing silence again restored Samson's calm. Fingering the hinges of the second door, he discovered that they were generously oiled. This came to seem especially logical after he re-examined the iron wheel. Its well-greased steel axle was fastened with arched pieces of tin to a wooden structure resembling a winch frame.

Samson's thoughts suddenly took a mechanical turn. He realised that what he was looking at was a winch that had been used to transport heavy items up from and down to the shop on the ground floor.

Everything fell into place. Samson grinned as he regained his self-confidence, which banished his involuntary fear. Jacobson had used this winch as an elevator. The door to the shop below had been nailed shut because he had no need of it – he went down via this cupboard instead. That meant he had been hiding out below.

And he was probably down there at this very moment. His bad leg would have kept him from travelling far. How had Samson not thought of this before?

The young policeman shook his head. And then another detail caught his attention: the wheel, perpendicular to the door, was closer to the left side of the shaft, leaving some space on the right, no more than a foot. There, in the corner of this space, leaning against the blue-painted wall, stood a pair of fluffy slippers, either felted or sewn, toes up. The poor lighting, which apparently came from below, through the dirty display windows, prevented him from examining the slippers more closely.

Samson leaned his head closer to the wheel and his gaze plummeted through a square hole in the floor, at least two feet by two feet, and hit the dusty top of a wardrobe.

To look deep down is almost always to look on death.

Nevertheless, the young policeman made up his mind and leaned further forward. He got a better look at the wardrobe, and also saw a stretch of worn parquet floor, the edge of a cabinet and, beneath the rope hanging down from the wheel, another mechanism with two large gears and a metal spiral about two-and-a-half inches wide. This mechanism held the rope taut – or, rather, held taut the wooden plank inserted between the split braids of the rope, which looked like a swing of the sort that parents sometimes make for their children at country homes.

Samson took another half-step forward, touched the grooved rim of the wheel and stroked the rope. Then he tried to turn the wheel towards himself, and it moved easily. The plank rose higher and higher, requiring no special effort on his part.

He stopped his hand and looked for a step onto which someone might jump in order to climb up into the cupboard, because the rope would only rise so far on the wheel – no further than where the braids began to split. Then he noticed two iron handles nailed to the floor along the edge of the opening. One could imagine a person grabbing hold of them, throwing one leg up and over, climbing out of the opening and leaving by the cupboard door.

"Jacobson!" shouted Samson, his every sense heightened in anticipation. He had no idea whether the enigmatic, silver-loving Belgian citizen was down there or not.

There was no answer. Total silence.

He must have found another hiding place, Samson thought. After all, the camp bed was gone.

Standing on the other side of the wheel, he looked down more boldly. In the part of the room visible from that vantage point, he saw dusty glass-fronted counters, all empty, moved up against the wall. There was no indication that the premises were in use.

Yet it occurred to Samson that there was more than one back room down there, and so he began to turn the wheel more resolutely, lifting up the plank. When the split rope stopped the wheel, he tried to work out how he might get onto the plank. Even if he did manage to stand or even to sit on the thing, it wasn't clear what he would need to do in order to descend. That said, if he gripped the handles nailed to the floor, it wouldn't be difficult to reach the plank with his feet.

Samson looked at the revolver in his right hand. He slipped it back into the holster, but didn't fasten the strap. Squatting down, he took hold of the handles and lowered his legs through the opening. His feet reached the plank. First, he placed the toe of his left boot on it, then the entire sole of his right boot. One hand at a time, he grabbed the braids of the rope. The plank began to sink down slowly, all on its own. The rhythmic clicking of the mechanism below was almost like the ticking of a tightly wound clock.

The worn parquet of the shop came closer and closer. Eight feet down and there was the chandelier – seven feet, six, five . . . The young policeman looked around. The open door to another room disturbed him. Not for nothing, it turned out. A figure holding a small pistol appeared in the doorframe and fired twice. Both bullets entered Samson's left forearm and he let go of the rope, crashing to the floor and raising a cloud of dust. The sound of hasty footsteps reached him from the direction of the open door. Ignoring the pain of his wounds, he began to crawl towards the wardrobe, realising that he could hide behind its right-hand corner. A plywood or walnut wardrobe was no real obstacle to a bullet, of course. Nevertheless, blind shooting was always less of a danger to the target.

Another shot sounded, but the bullet whizzed over Samson's head and, as it happened, disappeared inside the wardrobe, leaving a small hole in one of its doors.

Samson managed to crawl around the right-hand corner and immediately drew his revolver.

"Give up, Jacobson!" he cried. "You won't escape!"

"*Ik ben niet bang voor jou!*"* a sonorous voice answered.

"I don't know Belgian languages!" Samson shouted back. "Do you speak Russian? Polish? Ukrainian? Or German, damn it?"

Two more shots were fired in response. The bullets cracked through the plywood very near Samson's head.

"Jacobson! Why do you want to die?" Samson shouted, then said in German: "*Warum brauchen Sie den Tod?*"

"*Ik heb de dood niet nodig, ik heb leven nodig!*"† Jacobson shouted back. And, this time, he didn't fire.

"I don't understand," Samson complained desperately, suddenly experiencing a rush of pain to his forearm. "But you understand German! *Sie verstehen doch Deutsch!*"

"I understand Russian, too! *Ik versta Russisch!* Who you are? Why do you do this?"

The accent sounded comical, childlike, as if Jacobson was only pretending to be a foreigner. If not for the shoot-out, the

---

* "I'm not afraid of you!" (Flemish)

† "I don't need death, I need life!" (Flemish)

conversation might have proved amusing. But Samson didn't know how many bullets the Belgian had in his pistol or what was going on in his mind. He only knew that he had trouble with his left leg.

"I went to see Dr Trattner!" he cried. "Don't shoot! Let's talk! I know all about your leg!"

Silence. Jacobson neither spoke nor moved. Samson also froze and focused entirely on listening.

"I'm not a bandit, you understand? I'm with the police!"

No answer – but this time Samson picked up the sound of movement. It seemed to him that the small pistol's muzzle was trained on him from the very edge of the doorway. He raised his revolver and fired. There came a scream, and something like the rumble of a wooden barrel rolling across a wooden floor.

"Are you alive?" Samson shouted. "Jacobson! Are you alive?"

"I live!" Jacobson answered in his funny accent. "You wish I don't?"

"No! Give up! Drop your weapon!"

"But you will kill!"

"I won't kill you if you surrender! I need answers! Why would I kill you?"

"What answers?" Jacobson shouted, with pain in his voice.

"Did I hurt you?"

"Yes. Hurt."

"Drop your gun!"

"No! What answers?"

"I believe you were threatened by a Red Army soldier named Anton! Do you know him?"

"I know," the Belgian replied. "I owe him money and passaport!"

"For what? Silver?"

"Yes!"

"Why didn't you give him the money?"

"I do not have. When I came to mine uncle, I had no money. And I cannot make passaport . . ."

272

"But you'd made him a promise."

"Yes, I promise everyone. I need silver for mine health. I want to walk . . ."

"Who told you silver would help?"

"Dr Trattner. He said silver bone, they do not hurt. I need much silver – new skeleton . . ."

"And how did you manage to make that silver bone?" Samson asked, trying to ignore his pain.

"At Oleksandrivska, where they keep corpses, I asked one orderly to cut out one bone from one body, my size . . . He boil it, clean it, give it to me. Then I go to monastery, I find jeweller . . ."

"And how did you pay the jeweller?"

"I did not. I only promise. When I come here, I think mine uncle is rich, but no. He had no money . . ."

"Was you uncle – Balzer?"

"Yes."

"But you are Belgian and he was German."

"My mother was his sister – my father Flemish."

"Why did they keep bringing you silver, in exchange for nothing?" The picture of the case in Samson's mind was nearly complete, but it was safer to talk than to shoot, and Jacobson seemed to be answering almost eagerly now.

"I promise them. In your country, you believe the foreigneurs . . . You do not believe your people, but the foreigneurs – yes . . ."

"And that's why the soldiers went looking for you?"

"It is why he steal the patterns from mine uncle. A pledge. And why he kill him . . ."

"That was Anton, then?"

"Yes."

"How do you know?"

"I was here, below. The door was open. I hear. They was screaming. Then they shoot. And another bandit fall on mine uncle."

"That was no bandit!" Samson shouted. "That was another man Anton killed. Throw your gun this way!"

"No! If you want, crawl this way."

"Jacobson, you don't understand Russian very well. Trattner didn't say that a silver leg would solve your problems – he was joking."

"Doctors, they do not joke! He spoke truth! He did such operation!"

"This doctor was joking, I assure you. He told me everything. He can tell you himself. He remembers you well."

"To you he lie! To me he spoke truth!"

A long silence followed, perhaps as long as two minutes, after which three shots rang out in a row, and then a lady's small pistol fell to the floor with a heavy clang, three feet from where Samson had taken cover.

"Are you alive? Have you shot yourself?" Samson shouted, worried.

"No . . . I shoot in ceiling."

"Come out, I won't shoot," Samson promised, and then, to convince Jacobson thoroughly, he added, "I had your suit made. The one your uncle didn't live to finish."

Chapter 43

"Don't that beat all," Kholodny commented, shaking his head, when Samson had finished his tale.

The former priest sat on a stool beside the bed in the surgical ward of the Oleksandrivska Hospital. He had raised Samson up at his request, placing the pillow behind his back. The young policeman held his bandaged left forearm slightly lower than its undamaged counterpart.

"You should have brought me with you! We'd be drinking tea or beer right now, while this Jacobson of yours would be cooling in the morgue beside the other police corpses."

"That's exactly why I went alone," Samson admitted. "Want to hear something strange? When the Chinese Red Army soldiers brought Jacobson and me here that night, the doctor said there were only two surgeons on call in the entire city: Trattner and Gedroits! I told him straight away: 'Take the Belgian to Trattner; they know each other. I'll take Gedroits.'"

"And how's this Gedroits fellow better than Trattner?" Kholodny asked, hoisting up his bushy brows.

"Gedroits is a woman! A princess, actually. She had me over, recently. For tea and ham. And I thought a woman surgeon might treat me more gently," Samson said with a smile.

As if on cue, a stern-faced woman entered the ward in black heelless shoes and trousers that peeked out from under her surgical gown.

"Well, Samson Theophilovich? Accepting visitors, are we?"

"Dr Gedroits, this is my partner. In the service."

Kholodny jumped up from the stool and extended his hand. The look on his face revealed that he hadn't expected such a strong handshake. Vera Ignatyevna asked a few questions, then left the ward.

"Your Jacobson won't make a run for it, will he?"

"He's physically incapable of running," Samson answered. "He has tuberculosis of the left femur. And, besides, he has nowhere to run."

"Bad not to have anywhere to run," Kholodny pronounced gloomily.

"I feel sorry for him myself. Not very bright, and illiterate to boot . . ."

"Illiterate in what sense?"

"In the sense used by census-takers. That's how they described him. Of course, I would've used a shorter word: fool."

Samson's smile was almost too faint to notice.

Epilogue

A week later, Samson and Nadezhda worked diligently, side by side, to scrub Anton's and Grigory's blood from the floor of their living room. That chore took nearly an hour and a half to complete. Then they had dinner, during which they tried to speak only of the weather. Alas, they couldn't avoid mentioning the shortage of sugar and salt. Nadezhda especially missed the former, Samson the latter.

They went to bed together, in Samson's parents' room. But they did so calmly. They were tired.

"Don't make any sudden movements," said Nadezhda, tucking the edge of the blanket under Samson's left side.

He slept deeply for two hours before a strange noise woke him in the middle of the night. He thought he heard two sets of footsteps. Cautiously, he got up and checked the living room, his bedroom and his father's study. Only then did he realise that the sounds were reaching him through his second, severed ear.

Then he heard the creak of his father's desk drawer, and male voices.

"Look, an old passport. And a tin of some sort. What was the complaint again?"

"Offence committed in the line of duty," answered the second voice. "Apparently he claimed that a chest of stolen goods was his own property, mistakenly confiscated. He took it home. In addition, he used governmental funds to have a suit made for a foreign criminal."

"Clever bastard," said the first voice. "What's in the tin? Confiscated gold?"

The tin opened with a metallic clink.

"Parchment?"

"Don't you see? It's an ear! Quite the character . . . Probably did away with one of his enemies and kept it as a trophy. We could use a few of his sort."

"Yes. Hard as nails. So, shall we open a case?"

"No," the first one responded decisively. "Let's just keep an eye on him. He did nab those deserters, you know, and brought a ton of silver into the treasury. Just doesn't add up . . ."

"I don't get why he didn't allow the arrested foreigner to be taken to the prison hospital . . ."

"He must need something from him. He didn't have that suit made for nothing, right? But the fellow's locked up. They summoned the consul to see him. Looks to be a petty swindler, not a bandit . . . Wanted to cheat the thieves out of their take."

"Alright, let's get out of here. We still have to ride over to Priorka," the second voice declared. Then the tin was audibly closed and returned to the desk drawer, which creaked back into place. Footsteps receded, the door to the office slammed shut and a key rasped in the lock.

For a long time, Samson lay with his eyes open. He listened to the silence that reigned in his office after the strangers had departed – and also to the silence in his parents' bedroom, which sounded warmer and dearer because it contained the calm, even breathing of Nadezhda. Two ears, two silences.

The end. But to be continued.

Translator's Note

Andrey handed me an inscribed copy of Samson Kolechko's first adventure one sunny spring day in San Diego, almost exactly three years ago, and I breezed through it before the Kurkovs visited me in Los Angeles that summer. By then he was already wrapping up Samson's second investigation and sketching out the third. Neither of us could have predicted that, less than a year after that idyllic reunion in California, Russia would launch a full-scale invasion of Ukraine, forcing Andrey first to flee his home, then to return and devote all his strength to defending his country on the cultural front. For Samson's creator, the urgent demands of 2022 eclipsed the imaginative appeal of 1919.

For his translator, however, submersion in that earlier period of crisis and uncertainty proved cathartic. After all, I had as little control over the fate of Ukraine, which is also my homeland, in 2022 as Samson had over its fate in 1919, when the reins of power seemed to pass from hand to hand every few weeks. It was oddly reassuring to cling to Samson as he did his best to find his way through the fog of war and revolution, and even more reassuring to reflect on how far Ukraine had come since those dark days; the days would grow darker still under Soviet rule, before slowly, painfully lightening after 1991. The Ukraine Russia invaded in February 2022 is a far stronger country than it was in 1919, when it first made a bid for independence after centuries of imperial oppression. It is still a country full of resourceful, good-natured people like Samson – people determined to live full lives no matter what obstacles they encounter – only the Samsons of today have a far clearer sense of who they are and where they stand.

I found another pleasure in my work on these investigations. Having spent years lapping up the sensationally vivid, linguistically delicious works of Dashiell Hammett, Raymond Chandler, and other masters of early 20th-century US crime fiction, as well as translating the equally vivid and delicious stories of Isaac Babel, I was able to put all I'd learned to use on Andrey's sparkling 21st-century evocation of that period's literature. Of course, every sentence in this book bears signs of Andrey's own signature style – a style I've come to know just as well as I know that of Babel. It all made for a delightful meeting of the worlds in which I feel most at home.

A word about place names: In general, I have opted for standard contemporary Ukrainian transliterations. A few places are relatively well known by their English names, like Kyiv's Andrew's Descent, and so I have used those. Some streets and landmarks have changed names several times since 1919, and others no longer exist. In the case of a number of these long-forgotten tags – especially those with strong imperial connotations – I have abandoned the adjectival forms in favor of simpler substantive ones, e.g., Stolypin instead of Stolypinska for a street named after Pyotr Stolypin, who served as the Russian Empire's Minister of Internal Affairs from 1906 until he was assassinated in Kyiv in 1911.

I hope you find the first steps of our young investigator's journey as engrossing and, ultimately, as moving as I did. I, for one, can't wait for the next case.

Select Chronology of
Ukrainian History 1917–1921

8–16 March 1917: The "February" Revolution ends the reign of the Romanov dynasty, which is replaced by the Provisional Government, headed by Alexander Kerensky.

7 November 1917: In what has come to be called the October Revolution, the Bolsheviks seize power from the Provisional Government, sparking a civil war throughout the lands of the Russian Empire. Most of the forces opposed to the Bolsheviks are part of the White movement.

17 March 1917: A governing council called the Central Rada is set up in Kyiv.

22 January 1918: The Central Rada declares the independence of the Ukrainian People's Republic.

Spring and Summer 1918: German troops disarm Ukrainian forces in Kyiv, the Central Rada is deposed, and, on 29 April, Pavlo Skoropadskyi is declared Hetman of Ukraine. A number of forces vie for control of Kyiv and other parts of Ukraine.

Autumn 1918: The Great War draws to a close. The Treaty of Brest-Litovsk, signed on 9 February between the Central Powers (Germany, Austria-Hungary and the Ottoman Empire) and the Ukrainian People's Republic, recognises the latter's sovereignty. As Austria-Hungary, which had controlled much of Western Ukraine, declines on the way to its eventual collapse, the West Ukrainian People's Republic is established on 1 November, leading to conflicts with Poland.

November to December 1918: A new governing body, the Directorate of the Ukrainian People's Republic, is established on 13 November and, on 19 December, it overthrows Skoropadskyi's regime and takes power in Kyiv.

22 January 1919: Union is proclaimed in Kyiv between the West Ukrainian People's Republic and the Ukrainian People's Republic.

February 1919: The Bolsheviks take Kyiv, while Symon Petliura is named leader of the Directorate. He heads the Ukrainian People's Republic and its army, continuing to battle against the Bolsheviks.

August to September 1919: White forces drive the Bolsheviks out of Kyiv and most of Ukraine.

December 1919: Representatives of the Ukrainian People's Republic issue a declaration of their willingness to accept the Curzon Line, proposed by the then British Foreign Secretary, the 1st Earl Curzon of Kedleston, as the eastern border of Poland. The Bolsheviks retake Kyiv.

21–24 April 1920: The Directorate signs a pact with Poland, whose chief of state is Józef Piłsudski, ceding the western Ukrainian regions of Galicia and Volhynia in exchange for military aid. The Polish-Soviet War begins.

May 1920: Polish and Ukrainian forces retake Kyiv.

July to August 1920: The Red Army pushes Polish forces back, advancing on Warsaw, and the Directorate is evacuated to Western Europe.

18 October 1920: A ceasefire between Poland and the Bolsheviks comes into force.

18 March 1921: The Peace of Riga brings an official end to the Polish-Soviet War, dividing Ukraine and Belarus between the two powers. The Ukrainian Soviet Socialist Republic, which had been founded in Kharkiv in 1919 but not internationally recognised, becomes the official government of the portions of Ukraine controlled by Soviet forces.

ANDREY KURKOV was born near Leningrad in 1961. After working as prison guard and a journalist, he found renown as a novelist with *Death and the Penguin*, now translated into thirty languages. Since the Russian invasion of Ukraine, Kurkov, whose novel *Grey Bees* was set during an earlier stage of the conflict, has become a crucial voice for the people of his country. He published his *Diary of an Invasion* in 2022 and also appeared on BBC Radio 4's *Letter from Ukraine*. In 2023, his novel *Jimi Hendrix Live in Lviv* was longlisted for the International Booker Prize.

BORIS DRALYUK is an award-winning translator and poet. He has taught at UCLA and at the University of St Andrews, and is currently an Associate Professor of English and Creative Writing at the University of Tulsa. He is a co-editor (with Robert Chandler and Irina Mashinski) of the *Penguin Book of Russian Poetry*, and has translated Isaac Babel's *Red Cavalry* and *Odessa Stories*, as well as Kurkov's *The Bickford Fuse* and *Grey Bees*, which won the inaugural Gregg Barrios Book in Translation Prize from the National Book Critics Circle. In 2020 he received the inaugural Kukula Award for Excellence in Nonfiction Book Reviewing from the *Washington Monthly*.